COMMANDER IN CHIEF

POWER HAS NEVER

BEEN SEXIER

D1518325

KATY
EVANS

NEW YORK TIMES & USA TODAY
BESTSELLING AUTHOR

First paperback edition: January 2017

Cover design by James T. Egan, www.bookflydesign.com
Interior formatting by JT Formatting

10 9 8 7 6 5 4 2 1

Library of Congress Cataloguing-in-Publication Data is available

ISBN-13: 978-1539876014
ISBN-13: (ebook) 978-0-9972636-4-0

TABLE OF CONTENTS

11,08

PLAYLIST

"Gravity" by Alex & Sierra
"Better in Time" by Leona Lewis
"Love Me Harder" by Ariana Grande
"Reckless Love" by Bleachers
"Be Here Now" by Robert Shirey Kelly
"Real Love" by Clean Bandit
"If I Didn't Have You" by Thompson Square
"You and Me" by Lifehouse
"Holy War" by Alicia Keys
"The Ocean" by Mike Perry
(featuring Shy Martin)
"Dangerously in Love" by Beyoncé
"Better Love" by Hozier

"I do solemnly swear that I will faithfully execute the Office of President of the United States, and will to the best of my ability, preserve, protect and defend the Constitution of the United States."

OATH

Matt
Present Day

I suit up in black. Knot my tie. Add my cuff links. And step out to the living room of Blair House to greet the senior officer from White House Military, who's here to hand over the top-secret codes in case of a nuclear strike. With him is an aide with the nuclear football that will be passed on to me—as of noon, the man who carries it will be my shadow for the next four years.

"A true pleasure, Mr. President-Elect," the shadow tells me.

"Likewise." I shake his hand, then the senior officer's hand as the nuclear codes are handed to me, and they leave.

Customarily, the departing president holds a brunch for the incoming president on Inaugural Day. Not the case with Jacobs and me. I grab my long black coat and slip my arms into the sleeves, nodding at Wilson at the door.

It seemed fitting that I pay a visit to my father today. The day I become the forty-sixth president of the United States.

***

My father is buried at Arlington National Cemetery, one of three presidents there.

The wind is freezing, flapping my gabardine at my calves. As I walk up to my father's grave, I know the silence will soon be broken by the twenty-one rifle shots from the changing of the guard at the Tomb of the Unknown Soldier.

I kneel before his grave, scanning the name—*Lawrence "Law" Hamilton, President, husband, father, son*—on his tombstone.

He died a long time ago, tragically, in the kind of way that stays with you forever. Branding you.

"I take the oath today." My chest feels heavy when I think of how much he'd love to have seen this. "I want to promise you, Dad, that I'm going to fight for truth and justice, freedom and opportunity for us all. Including finding who did this to you."

The day is fresh in my mind: my father's lifeless eyes, Wilson cowering over me, and me, fighting to pull free so I could run to him. The last thing he'd said to me was that I was too stubborn. He'd been wanting me to go into politics; I'd insisted that I wanted to carve my own path.

It took a decade for me to feel the need to do what my father had always hoped for me.

I'm proud, today, to come visit with the sort of news that would make him as pleased as any father could be.

It seems at times that I talk more to my father here than I did those last few years we were in the White House.

"Mother's well. She misses you. She's never been the same since that day. She's haunted by what happened—and by whoever did this to you still being out there. I think she mourns the years she wanted to build back your marriage. She'd always hoped once we left there that she'd get her husband back. Yeah, we both know how that went."

I shake my head mournfully and spot the frozen flowers resting at the foot of the grave.

"I see she came to see you."

I once again feel the protective instinct of a son wanting to prevent his mother from hurting.

I think of how my father would tell me *you're meant for greatness; don't cheat the world of you.* And today, out of every day since he's been gone, I miss him the most.

"I have met the most wonderful girl. Do you remember I told you about her on my last visit? I let her go. I let the woman I love go because I didn't want her to go through what Mom went through. And I've realized that I can't do this without her. That I need her. That she makes me stronger. I don't want to hurt her if it's my turn to end up here—I don't want her to cry every night like Mother does because I'm no longer here with her. Or cry because I'm across the country and she needs me and turns around to find out I'm gone. But I can't give her up. I'm fucking selfish, but I can't give her up."

Frustration simmers in me and I finally admit, "I'm going out there to take my oath, and I'll devote my every waking breath to this country. I'll do what you couldn't and a thousand other things that need to be done. And I'm going to win her back. I'll make you proud."

I rap my knuckles on the headstone as I stand, my eyes locking with Wilson's as he nods to the rest of my detail.

We head back to the cars, and I stop to level a look at Wilson before I board.

"Hey, I checked up on her, like you asked," Wilson says.

I inhale the cold air, shaking my head and shoving my hands into the pockets of my black gabardine.

She is the one relentless, constant thought in my head and tug in my damn chest. The only *she* that has ever existed in my life.

She left for Europe after Election Day. I know because I went to see her when the voting results became official. I kissed her. She kissed me. I told her I wanted her in the White House. She told me she was leaving for a few months in Europe with her best friend, Kayla. "It's better this way," she said. "I'm not going to keep my cell number. I think—we need to do this."

It cost me everything not to go after her. To stay away. She changed her number. I found it. Tried not to call. Barely succeeded. I couldn't keep from having my staff check up on when she'd be returning to the States.

She wants to be done with you, Hamilton. Do the good thing here.

I know that, but I can't give her up. Two months without her is two months too long.

And I've had enough.

"What did you find out?"

"She's back from her trip and she RSVPed to one of the balls tonight, Mr. President-Elect."

She's back from Europe just in time for my inauguration.

My chest tightens. I've stayed away and every inch of me wants to see her. I'll have the keys to the world, but turned my back on the key to the woman I love's heart. How can I be proud of that? She shed one tear that day. Just one. And it was for me.

"Good. You'll be taking me there tonight."

I climb into the back of the car, the Secret Service hot on our tail, and I drum my fingers restlessly on my thigh—my blood simmering at the prospect of seeing her tonight, already envisioning the red hair and blue eyes of my woman as she greets her new president.

Charlotte

It's a historic day.

Matthew Hamilton, the youngest president of the United States of America.

I'm amidst a crowd of hundreds of thousands gathered at the U.S. Capitol. I was sent a seated invitation, along with a plus-one. So I brought Kayla. I sit tightly in my seat. One where Matt will be so much closer than he will be to the crowd below.

They opened up the National Mall to the citizen spectators, something that had never been done until his father won—and now. The country is simply too invested in this outcome, too eager to celebrate him, to stay away.

A chorus of children have been singing "America the Beautiful," and I sit on a bag of nerves, excitement, and feelings as the song ends and the U.S. Marine Band picks up with a wildly happy, patriotic tune.

Trumpets start blaring.

Through the speakers, we hear the presenter introduce the departing president, along with his wife and other members of our political engine. Claps erupt across the crowd as people file into place, taking their seats. And then, to the crowd's mounting excitement, after a trail of high-profile names are announced, the presenter finally announces, "Ladies and gentlemen, the President-elect of the United States, MATTHEW HAMILTON!"

Okay, breathe.

BREATHE, CHARLOTTE!

But it feels like some invisible rope is wound tightly around my windpipe as Matt walks down a blue carpet to the platform, the people chanting at the top of their lungs: "HAMILTON! HAMILTON! HAMILTON!"

He's greeting all the cabinet members as well as his mother, shaking their hands. His mother is seated to the left of the microphone, and after greeting the crowd with a huge smile and a sweep of his hand, Matt settles his big body next to hers.

I'm wringing my cold fingers, my eyes so starved for him they hurt.

He looks imposing in his seat as Vice-President-elect Louis Frederickson from New York takes his oath.

He looks just like I remember. His hair a little longer, maybe. His expression calm and sober. I watch him duck his head to listen to something his mother tells him—and a frown creases his forehead, but then a smile tips his lips and he nods.

Butterflies.

Mean, evil little butterflies are flapping in the very core of me.

I inhale and stare at my lap, at my reddened, freezing fingers.

It's bone-chillingly cold outside, but when Matt is called up, and his baritone voice comes on suddenly over the microphone, it warms me like a bowl of my favorite soup. Like liquid fire in my veins. Like a blanket around my heart.

I lift my head. He's standing on the platform. Calm and towering in a black gabardine and a perfect suit and red tie, his sable hair blowing in the wind, his expression somber as he places his hand on the Bible, the other hand raised.

"I, Matthew Hamilton, do solemnly swear that I will faithfully execute the Office of President of the United States, and will to the best of my ability, preserve, protect and defend the Constitution of the United States."

"Congratulations, Mr. President," the presenter says.

My head spins.

Holy.

FUCK.

Matt is now *president of the United States.*

The cheers erupt like a wave crashing upon us. People stand. Everyone claps and revels in the euphoria, the country welcoming their new commander in chief.

My body jerks from the sound of the twenty-one guns exploding—one after the other.

Trumpets blare.

The crowd waves small U.S. flags side to side.

People are crying.

The music of the orchestra plays, louder and louder across the U.S. Capitol and National Mall.

All while Matt salutes his crowd. His smile the most dazzling thing I've ever seen. His gaze sweeping across the hundreds of thousands of people here. People who've loved him for decades, since he was their president's son. And now he's simply their president.

The youngest, hottest president in the world.

The people in the crowd below keep waving their small flags.

Once the gun salute is over, the presenter leans in to say, "It is my deep pleasure to present the forty-sixth president of the United States, Matthew Hamilton."

He steps up to the microphone. Hands braced on the stand, he leans into the mic, and his voice rings out, powerful and deep. Just the sound of it affects me intensely. Causing both a pang of nostalgia and a surge of excitement in me.

"Thank you. Fellow citizens ... Vice President Frederickson," he greets. "I stand with you today, humbled and in awe of the true change we can set forth in this country when we as a collective contribute to putting it in motion." Claps interrupt him and he pauses. "Citizens, I am thankful for the opportunity." He nods somberly, glancing one way, then the other, his powerful shoulders straining the fabric of his gabardine.

"In our country, we fight for truth and justice." Pause. "We fight for freedom, for what's right." Pause. "We fight for it, and we die for it—and if we're lucky, we die having those on our side ..." Pause.

"These aren't times to stand back and hope for the best. These are the times where we make it the best. Giving back to our country. Putting the best pieces of ourselves out there. America was formed on the principle of freedom, has embraced the promise of unity, peace, justice, and truth. It is only by preserving and honoring who we are that we can do justice to the very core of what we stand for. And what we will continue to stand for. A beacon to other countries across the globe. The land of the free. The home of the brave. Let's fulfill our full potential, and ensure our enjoyment of that which our ancestors have so fiercely fought for, not just for ourselves, but for our generations to come. You wanted a leader to take you into this new era with courage. With conviction. And with an eye for getting things done. Citizens." Pause. "I will NOT. LET YOU DOWN."

A roar goes out across the crowd. HAMILTON is the name they call. HAMILTON is the man of the hour. The year. Their lifetime. He smiles at that warm welcome, and he closes with a deep, gruff, "God bless you. And God bless the United States of America."

A warm glow flows through me and a ball full of spikes sort of gets stuck in the middle of my throat.

They play the national anthem, and as the chorus of the singing citizens rings across the U.S. Capitol and households around the world, I'm placing my hand on my heart and attempting to get the words of the anthem out—but that doesn't help to ease this deep, unaccustomed pain in my chest. This is simply such a monumental day for me. Not only as a citizen; as a person this day is directly proportionate to the depth of my feelings for the new president. And the depth is endless,

fathomless,

eternal.

This is what he wanted. This is what *we* wanted. What the whole country did. It's the first day of the changes that are about to come—and I'm burning with the wish to have just one tiny moment to talk to Matt. Tell him how proud of him I am. How much it hurts to not have him, but how safe I feel knowing he'll be fighting for our interests.

I sit there among the crowd, my eyes stinging as emotion wells in my chest. We finish the anthem.

"Hey, come on, let's go get you pretty for the inaugural ball," Kayla says, slipping her arm around mine as she tugs me away.

I stand, but resist a little. My legs feel leaden, as if I don't want to go in this direction—but instead, I want to go in the direction where he's saying goodbye to those around him and heading up the platform to leave the grounds.

I watch Matthew stop at the top of the blue-carpeted stairs.

Matt cants his head back to the crowd and sweeps it with one powerful gaze.

I hold my breath, then shake my head.

He's not looking for you, Charlotte; you can start breathing now.

I sigh and rub my temples, shaking my head as we wait for the motorcade parade down Pennsylvania Avenue. "I'm not sure that I should go."

"Come on." Kayla nudges me, her expression questioning. "We came back just in time for inauguration because you wanted to be here. You cannot turn down an invite to the inaugural ball."

I keep my eyes on Matthew.

Matthew

Hamilton.

My love.

I remember the sounds he makes when he makes love, the way his breath hitches, the way his eyes cloud. I remember the taste of his sweat as he drives inside me, the way I kiss and lick him and want more, want him, anything he can give.

Intimate moments.

Moments between a man and a woman.

Moments that seem so long ago but at the same time, I can never forget, because we had them. I cling to those moments because I never *want* to forget them. When I see the man—the president—I want to remember what his chest feels like under his tie and suit, all that power rippling in his muscles. I want to remember the size of him, when he's joined to me, as big as the name he now wears, and I want to remember what it felt like to have him come inside me. I never want to forget the sound of his voice in the dark, when nobody is watching, and how tender it sounds.

I don't want to forget that for a little while, Matt Hamilton—forty-sixth president of the United States—was mine.

I head back to my apartment to shower and blow-dry my hair and prep for tonight.

I spent the last two months in Europe. It was freezing cold and we spent more time at the hotel than touring, but it didn't matter. I wasn't in the United States, the country I love, close to the man I love, simply because I needed to heal.

I didn't want to be tempted to call. I was afraid if I stayed, I'd see him in every headline; that the very air in D.C. would smell of him. That I'd bump into him or simply have too many memories everywhere I went to be able to breathe right. Europe was good. It centered me, and yet I was anxious to come back home. I couldn't bring myself not to be home by the time Matt had his Inauguration Day.

I told Kayla I fell in love with him while campaigning. I didn't give her more details. She pressed, but I didn't budge. I understand now that when you're as high-profile a person as Matt is, you cannot trust even those you're supposed to trust. Not with everything. I'm afraid one drunken night she'd spill the beans of the affair. So I kept it to myself and nursed it quietly in my heart, even as Kayla kept telling me that it was a crush and I'd get over it in Paris, the city of love.

I didn't.

My heart hurts right now no matter how much I will it to stay strong.

God.

How will I bear to look him in the eye tonight?

He will see right through me.

I'm hoping that with the several balls going on, his visit to the one I'm attending will be brief. That we'll just say a quick hello and he'll have to continue down the line of people eager to greet their new president.

Still, I dress with the same care that a bride might on her wedding day.

I'm seeing the man I love, and it might be the last time, and the girl inside me wants him to remember me looking as stunning as I can possibly look.

As desirable as he previously found me to be.

I brush my red hair and let it fall down my shoulders. I go for a strapless blue dress that matches my eyes. I paint my lips a deep shade of red, and I ask my mother if I can borrow my grandmother's fur coat. I've never bought a single fur thing in my life due to animal cruelty—but that coat has sentimental value to me, and it's freezing outside.

My parents are attending a different ball than I am. "You really should consider coming with us," my mother said this morning.

"I'm going with Alison—she's the new White House photographer and she's got to be at this event to capture the moment."

"Oh, all right. Charlotte?"

"Yes?"

"Are you sure you're ready?"

I knew what she was asking. She knows that there was something between Matthew and me, though I never gave her details. She knows I fell in love—and having a daughter in love with the hot, young president is enough to make any concerned mother worry.

Emotion makes it difficult to speak, but I nod, then I realize my mother cannot see me. "Yes."

I know it won't be easy. But I need to see him today.

I want to congratulate him. I want him to know that I'm okay, that I'm proud of him, that I'm going to move forward, and that I want him to do the same.

INAUGURAL BALL

Matt

"President Hamilton. Mr. President."

I pull my gaze to the man drawing my attention. I'm at the luncheon, and my damn mind keeps wandering to tonight.

"I apologize; it's been a long day already." I grin and run my hand restlessly along the back of my hair, leaning to speak to the Senate majority leader.

It's incredible how we never rest. Even at social events, we're discussing policy.

I try to pick the brains of most men there; it's in my and the country's best interest that my ideas for change are aligned with those of Congress and the Senate. Whether they'll be easy to align remains to be seen.

"I asked if the first bill on your agenda will be the clean energy bill?"

"It's one of my priorities, but not necessarily at the top," is all I give him for now.

All in due time, old man. All in due time.

I'm relieved when we get ready for the parade down Pennsylvania Avenue. We walk surrounded by black presidential state cars. I'm flanked by my grandfather and my mother as we head to the most famous address in the country. Hundreds of thousands of people line the streets to watch the parade. U.S. flags flap in the wind.

It's an honor to be the one heading to 1600 Penn.

Grandfather is marching like a proud king, grinning from ear to ear. "I'm proud of you, son. Now you need to get in line with the parties or you won't do shit."

My grandfather isn't necessarily my hero, but I know when to listen. And when to brush him aside. "The parties will get in line with me." I wave at the crowd.

To my right, my mother is silent.

"You have a room in the White House," I tell her, reaching out and squeezing her hand.

"Oh no." She laughs, looking like a young girl for that fleeting moment of happiness. "Seven years was enough."

I release her hand so we can greet the crowd again. I know she's remembering a day like this a decade ago. Not only the day she rode the motorcade parade for the first time with my dad. But the day he died ... and the motorcade that carried his coffin.

"Besides, I have a feeling it'll soon be occupied," she adds.

It takes me a moment to realize she's referring to her room in the White House.

"Why do you say that?"

"Because I know you. You won't let that girl go. You haven't. I've never seen you ... look sadder, Matt. Even after you won."

I'm so blown away by how well she knows me, I can't think of a reply. That she knows it's taken every ounce of my restraint not to call Charlotte. That for months I've told myself it's for the best, that I can't do it all, that I will fail if I try. But I don't buy it. I want my girl, and I will have her.

"She's the light. Walks on water," I tell my mother.

We reach 1600 Pennsylvania Avenue.

The gates open, the red carpet is rolled out. From within the house, my dog Jack, who was transported from Blair House earlier today, bounds down the steps to greet us.

My mother is dressed to impress. You'd think she was thrilled that I'm back in the White House. Maybe a part of her is. I know that another part is full of fear that I'll meet the same end my father did.

We walk up the red-carpeted steps of the North Portico entrance.

"Mr. President," the chief usher greets me. I shake his hand. "Welcome to your new home," he says.

"Thank you, Tom. I'd like to meet the staff tomorrow. Help me arrange that."

"Yes, sir, Mr. President."

"*Tom*," I hear my mother say, pulling him into a hug.

Jack is leading the way as we step through the wide-open front doors.

"Mr. President, sir," one of the ushers announces. "There's a buffet set up for you and your guests in the Old Family Dining Room while you prepare for the balls tonight."

"Thank you. Nice to meet you …?"

"Charles."

"A pleasure, Charles." I shake the man's hand, then head to the West Wing. I find Portia, my assistant, already organizing her desk outside the Oval Office.

"How's it going, Portia?"

"Uff," she huffs. "It's going. This house is immense. Your chief of staff, Dale Coin, told me I could call the ushers' office if anything seemed out of reach."

"Good. Do that."

I walk into the Oval, Jack trailing behind me.

I had my father's desk returned—it had been in storage. I walk to it now, glancing down at the presidential seal on the rug beneath my feet. I run my fingers over the wood. The U.S. flag behind me. The presidential seal flag beside it. Then I rap the desk and take my chair and go through the documents readied for me. Jack is sniffing every nook and cranny of the room as I flip the pages.

Today I've become privy to confidential information—deals with other countries, high-security risks, things our CIA and FBI are engaged in that will proceed as usual unless I indicate otherwise. Intel on the situation with China. Russia's playing with fire. Cyberterrorism on the rise.

So fucking much to do and I'm ready to get started.

I set the files aside an hour later, but instead of heading back to the buffet, I proceed to the residence to get ready for the inaugural balls.

The White House is never truly quiet, but this evening the top floors are quieter than I remember. No sound of my father or mother, just me. In the place of forty-five men before me.

Jack is sniffing around like there's no tomorrow as I head to the Lincoln Bedroom, the room I've chosen to stay in. "Welcome to the White House, buddy. Like Truman said, the great white jail."

Crossing the room, I stare out the window at the acres of land surrounding the White House, the District still foggy and cold outside.

Ready to go see her, I shower and change for tonight's inaugural balls. My hands easily working on my cufflinks as I think about finally, finally looking into her beautiful blue eyes again.

"You miss her?"

Jack raises his head from where he was watching me from the foot of the bed. As if there is only one *her* in the whole goddamn world.

I smile, then I reach down and I stroke the top of his head while I reach for the tuxedo jacket. "I miss her too." I shove my arms into the sleeves, then glance down at him. "We won't have to miss her for long."

Charlotte

"**L**adies and gentlemen, the President of the United States!!"

I almost spill my drink when the announcement echoes across the ballroom.

I stand with Alison, who's thrilled to be one of the White House photographers. While she was snapping pictures of the partygoers, I was mingling by her side, a drink in hand, when those words rang out.

And if someone had just grabbed a bat and smashed the air out of my lungs, I would absolutely believe it.

This is the smallest ball among all five being held tonight. Everyone expected the president to make it to the other grand balls first. I was barely prepared to see him—I'd only drunk one glass of wine so far!—and now he's *here*.

Oh god.

I'm ten times more nervous than all the women in the room. Hundreds of them, all important, highly intelligent or highly beautiful women, all tittering excitedly as Matt Hamilton, *my* Matt Hamilton, walks into the room.

Um. No. He's not yours, Charlotte, so you'd better stop feeling possessive over the man.

But I can't help it.

The sight of him makes me yearn to be walking by his side, with my arm hooked into his, no matter how ludicrous the idea is. It was one thing looking at him at a podium. Farther away.

But it's another thing being in the room he's now occupying.

In a tux.

A hot black tux.

So much closer to me than he's been in two months.

I can almost smell him, expensive and clean and male.

Alison is snapping pictures at my side.

Snap, snap, snap.

Matt takes over the room with his long, confident walk, briskly greeting those who greet him. Is he taller today? He really is towering over everyone. And are his shoulders broader? He looks so much larger than life. His very posture and stride that of a man who knows the whole world revolves around him. Which wouldn't be entirely false.

"You know what I like about Matt? That he actually backs up the hotness with brains," she says, making an *O* with her mouth and exhaling, then licking her lips with a mischievous sparkle in her eye. "Yum."

Before I realize what I'm doing, I'm licking my lips too. *I really need to never do that again.*

Alison shifts positions to capture a dozen different shots—not only of Matt but of people's awed and ecstatic reactions to him.

His eyes are sparkling as he greets one person after the next. They crinkle at the corners when he smiles, and I remember that crinkle. I remember the feel of the stubble on his jaw in the mornings even though his jaw is smooth and perfectly clean-shaven now, his lips curved upward.

His hair is combed back, his features chiseled and beautiful. My whole body spasms uncontrollably. It's as if every pore and every inch of me remembers him. Still wants him.

I lift my fingers to stroke the place where I used to wear his father's commemorative pin—but all I touch is my bare skin, revealed by the long, strapless gown I'm wearing.

My heart thuds crazily as he continues greeting the people he passes, approaching where I stand with my drink frozen in my hand. He looks so happy. My stomach clutches with a mix of emotions. Happiness, yes. But his presence is also a reminder of what I'd lost.

Did I lose him?

He was never really mine.

But I was all his. His to take. Body and soul. And I would have done anything he wanted me to. But I've tried to regain my sense of self. While traveling through Europe, I've tried to see the reasons why it could never have worked, among them that I'm inexperienced and young and not the kind of woman a president needs. I am not ready for what he is. No matter how much I wish I were older, more experienced, more fit to be by his side.

Not that he wanted me there.

I am torn when the crowd keeps parting and he keeps advancing.

"I'm going to the restroom," I breathe, and I head off, wondering why I came here. Why I said yes. It was his important day. I didn't want to miss it. But it hurts anew, as if today were the day he was elected, the day I walked away from him—booked a flight to Europe and spent two months there with Kayla, freezing our asses off, drinking hot chocolate. I came back in time for his inauguration—I could not miss it.

But landing in the USA felt bittersweet—it's the home I love, where I was born and want to die, and fell in love, but also the country that's led by the man I love and am trying desperately to get over.

So I steal into the ladies' room to find it vacant. And I just look at myself in the mirror—and whisper, "Breathe." I shut my eyes, lean forward, and breathe again. Then I open my eyes. "Now get out there, and say hello to him, and smile."

It's the hardest thing I've ever told myself to do.

But I exit the room, and watch him with every step I take as I head back to the crowd—everyone waiting to greet him. To be greeted. Acknowledged.

Alison spots me and snaps my picture. "You've got it bad. Can't say I blame you," she says.

"I don't want to," I whisper.

She smiles and continues snapping pictures.

I drink him up like a starved woman, six feet plus of pure fantasy, all packaged in a real man—beautiful beyond belief. So beautiful, I can't believe beauty like that exists.

And then he's three steps closer, his voice so near. "Thanks for coming."

Two steps. "Good to see you."

One step.

I try to smile when he stops before me, towering over me, dark and gorgeous. Everyone is holding their breath. A silence settles over the room. I blink in disbelief.

Matt Hamilton.

God. He looks hot as sin, his eyebrows slanted as he looks piercingly into my eyes, a half smile playing on his beautiful lips—lips that are full and lush, and very, very wicked.

There's a catch in my breath, and so much pride welling in my chest as I duck my head in a slight nod.

"Mr. President."

He reaches out to take my hand in his grasp, his fingers sliding over mine.

"It's good to see you." His voice is especially low.

I remember him telling me he'd get hard when I called him Mr. President, and now I can't stop blushing. But it's not like I'm going to bring it up now.

His fingers are warm and strong. His grip just right.

His hand *so* right.

We're not even shaking hands. He's practically holding my hand. And every part of me remembers this hand. This touch on me.

When he lowers my hand to my side, he slips something into my palm and ducks to murmur in my ear, "Be discreet," and I grip what feels like a small piece of paper in my fist as he proceeds to greet the other guests.

Slack-jawed, I watch him retreat, then I discreetly open the paper. It reads:

10 minutes
South exit
up the elevator
take the double doors down the hall.

He's expecting me.

I count the minutes as the live performance by Alicia Keys begins, and Matt opens up the dance floor with his mother.

The most handsome president I've ever beheld.

Where did he learn how to dance like that?

I'm holding a glass of wine as I watch him twirl her on the dance floor. She's laughing, looking younger than her years, though the pain in her eyes never really fades. Matt is grinning down at her, trying his damnedest to relieve that pain.

I love this stupid man so much I want to punch something.

When the dance ends, other couples join, and I see Matt —who's still causing titters in the room—excuse himself from his mother and head out a different exit than the one he indicated for me.

He's tugging on his cufflinks as he crosses the room, his agents already moving at the sides of the room, toward the same exit, and I set my wine aside. I'm telling myself it's no good—that if I go there, it'll just be to get my heart broken a thousand times again. But a part of me … just doesn't care.

This is Matt.

I crossed an ocean to forget him, but I'd swim across thousands for this man.

My heart will always beat for him.

The heart that had to put a whole ocean between us for fear of seeking him out.

The heart that beats like a mad thing in my chest as I go meet him.

I follow instructions to the *T*. I spot Wilson outside the room, along with an army of other agents of the Secret Service.

Wilson whispers something into his receiver as he nods at me and reaches for the doorknob.

"Hi, Wilson."

"Miss Wells." He nods briefly as he opens the door. "The president is inside."

"Thank you."

I suppose my heart is whacking so loudly because I'm seeing him again, and also because I don't know what to expect.

I walk into the room, the door shutting with a soft click behind me.

The air is sucked out of me as if by a vacuum.

A Hamilton vacuum.

It feels as if the whole room is just a backdrop for him. He's so … imposing. Electrifying. I have eyes only for the tall, dark-haired, broad-shouldered man at its center. His stance confident but easy, one hand inside the pocket of his slacks. The bow tie he wears is perfect. Even his hair is perfect, not a strand out of place, and I ache to run my fingers through it.

But inside his eyes there is a whole universe, dark and endless, an intensity in his gaze that pulls at every fiber of my being as he slowly drinks me in—every inch of me in this dress, from my eyes, to my nose, to my lips, my throat, my shoulders, my chest, my abdomen, down my legs.

It's hard to speak. The way he's looking at me is thawing my resolve to be strong, and I need to pull his attention away from stripping me naked with his eyes. "Being president looks good on you," I can't help but say, because as he undresses me with his eyes, I sort of get an eyeful of him too. His athletic, muscular frame and how the tux hugs his shoulders.

At my words, Matthew's eyes leisurely trek back to my face to lock on mine again. He responds simply, his voice as deep as I remember, the tone firm and completely unapologetic. "You're beautiful."

I inhale sharply, his words like a punch at the very core of my being. Warmth blooms in my cheeks. It's as if he's lit me up, this man. And nothing I do can dampen the fire he ignites in me. "I didn't go into this for a happily ever after," I whisper.

"But you deserve a happily ever after."

Matt is not smiling. His eyes are dark and somber as he continues to stare at me intently. "I've stayed away from you," he says, taking a step, withdrawing his hand from his pocket.

"I've noticed." My voice sounds raw, and I'm so overcome with his presence as he prowls around the room that I drop my eyes, my emotions all over the place. I raise them after a second and meet his unflinching gaze—which he hasn't removed from me. Not for a second. "Is it getting easier for you?" I ask.

"Fuck no. It's taking everything in me not to touch you right now."

He drags a restless hand over his face, a tinge of regret in his voice as he stops a few feet away. "Being with me could hurt you—you know that's why you wanted me to stay away. You know that if I'm with you, I'm going to hurt you even when that won't be my intention. Not at all. I know that wasn't my father's intention when he hurt my mother for years."

"Seeing you is hurting me now."

He clamps his jaw, then reaches out to tilt my head back. "Look at me," he says, his voice gruff and low, his dark gaze carving into me. "I can't give you what you deserve. I can't give you a house and I can't even take you out on a normal date. But I want you. I fucking need you in my life, Charlotte."

His touch is making my knees quake. I breathe, "I've accepted that I can't have more and that's okay with me. It's not worth it. You're doing more important things than being with me."

He frowns thoughtfully as he curls his hand and drags his knuckles down my cheek, grazing my skin. "The bigger risk is you getting hurt because I can't give you what you need. But I want to. I want to give you everything."

I battle a tremor, lick my lips nervously, craving more of his touch, more words, more Matt. "That's not why I came here. I want you to have the best presidency, and I wanted you to know I'm okay that this is over between us."

"I don't want this to be over." His eyes glimmer mercilessly as he drops his hand and just looks down at me. "I'm fucking selfish. I want you all to myself. Jesus! Every day, I wonder what you're doing, who you're talking to, who you're smiling at, and I want it to be me."

"I don't want this to be over either. But it has to, Matt."

He shakes his head, smiling ruefully. "It doesn't have to. Fuck trying to stay away from you. That's not what I want. What do you want from me? Do you want this?"

"What's 'this'?" I ask uncertainly.

"Everything."

My stomach feels as if I'm riding a roller coaster, so many dips and tugs I can't stand still as Matt waits for my answer.

I've never been able to lie to him, and I don't think I ever will be. "I don't want you to stay away from me."

"I asked you a question. Do you want everything I can give you?"

God. The pull he has on me, his magnetism tugging at me. The pain in his eyes only reminding me of my own.

He's the president now, but he's still Matt. My first crush, my first love. And I know that after Matt, I'll never want or love another man again.

"I don't know what 'everything' means. I want to start slowly," I begin.

"How slowly?"

"*Slow*, Matthew," I say.

He exhales, his eyes softening.

"It's too much. *You're* too much," I groan. "But I don't care about anything else. I don't want you to stay away from me."

His gaze is alive with heat as he gazes down at me.

"I just don't see how this can even work without a media explosion I don't want," I add. "It's too close to the campaign —people will think we had an affair all that time."

"We did."

I feel my cheeks heat at both the memory and the gruffness in his voice.

The times I spent with him are too valuable to me to willingly give them up as fodder to the media. "Yes, but those were *our* moments." I flush even more at the look in his eyes, as if he remembers too. "I don't want the world to use them against you. Or me."

He's silent for a moment, simply staring at me, everything about him making my mouth water—his achingly familiar espresso eyes, warm and liquid as he looks down at me. And when he lifts his hand to hold me by the chin, my whole body jerks in response. Wanton. Aching. Swaying toward him. "Come to the White House. Be my acting first lady," he says, his voice husky.

"Matt, I couldn't possibly."

"You can very possibly."

I'm stunned to realize he means it—his eyes steely with determination and certainty.

"You can do whatever you want with the role, it's self-defined."

"But your mother would be so much better at it," I insist.

"And yet I've got my eye on you for the part."

"Why?"

That lovely playful sparkle I remember so well appears in his eyes again. "Because you look good on my arm."

"Haha." I'm suddenly smiling, I can't help it.

His lips are curved too, but his stare is deathly serious. "Because I can't see any other woman standing next to me. And because no one could do the job that you could."

My heart flips in my chest.

"We'll figure this out. You try the role on for size. Let me date you out in the public eye without hiding this time. We'll take it as slow as you need."

"The media will begin to speculate."

"They can speculate all they like. As acting first lady you sleep in the White House, you're on the president's arm, and you can do so many things, Charlotte. I want to see you spread your wings and fly high, and I want to give you the platform to do it."

"I don't see myself as one of those ladies. I'm not posh enough."

"You're a countess; your grace is innate."

"Stop flirting with me. You're a cad, Mr. President."

He laughs, and I scowl, and then he reaches out. "I'll take this"—he leans over and pecks my lips—"as a yes." He sets his forehead on mine. "A team will stop by to get your belongings, set them all in your room in the White House, and your new detail will pick you up tomorrow and bring you here."

"I can't move, Matthew—"

"Listen, I know you don't want a media circus outside your apartment building every day for four years. I want you to be safe, and you're safer with me."

"I ..." I can't even think of an argument, and I definitely don't think my neighbors deserve a media circus and Secret Service around 24/7. "Well, see, that's something I really don't need, a detail—"

He interrupts me as he crosses the room to leave. "We can talk more tomorrow. Expect them early."

I watch him step outside to a trail of Secret Service agents behind him. I stay back for bit until he disappears out the door

—and, it seems, until that moment when I can finally breathe. When I start to follow, he suddenly fills the doorway again.

"I forgot something—wait a minute."

He pulls me back into the room, and then his lips are pressing firmly down on mine. I gasp at the contact, having missed it too much. *Him* too much. His taste, the way his tongue massages mine. And it's massaging mine so wickedly as I open up instinctively, a moan leaving me and muffled by him as our tongues rub, tangle, twirl. Taste. Taste. Oh god, his taste. It's divine ecstasy when he kisses me. Impulsively. Ravenously.

Head slanting, going as deep as he can go in the precious minute the kiss lasts. He groans as he pulls back, my face engulfed by both his warm hands as he drops his forehead on mine, his tone fierce.

"This isn't over yet."

"Matt—"

"It's not over."

Trying to pretend that a thousand and one things didn't just awaken in my stomach, I push at his chest, urging him out the door. He doesn't budge.

He takes a long moment to look down at my kissed lips—at me. In the way only he sees me, as if he knows my every dream and fear and nightmare, and all I have been and will ever be.

As if he knows that I … was and am and will always be his.

He smiles, and after one last glance at my wet lips, he steps out and leaves me with knees that just turned to putty.

"Mr. President," says Wilson as Matt buttons his jacket, which I seemed to cause to come loose.

Matthew just nods and strides confidently down the hall with the men after him.

"Jackie Kennedy, Princess Diana—all young and beautiful and loved."

"I just cannot believe you're comparing me to them," I tell Kayla as she sits on my small couch that night.

"Why?"

"I don't see myself like one of them. I don't know the first thing about it. I'm not my mother—it's easy for her, smooth-talking, cool, and collected. My palms sweat, thinking of all these important people looking for reasons why I don't fit the part."

"You *are* the part. The president has asked you. The people have been fascinated by you and Matt since the whole campaign began. You go out there and show them Matt was right in picking you. He's an intelligent man; let them see what he sees."

I exhale.

"You don't need to do it all at once," she says.

"Oh, I'm definitely not doing it all at once. Small steps. Jessa would tell me that when I was little. Small steps take you farther, and one at a time."

She continues gaping across the room, clearly still mind-blown. "Wow. God, I still can't believe it."

"Don't tell Sam, or Alan, anyone, until he makes the official announcement, please."

"Of course."

I stare out the window, as mind-blown as she. I wanted a man to love and to make a difference. Does this mean I can have both?

Why is it that when the opportunity finally comes, the fear is so great, you almost want to back down?

"Whenever you doubt whether you belong there, know that you do. Jackie and Di. Both very beloved. They brought something new, something you cannot buy with experience. Tell yourself, Charlotte, 'I have been asked by the president to be his acting first lady. And I've accepted.'"

I swallow, nodding. I've missed him too much. I'd do anything to be close to him. Anything. They say to grow as a person you need to challenge yourself, go for something higher, something that you might fail at, even.

There is nothing higher or greater for me than this.

To try to be with the man I love, no matter how big he is, how grand, how larger than life. Try to make a difference, not a small one, but one that reaches across cities, states, continents.

Oh god.

I'm going to be Matthew Hamilton's acting first lady.

I'm afraid of it, and at the same time, I'm scared of how much I want it. To be his true first lady. His only love. His girl, his wife, just ... *his*. His in public, his at night, his every morning, his by right.

Is he thinking he wants something like that in the future? *Everything* ... he said.

But I don't want to ask what he meant yet. Because ... baby steps. I cannot handle more right now.

I don't sleep that night. I lie awake in bed in my small apartment, touching my lips. Squeezing my eyes shut as all the memories come washing down on me. As Matt's eyes come back to haunt me. Matt telling me he wants me at the White House. Matt once telling me of the woman he'll settle down with someday:

"One day I'll do all the things I need to. And she'll be mine. Mark my words."
"Does she know this yet?" I ask, quietly.
"I just told her," he says.

Warmth races through my bloodstream as I remember. I want to prove myself worthy. That I deserve to be there. That I deserve to be the woman by Matt Hamilton's side.

I know it won't be easy, winning the public. But I know that despite the fear, the uncertainty, the self-doubt, I am still that girl. The one who wants to make a difference. The one who offered to help him with his campaign. The one who fell irrevocably in love with him.

THE OVAL

Matt

I
f you want to make a difference, you need to start today.

Four years sounds like a lot, eight an eternity, but it's really not. I learned that from my father. Things that were postponed never got done. Changes never set in motion remained stagnant, dead dreams never to be fulfilled, not with the new management and every president having his own agenda.

I tackle confidential information for the entire night, reading—sometimes filled with respect for my predecessors and the calls they made, sometimes with disgust. A lot of times, all I can really say is *fuck*.

I meet with my chief of staff, several issues on the board.

I meet with my press secretary, Lola Stevens, and strategize for a press conference tomorrow when I will introduce Charlotte to the world.

"I want the drafts for the Clean Energy bill. The Healthcare bill to fix what's broken in our healthcare system. I want to look into a bill for equal pay and opportunity for working mothers," I tell Dale as we head down the halls of the West Wing to the Cabinet Room—I walk inside, and everybody stands. "Good morning," I tell my cabinet members.

"Mr. President."

"Good morning, Mr. President," Vice President Louis Frederickson greets me.

I chose him as my running mate because he's honest, humble, no-nonsense, and a no-kiss-ass kind of man—exactly what we need to get real changes in our country.

I take my seat, then glance at the press corps standing behind the members of my cabinet.

"This meeting will be closed to all members of the press," I say.

"A quick picture, Mr. President?" one coaxes.

"We have work to do here. But I'm aware, so do you. Make it fast, guys," I say as I flip to the first page of the thick file before me, an identical one seated before each cabinet member.

Flashes erupt for the next ten seconds, and then Dale opens the door.

"That's enough," he says, waving them out.

The door shuts and I look at all the members of my cabinet, letting the taste of the silence sink in.

"We're going to have so much work, there'll be days when we sleep very little, eat very little, and can think of very little else but the things we're going to do. I want to be sure everyone understands, I'm taking no prisoners for the next four years. What I aim to do is vast, extensive, and very concrete. Let's get started, then." I slip on my glasses, take a sip of my water, and we begin

WHITE HOUSE

Charlotte

There is a majesty about the White House that envelops you even from miles away. Today, though, I cannot help but be overwhelmed by its size, its splendor, its very whiteness as I'm led by my new chief of staff, Clarissa Sotomayor, into the White House and along the second floor of the residence—more specifically, to my bedroom. If being transferred from my apartment to the White House in a black car by men with guns wasn't enough to blow my mind, walking down the White House's endless wings certainly is.

I'm going to be the youngest first lady in history—as Matt is the youngest POTUS in history. Speaking to Kayla about Jackie and Lady Di last night, I sort of blow my *own* mind that I'm even comparing myself to these women—is this really my life?

I'm in love with the president, for god's sake!

And Matthew asked me to be here, asked to see me, asked me to take on this role.

It's actually happening—and I can hardly believe that it is.

It's barely after lunch, and *here* I am.

"And this will be your bedroom," Clarissa declares as she swings the door open.

My jaw just ...

Drops.

I didn't have to lift a finger—every one of my belongings that I wanted to take was transferred from my "shitty, unsafe" apartment (as my mother called it) to the secure, huge, and glamorous White House.

To this room.

My room.

My room in the *White House*.

"Charlotte, are you sure about this?" my mother asked this morning.

"Yes," I lied, as I packed, nervous, excited, knowing only that I'd do anything to make a difference, and that this is the best chance I'll ever get to make a mark. Knowing, also, that I'll do anything for *him*—to be close to him.

As I spoke, I was fully aware of a group of Secret Service agents, my new detail, outside my door.

"Charlotte," my mother said tearfully.

"Don't tell anyone yet, not until the president gives the press conference."

She hesitated. "I don't know if I'm terribly proud or terribly concerned right now."

"It's okay, you can be both." I exhaled. "I won't disappoint you."

"You never could."

Oh yes, I thought to myself, *I could*, but I didn't want to think of the one selfish act that, if discovered, could have shamed my mother terribly. The one thing I took for myself, without concern for anyone else. The affair I had with Matthew Hamilton before he became president. I was so afraid of a scandal.

I still am. He made it clear from the start that he didn't want a family, and I'm not sure I'll bear my heart getting broken twice. Still, not for a second would I think of denying him. I guess I'm hoping.

Hoping we can make things work. Hoping that maybe … I belong here. Determined to try.

Matt began his presidency without a wife. I know his greatest fear is not being able to have both, and he sacrificed his personal needs for those of his country. I admire him for it. If he can put his country first, so can I.

We can take things slow. I can try this role on for size—and even though it already feels gargantuan, I'm excited. The only other time I've ever been this excited was when he asked me to join his campaign.

But for slow, things sure are moving fast. The Secret Service at my door, very early this morning. Now here I am, inhaling as I take in the room.

"It's the Queens' Bedroom," she explains.

I clear my throat as I take in the luxurious bedroom before me. Oh god, the man I love is … *sleeping somewhere near. Night after night after night.*

"The president will be right across the hall. His chief of staff asked me to take you to see him, once you were ready."

I inhale, stepping into my room in the most photographed residence in the land, overwhelmed, happy, honored … and afraid that I won't be able to fit the shoes of all the first ladies before me. I set my things down, then I look at Clarissa and smile, nodding, terribly humbled as I stride down the long, busy halls and toward the West Wing.

"Miss Charlotte Wells, here to see the president," Clarissa tells Matt's assistant. She worked with us on the campaign, but she was stationed in San Francisco and I didn't have the opportunity to talk to her. I say hello now, and she smiles and quickly steps away from her desk.

"He's expecting you. I'm Portia. It's very nice to meet the first lady."

"Thank you." I'm a little light-headed. She opens the door of the Oval Office after a few raps.

I gulp as I see the regal curtains framing the windows at the end. And the desk.

And ... Matt. In a suit.

I walk into the Oval. Matt stands leaning on his desk, arms crossed, while five other men and his chief of staff are there. I spot Hessler and Carlisle among the group, and I smile, my eyes sliding back helplessly to a pair of dark espresso ones.

"Charlotte," he greets, his lips curving.

"Mr. President."

"So nice to see this lady right here." Carlisle gives me a brief hug, and Hessler a nod and a rare smile, before Matt motions with his head and they all start leaving.

The door shuts, and I'm alone with him.

With *him*.

And he is everything.

All of him.

All of this place. This room.

He smiles a little. "Welcome home, beautiful."

I swallow. I laugh, aware of his eyes sort of quietly, intensely caressing me. "This room is bigger than I imagined."

He just smiles at me, motioning to the sitting area. I follow and sit across from him, licking my lips nervously.

"I'm so happy to see Carlisle and Hessler. I thought you'd ask Carlisle to be your chief of staff?" I breathe.

"I did. He declined due to health. Besides, he likes campaigning. He wants to be ready in four years when we run again." His voice so close is soothing, yet quietly arousing, too. "He's part of my kitchen cabinet—him, Beckett, and Hessler."

"Hessler won't be joining you either?"

"He wanted experience before attacking the position of chief of staff himself. They both seem more inclined to be ready for when I run again in four years." There's a trace of laughter in his voice. "I know—seems so far away. But that's the way their minds are working."

"How do you feel, Matthew?"

"Ready. I'm ready." His expression stills and grows serious, and he glances around the Oval, at the George Washington portrait, then at me. "I'm making big changes and it's going to take time, but I'm getting them done no matter what I have to do." He frowns, his eyes level under drawn brows. "How do *you* feel?"

"Scared. Happy. *Scared*," I repeat, laughing. Then I shrug, and meet his watchful, intent gaze. "I couldn't sleep, thinking of this opportunity. I want to open the White House a bit more, for citizens to experience it in a different way, not just as a museum they walk into. I'd like to do things for women and children, too."

"Do it," he says, no questions asked.

"Okay. I will." I exhale, smiling. "I'm excited. So many things I want to do, I don't know where to start."

"Are you all right so far? Do you need anything?"

I shake my head. "All this is so much more than I need."

"I want you to feel at home."

"I'm trying." I shoot him an honest smile. "I don't want to make a mistake when it's simply too easy to make one ... All this is too new. So I'll just take it one day at a time."

Matt smiles. "When you love something as much as you love our country, you take care of it—you do anything for it. I have no doubt in my mind I've picked the right first lady."

I'm flushing. Head to toe.

He sets his elbows on his knees as he shifts forward. "I hope you know, baby, asking you to act as first lady is not only an excuse for me to see you. I believe you have a lot to offer our citizens. Regardless of our relationship, I want you to have a salary, and you will be directly compensated for your time by me," Matt says.

"What? I couldn't possibly." I shake my head. "I don't want a salary."

"Everyone working here has a salary—except the first lady. Is that fair?" He grins.

"I wasn't elected to office."

"Not everyone here was elected."

I look around, awed by the sumptuous surroundings, the plush upholstered couch beneath me, and I glance at Matt. "I get to do what I most want, sleep safe in the grandest home in the land," *close to you*, I don't add. "I don't want a salary. If you insist, then we can donate it to Women of the World, help women who can't find jobs get on their feet."

"All right then." He smiles his mercurial smile, one that makes his chiseled face look even more handsome.

I wring my hands. "I never slept with you to get a position in the White House."

"I know. I need trustworthy people on my team, and I trust you."

"Thank you, Mr. President."

"Matt," he says softly.

I smile, but I can't say it.

"I rather like the sound of Mr. President on your lips." His smile curves a bit more. "But I miss hearing you say my name."

"Don't," I whisper. "Matt."

"Come here, baby." He pats his side.

I swallow, rising to my feet and crossing the room to take a seat beside him.

He reaches out and slips his fingers into the fall of my hair at the back of my neck, seizing me gently as his dark gaze holds mine in its grip, his forehead to mine. "I'll give you time to get used to all this, but I want to make it clear that you're still mine. You never stopped being mine, and you never will," he says.

A promise.

A promise I'm afraid to believe for fear of losing him— never really having him, like before.

I inhale deeply, breathing him in, letting everything Matt surround me, when I feel him tug me closer and brush my lips with his.

I gasp, and Matt flicks his tongue out to taste me.

I groan. Matt groans too and slides his arm around me, taking my mouth fiercely. He pours every ounce of fire into that kiss—his lips the flame, his tongue the accelerant, and I feel the burn. I feel the burn at the tips of my nipples, my fingers, my toes. At the center of my being.

I'm breathing in fast, shallow breaths when we ease apart. "What are we doing here?" I ask, breathless.

He frowns. "Are you asking me or are you asking yourself?"

"Myself. I think. Because I can't stay away from you."

"I can't stay away from you either."

"We said slow."

"This … is slow." He cups my face and kisses me again, his tongue plunging into my mouth. "I missed you. See, two months without you was two months too long. I don't want another day where I don't see this face. That smile. It has to be here somewhere." He peers down at my lips, tugging the corners with his thumbs.

"Matt, stop."

He smiles as I laugh softly—and his smile begins to fade.

The way he stares at my mouth makes me tremble deep inside.

A quiet intensity creeps into his eyes—and they blaze with heat. With emotion. With a possessiveness I've never, ever seen there to this degree. Until now. Sixty-eight days after seeing him last.

Sixty-eight days where I thought I couldn't even breathe knowing I'd lost him. That I could never, ever have him.

My sex ripples.

I groan and I pull him close as he gathers me in his arms.

His mouth is hot and wet and more possessive than it's ever been, fitting perfectly over mine.

He pulls me closer. I'm shivering on his lap, wanting him to never take his mouth away.

I'm a normal girl. One who fell in love when she shouldn't have. I'm a daughter, a friend, a working girl. I know my name, somewhere in the back of my mind, but I can't really remember it. Not now, when the heat of his mouth is working over mine.

We're starved for each other. My nails sink into the muscles of his back.

Matt's body shifts beneath me, hard, as he runs his hands over my body as if memorizing every contour, squeezing and shaping my every muscle.

"I want you in the White House. I want you wherever I am." He's breathing hard, his voice thick. I'm panting as I kiss his jaw, missing this, missing *him.*

"I want you coming all over the president's cock, you little wanton. You delicious little kitten, huh."

He palms my sex, stroking a finger along my opening over the fabric of my slacks. I mewl softly, grabbing his hard shoulders for support. "Don't …" I warm as pleasure shoots across my body—through every nerve and muscle and atom. "I want you … too much …" A groan leaves me.

He smiles and kisses me a little harder and doesn't stop. He rubs me over my slacks a little faster. I clutch my arms tighter around his neck and push my hips up to his hand, losing it.

"Who are you coming for? Huh? Tell me now," he presses.

I tell him who.

The president of the United States.

My love.

PRESS CONFERENCE

Charlotte

There's excitement in the air of the White House press room as Matt addresses the reporters. Several dozen flashes snap as he stands at the podium.

"I realize this is a little unorthodox. Usually the president of the United States is married, which I'm not, or has a close family member acting as first lady; in my case that also won't be the case. I've asked a woman whom I've come to deeply respect and admire for many reasons—among them, her passion for this country that equals mine, and a heart as big as that smile she's now wearing. Ladies and gentlemen, may I present the Acting First Lady of the United States of America, Charlotte Wells."

Breathe, breathe, breathe.

Matt motions me to the podium.

Cameras keep snapping. I marvel that I can walk—with Matt's direct gaze on me, with the whole room's eyes on me. I marvel how I can act composed. How I can manage to open my mouth and say what I rehearsed with Lola, the press secretary, just an hour ago.

"Thank you, Mr. President." I inhale his scent as he passes me, and I cling to it for strength. I make eye contact with as many sitting reporters as possible even though it makes me doubly nervous. "I'm honored to be standing here. I'm not ashamed to admit when Matt—the president—asked me to take on this task, I didn't think I could possibly say yes. Turns out it's not easy to decline the president, especially this one …"

I shoot him a look, and when he raises one eyebrow, there's laughter, and my nerves start easing.

"And although I still feel completely undeserving to be standing here, I will do my best and more than that to represent our country as best I can and do justice to President Hamilton's presidency. Thank you."

Applause. *"Miss Wells—!"*

"Miss Wells, could you give us any specifics on the kind of relationship you and the president—"

Lola takes my place behind the podium and murmurs, "No questions at this time, thank you."

And with that, she wraps up the press conference and I follow Matt out of the room.

"That went well, Miss Wells! Now if you'll review the schedule—Oh! Mr. President."

My chief of staff steps back when she realizes Matt is still there, and we walk together down the hall, his gaze on *his* chief of staff, who seems to be waiting for him at the end.

"You looked great out there." His eyes slide to mine.

The impact of feeling his eyes on me never seems to diminish.

"Probably because I was standing next to you."

"Trust me, I had nothing to do with it." His eyes start twinkling.

"I expected a little booing, really. But they love you so much that anything you do, they'd agree with."

"No, they wouldn't." His eyes rove over my features. "But whoever said Americans don't have exquisite taste was very, very wrong." He raises both his brows meaningfully, and even that maddening smile he wears, just a little arrogant, is sexy beyond belief.

There's so much intimacy in his gaze, I'm transported to our nights together—his kisses, his words.

I want him to touch me. I want to touch him. But something as simple as a touch would cause an uproar and a scandal—that's not what we want his first months in the White House to be about.

He leaves me with a smile and heads off, his chief of staff already listing a thousand things on his plate, and I sort of have trouble moving my eyes away from his retreating back—and how well he looks in that suit—to the woman before me.

"So if you'd like to review your duties as first lady," she's saying as she leads me to my wing, "it's really up to you how much you want to get involved, but if you'd like to be very active, there's always the menus to look at, the social events to plan and host ..."

Waiting naked in the president's bedroom, I think to myself, aware of a warmth flooding my cheeks as I do. No. That can come later. We need to be sure about what we're doing first.

I don't want to fail this country, or my parents, or myself. Or Matt.

I sleep alone in the Queens' Bedroom. So aware of Matt—the president—just across the hall. I hear him walk into his room late at night. I tiptoe to my door, sort of listening as I decide whether I should go see him.

Touch him. Kiss him.

I'm pressing my ear to the door when I hear footsteps approach.

My breath catches, and I quickly hurry back to my bed and slip under the covers as the door opens. Matt looms in my doorway. I hear the door click shut and his figure walking in the shadows.

I prop myself up on my arms, alarmed. "You can't spend the night—the staff will talk, and it's too soon to give the media the gossip-fest they'll get with this."

He lowers himself into a chair by the window, feet away from the bed.

I frown. "What are you doing?"

"Looking at you."

TODAY SHOW

Charlotte

"*T*oday we are honored to welcome the first lady on the Today Show, *Miss Charlotte Wells!*

"*Miss Wells, you were surprised when President Hamilton asked you to act as first lady?*"

"*Very.*"

"*Why were you surprised?*"

"*I don't own a pretty pair of white gloves.*"

Laughter.

"*The country was feeling pretty disappointed when hopes of a romance between then candidate Hamilton and yourself seemed dispelled. Any dirty secrets between yourself and President Hamilton, breadcrumbs for the crowd?*"

"*Oh, I do have a few. Mainly I just like looking at him. In a very professional way.*"

Laughter.

"*You're very refreshing. And President Hamilton seems to enjoy looking back at you, Miss Wells. Here's for us to keep hoping.*"

A hot little blush runs up my body as I think of last night. I slept like a baby, feeling him close. Though I woke up to find his chair empty, I could smell him on my pillow. And I wonder if he spooned me during the night.

"I'm fully committed to my role as first lady, as he is to being the president," I force myself to say.

I go out of the filming studio to screams and placards raised.

I laugh and wave, biting back a smile as I'm led to the car by Stacey, one of the agents appointed to protect me.

She climbs into the back of the car with me and we head off in one of the presidential limos.

"What just happened?" I ask her.

"You're America's sweetheart. They love you, miss."

"Charlotte," I correct. I stare wide-eyed out the window, never having imagined the people would embrace me like this.

Matt

"The first lady on the *Today Show*," Dale says.

I walk forward, lean on the couch, and watch her.

"She's the darling of the country," Dale adds.

I watch the TV as she blows them away, every single person she walks by. "Look at you," I purr.

GLOVES

Charlotte

I received a book with the pictures and names of everyone working in the White House—it's a security measure, I was told, in case I spot someone who seems unfamiliar—and I've been poring over the book to be sure I know them all.

I'm eyeing it a second time the next morning when I hear Clarissa's voice at my East Wing office door.

"The president sent this."

She's holding a silver box with a white ribbon.

I feel my lips part involuntarily.

I resist the urge to tear into the package. That's just not how a first lady would act. So I stand up and accept the box, then set it on my desk and open it carefully, removing the ribbon, unfolding every corner of the wrapping, and lifting the lid.

Inside are two beautiful elbow-length white satin gloves.

In all seriousness?

I've never been so turned on. It's not the fact that he sent a gift that is sexy in itself, but the fact that he wants me to feel like I belong here. As his first lady.

I'm done. I'm a goner. Is it possible to fall in love with a man all over again? I think I just did. Even when I've never, for a moment, stopped loving him.

I spot him later that day as I head down the hall, trying to memorize where everything is and personally greet the staffers by name.

The sight of the tall, dark-haired man walking with an entourage of four men around him makes my heart stop in my chest.

He stops walking when he spots me, then plunges a hand into his slacks pocket, gives a half smile, and starts forward.

He's wearing his glasses.

My mouth is dry and the part between my thighs, way too wet.

"Charlotte. I'd like to invite you to dinner in the Old Family Dining Room tonight. If you wouldn't mind looking at the menu."

Our eyes meet, and I'm hot all over. "If I can *find* the dining room," I say.

Under the rim of those gold-rimmed Ray-Ban glasses, the smile touches his eyes. "Someone will make sure you do so."

"I know. They always do." I smile and glance around as the men wait in standby, and the staffers continue bustling past and carrying out their respective duties. "I'm actually supposed to go meet the chef this afternoon—I'm to review the menus for the week."

"That's very considerate of you, Miss Wells."

I know he's teasing me—and it feels good. I miss him. I want to flirt more. To talk and hear about everything he's doing. But now is not the time. "I feel so bad having so many people wait on us," I whisper.

His gaze turns somber. "They're trying to make our lives easier, get the little things perfect so we can focus on the big ones."

I nod, smiling. "I'll see you tonight."

He nods and heads to the West Wing.

The Old Family Dining Room, it turns out, is the smaller dining room in the White House, and I'm grateful to be seated at a normal-sized table that seats up to six—one from Matt's personal, more modern furniture collection. He sits at the head, my place setting to his right, and we dine on the White House chef's version of a personal favorite meal of mine.

"I wasn't sure what you liked, so I had them make Mom's special quinoa, which my mother and Jessa had made for you and your dad. The first time we met."

"I remember. You were a cute little thing. Full of fire."

"Full of fire for you," I mumble, rolling my eyes.

His eyes widen in surprise over my comment, and then a laugh rumbles up his chest, but that delicious laugh doesn't last long, and then he's frowning darkly. "You were too young, baby."

"With big feelings awakening," I groan, shaking my head over the pain he caused me and my "awakening" years.

He shoots me a chiding smirk, his gaze dropping to my lips.

"Matt ..." I breathe, recognizing the look in his eyes.

He leans forward, our eyes inches apart. His voice is so rough and raw it cuts me up on the inside. "I miss you. I miss touching you. I want to be able to kiss you anywhere, anytime I want."

My thighs press together under the table. "I want that too, but this is such a big change for me."

"Do I get a kiss for the gloves, at least?"

My body keeps tightening with yearning, but I manage to control myself and say, "Yes, but not here. Tonight when we're alone."

His eyes darken intensely. "Mmm. I look forward to that." He scoops an especially large forkful of quinoa into his mouth.

After dinner, we sit in the Yellow Oval Room on the second floor for drinks. He nods at Wilson in some sort of silent indication, and we get the privacy that we want as the agents scatter. I turn to Matt on the couch, his posture relaxed, but his gaze about as relaxed as an inferno in full blaze.

"Don't move," I warn. "It's just a little kiss. If you move then I won't be able to control myself."

His raspy laugh surrounds me. "Baby, I can't control myself when you look at me like that ..." He strokes his hand down my cheek, his stare crackling with raw intensity.

"*Shh.* Close your eyes."

I straddle him, and Matt slides his hands to cup my butt rebelliously but closes his eyes. And oh, how close I feel, how safe I feel, how *hot* I feel.

I look at his face and I feel like exploding from the inside out and imploding from the outside in. I love him so much. I trace his lips with my fingertip. He bites me. "Don't," I giggle.

He groans, his eyes still closed.

"Stay still," I say.

He stills, lips quirked.

I lean my head and press my lips to his. A thousand shots of lightning course through my veins when he parts his mouth. I lick into him, and his hands slide down the small of my back, grinding me to his hard cock as he plunges his wet tongue into my mouth. He holds my ass in both hands, and his touch sets the butterflies off in my stomach. Memories of us threaten to drown me—every moment, every kiss.

I link my hands behind his neck, and though Matt isn't moving, I feel his power, his hold on me and my heart.

"Thank you for my gloves," I say, breathless, as I ease back.

He smiles, shifting forward as I get up on trembling feet, his mouth red, his hair mussed. "You're welcome. Thank you for putting in all that effort for our dinner."

"I enjoyed it." I exhale. "I'd better go. We both need to be ready for tomorrow."

He just smiles, watching me in silence as I leave.

The French president is holding a state dinner in Matt's honor, and all the arrangements to my schedule were automatically made to be sure I could accompany him.

I'm excited, nervous, and still aroused from that silly little kiss.

So excited and aroused that I just can't sleep. I know that Matt doesn't sleep, because the door to his bedroom never shuts all night.

AIR FORCE ONE

Charlotte

The last time I crossed the Atlantic, it was to try to put distance between us. Today I'm crossing it by his side. We board Marine One on the South Lawn of the White House. The motorcade creates too much traffic for people's everyday commute.

Soon we reach the airport and are escorted to the long, open steps leading up to Air Force One, the American flag proudly on its tail.

The president motions me to go ahead, and my heart is pounding as I walk onto the biggest private plane I've ever beheld. It's beyond luxurious, tastefully decorated in beige tones and dark woods.

I wander down the hall and peer into the rooms and separate seating areas.

I can't believe we're on Air Force One. I'm sort of embarrassed by how blown away I feel and how calm everyone else seems as Matthew's staff heads to the main seating area. I try to keep a grip as I walk down the plane aisle when I notice Matt two steps behind me. He's wearing a navy-blue bomber jacket with the presidential seal and I want to rip it off him.

"Big change from our days campaigning, huh?" I whisper, eyeing everything with admiration, gasping when the rooms continue. "Oh god, it's like a hotel in the air, conference room, office …" I add. I open one door and gasp again. "Bedroom?" I ask him over my shoulder.

"Yep."

I walk in to see, and then I hear the door shut behind us.

I whirl around, and Matt is shrugging off his jacket.

I open my mouth but no words come out. The only things working really are my sexy parts, the flood of liquid heat between my thighs, the hard beads of my nipples pressing against the soft cashmere of my sweater and the lace of my bra.

Matt sees.

He *sees*—my pointed nipples, poking in salute, my breasts feeling sensitive, my cheeks flushing as I start to pant.

"I've got to get some work done. But nothing will get done until I do this."

The whispers trigger a tremor down my spine as he approaches.

Matt tugs his button-down shirt from the waistband of his slacks, and takes my hands and slides them up his chest. Then he steals his own under my cashmere sweater, pulling me flush to him—our fingers touching each other's bare skin. His eyes a whole world of fire.

"Your enthusiasm for all this affects me deeply, baby," he rasps, rubbing his thumb over my lower lip.

I moan in anticipation as he leans down and sets a kiss on my forehead. "I know we said slow. So I'm going to kiss you. Very, very slow. Because when you ooh and ahh all over Air Force One, and all over Élysée Palace when we arrive, I want you to have my taste in your mouth, and I want every ooh and ahh to taste like me," he rasps, and his lips slide, ever so slowly, torturously slowly, down my nose. My breath catches, and Matt inhales deeply, as if breathing me in, prolonging my torture and his own, before he whispers, "Now kiss me back, C, like you mean it. Like you miss me," as he presses his lips directly to my mouth.

I shudder at the contact, parting my mouth. Flicking my tongue out. Pressing closer to him. His groan is about as drugging as his kiss.

And his kiss.

It's not just drugging. It's soul-shattering, chest-imploding. Wet and *hard*. My hands are on his shoulders. His arm is sliding around my waist, pressing our upper halves flush. Our lips are fusing, moving, Matt's so strong and hungry.

He runs his tongue around mine, then suckles me into his mouth.

We kiss for what feels like forever and at the same time, not long enough. We ease apart, but Matt remains too close, intently looking down at me. I run my tongue over my lips, and they feel swollen and sensitive because of his kiss.

His gaze is hot, and god how I miss him.

Matt is gazing at me with eyes that look very dark.

He clenches his jaw. He uses his thumb to rub my lower lip and part it from the top.

I meet him halfway; I reach up and grab his hair, parting my mouth and flicking my tongue out.

I sink a little into his body, into his kiss.

He holds my face in one hand until he tears his lips away, glancing at my mouth. "If I don't stop now, everyone will know you've been kissed senseless."

He looks at my kissed lips with male pride and not one bit of apology.

I swallow, out of breath.

He slips his hand up my back, under my sweater, touching my bare skin.

I moan and leave my hands on his shoulders for a bit.

There's something predatory as he looks down at me, releasing me only when the pilots announce that we will be taking off shortly.

He grins. "Settle down somewhere for takeoff. Take a nap if you feel like it. I'm reviewing policy in the effort to enjoy you as much as possible in Paris."

I swallow as a bolt of excitement at the prospect rushes through me, and nod.

I find a place to sit and strap down, watching D.C. beneath us as we take off and cross the ocean, and for a strange reason, I feel humbled and undeserving to be flying here, with the president, the whole United States depending on us to represent our country the way it deserves.

I have no doubt Matt will—he does it effortlessly; he's got red, white, and blue in his veins. I'm just a girl who used to work at Women of the World, a senator's daughter who wanted to make a difference but never dreamed she could make one on this scale. And I'm faced with the doubts I suppose we're all faced with, wondering if we're enough, if we have the mettle to back up the shiny illusion of our best version of ourselves in our minds. But that's the point, isn't it? To try to chase it, even if it may always feel elusive.

Except this dream is too big for me to fail at. I want to be a great first lady; I want to be a great woman deserving of a great man. The man I love.

ÉLYSÉE PALACE

Charlotte

"*Président Hamilton!*"

We're greeted by the French paparazzi piling outside Élysée Palace, and inside the gates and out on the steps, the President and First Lady of France await us with a grand welcome and give us a tour of the palace. I walk along the gardens with the first lady as the presidents head to do state business and talk about the mutual problems we're facing—among them, ISIS. Once they're finished, Matt meets me and an usher leads us to our bedroom before the state dinner they're holding in his honor.

"President Hamilton, if you please, our grandest guest room." The usher motions for Matt to step inside, and adds, "And First Lady," nodding as he motions for me to follow Matthew, and then departs.

I feel the blood in my veins sizzle a little bit as the realization hits me.

Matt

Charlotte looks confused. She follows me inside and as soon as she walks in, I reach out with one arm and shut the door behind her.

"One room?" she asks.

"They don't need to know the details of our arrangement."

She scowls, possibly noticing how happy I am about this setup. I'm exhausted, but the thought of having her all to myself shoots pure adrenaline into my veins.

She changed on the plane. She's wearing a prim ivory-colored skirt and jacket, and the gloves I sent. I peel the glove off her right hand, exposing her fingers, and lift them to my mouth. I take her middle finger between my lips and teeth. I taste her. Suck gently. Watching her eyes shutter and her breasts rise as her breath catches. "I want you. Tell me you want me. You want this."

Her eyes glaze over.

"Tell me you miss this," I press.

"I …"

I don't let her find the words. Immediately I remove her other glove and lift her hand to my mouth. This time I drop a kiss in the center of her soft palm.

"You don't miss any of it?" My voice is hoarse from my need. "Not even this?" I lick her palm, then kiss the inside of her wrist. Nibbling and tasting her skin.

Her eyelids become heavy. Her pupils dilate as she watches me drag my lips all along the sensitive skin on the inside of her arm. Against her skin, I whisper, "Maybe you just forgot. Maybe we need to figure out if you remember anything. Anything at all."

I pluck open the top button of her jacket.

At this point she's panting visibly. I like it.

Hell, I like it too much.

My own lungs feel constricted in my chest, and my cock is swelled to maximum capacity. One flick of her eyes in that direction makes her notice. And blush.

"I remember," she says, swallowing thickly.

I undo the next two buttons and spread her jacket open. "What do you remember, Charlotte?" My voice has thickened. My own eyes feel heavy but I can't take them away from her, from this girl—this woman, this lady. My first lady. "Do you remember this?" I ease my hand between her thighs, under her skirt, and caress her over her panties.

I find her wet for me—ready for me—and I feel my heartbeat accelerate. The need to feel her around me, to be inside her, make love to her, fuck this need inside of her simmers in my veins.

She swallows audibly.

I push up her skirt and look at her—swollen and wet, her panties tight over her sex, the fabric damp, and my eyes fucking hurt.

I lean over, my forehead touching hers, my eyes fixed on hers as I pull down her panties until they fall at her ankles. She steps away from them—closer to me. I insert one finger into her opening, seeking her depths. And god, she's so snug. So wet she's soaking me down to the base of my finger.

"Do you remember?" I press, doing nothing but touching her between her legs, watching her pant as I slide my finger in and almost out, deeper in and almost out. Her eyes drift shut as she fights this, fights me.

I use my free hand to undo the top buttons of the silk blouse she's wearing under her jacket, part it open, and I duck my head. I coast my breath over the swell of her breast, the move designed to break her defenses, make her mine again. "Do you remember this?" I kiss the top swell of her breast.

She inhales and moves her hips to my finger. I move my mouth downward, to her nipple, and circle the tip with my tongue over the silk of her bra, marking the spot wetly. I suck her into my mouth then, fabric and all, and find her nub with my thumb. I circle it, watching the pleasure take her over—and I'm high on it. I'm high on her. High on the act of giving her pleasure alone.

"Tell me you remember this, baby," I croon, unbuttoning the rest of her blouse. I lower the fabric of her bra so that I can take that hard tip of her nipple into my mouth and suck her, suck her like I need to. I groan when she shudders and her body softens against me.

I lift her and set her down on the side console, making room between her legs as I continue with my caresses, brushing my lips over hers.

"Matt, don't …"

"That's not the word I want to hear. That's not the word you want to say to me—don't tell me you don't remember this, want this. Want *me*."

She parts her lips and I slip my tongue inside, grabbing the back of her head and fitting my mouth to hers as I kiss her.

I've never been so gentle and so rough with a woman at the same time. I've never wanted to make love and fuck at the same time. She makes me want to do both—do her every way to Sunday, draw out every moan in her, every gasp, every breath, all of them mine, all of her mine.

She moves her body and tries to get closer, squirming, her lower lip trapped under her teeth as she bites down hard to keep from telling me.

I place a kiss on her top lip, softly, causing her to release her lower lip, allowing me to fit my lips on hers perfectly now. And she opens up and I'm drowning in the taste of her, the smell of her—so sweet and pure, she is. I'm here because of her. I'm trying to do my best because of her. Hell, I'm trying to do more—she's opened my eyes, made me realize this isn't enough. I want more. I want this. Her. And I want to do right by her.

I'm determined to make it happen at any cost.

Slowly, today, day by day, touch by touch, breaking down her walls—she'll be mine again, her body first, her soul, and then her heart. I'm not letting her go.

"Open up to me, baby. Do you remember how you used to? Hmm? Tell me I'm still here," I beg, cupping her breast, squeezing gently as I rub inside her. "And here. Tell me, beautiful. Tell me C is for Charlotte, my Charlotte, coming in my arms again."

She goes off, breathing fast beneath me, clinging to my shoulders as if I'm all that holds her upright. "Oh god!" She presses her cheek to my neck, then pushes me back.

Then laughs. "Matt … you're pretty good at this sort of thing. Seducing and pleasuring me."

I lick my finger. "Hmm. At your service, Miss Wells."

"Mr. President, you're a cad."

"I'm *your* cad."

She swallows, her eyes wide. I pull her skirt down and lower her to her feet. "We need to get ready."

"I can't go without panties!"

"Live a little," I say. "You're a filthy first lady, a very wicked, naughty, hot first lady," I say, raising her back to the console and ordering, "Part your legs."

She does. I'm testing her; there's no fucking way I'll let her go anywhere without panties. I'm fucked up enough by the thought alone.

I ease the panties back up her legs, then lift her up and set her on her feet, kissing her leisurely as I tug them all the way up her sweet little pussy and round little ass.

Charlotte

We end up showering—separately. I don't think either of us could take the heat of a joint shower, but I was still so aroused rubbing the loofah over my skin, thinking of Matt waiting outside the room.

I dressed while he showered, putting on a long blue silk taffeta gown with layers upon layers on its skirt, and I try not to drool too much when Matt walks out drying himself, fully naked, giving me a glimpse of everything I adore and want and miss as he gets dressed.

The state dinner is a lavish affair. French influentials gravitate toward Matt. That effortless grace; he's in a room and it feels as if there's no one else, and never was, and never will be.

There is just a natural charm about him—and the women, especially, don't seem to miss it. I have my own admirers and try not to get jealous, especially because Matthew keeps glancing in my direction, and I can't stop myself from stealing covert glances at him as well.

After all the guests depart, we remain chatting over after-dinner drinks with the French president and first lady.

"You two." He motions toward Matt and me, then presses his fingers to his eyes. "The eyes don't lie, eh? You are guests here; my wife and I hope you're comfortable in one room rather than the two—in fact, I believe all the other rooms in the Élysée Palace were taken, weren't they, *chéri*."

Matt's laugh is low and very masculine.

And very, very sexy.

"What happens in Paris stays in Paris," the French president adds with a wink.

"I wouldn't mind the opportunity to spend some private time with my first lady," Matt admits. He shifts forward and eyes me challengingly.

"Opportunities like these are rare, eh?" The French president chuckles and lifts his glass. "To President Hamilton, and his enchanting first lady."

Matt raises his glass and looks at me, and I clench my thighs together and take a sip. Only after that do I arch an eyebrow.

The French president's wife smiles at me and sips from her wineglass.

Finally, after the longest day ever, we head to our room.

We close the door, and the surroundings are so alien, I feel a little homesick—but home stands before me, over six feet tall and virile, and I'm sunk into those knowing dark eyes and that half smile of his as he watches me take off my shoes.

I don't even know what to do with my hands as Matt plucks his cufflinks open and sets them aside, his eyes never leaving mine.

Something about this aloneness—about having him all to myself, in this city—feels like another stolen moment. Like I'm taking something that doesn't belong to me but I very much want to.

"Come here."

I shiver at his gruff whisper. I know that he senses my homesickness, my longing. My homesickness for him. Home. And when he opens his arms, I go. I press myself to his side and bury my face in his neck and let him engulf me. God, I've wanted this so much.

"Come here," he says again, as if he needs me closer still.

He drags me onto the bed and slips his arm under the opening at the back of my dress, gathering me to him, his hands spread on my bare back, my whole body pressed against Matt's hard one in the most protective embrace I've ever felt in my life—it's a wall of muscle and flesh and warmth and I bury myself even more into it, as close as physically possible.

Matt tightens his hold too.

I'm shivering and overwhelmed. His smell all around me. His hands on my back. The weight of his eyes on me. Matt's hand brushing my hair back as he tries to peer into my face even though I'm trying to hide it because this urge to cry has to be jet lag. I can't just break down for no reason. But I bury my face into his neck and fist the fabric of his open shirt, trying to get a grip on myself, letting the soothing motions of his hands massaging down the length of my back comfort me.

"I still love you."

"I know." His voice is low and thick and textured with emotion.

"I still want you like nothing in my life."

"I know. Come here." He drags me over him, holding me by the back of the head as he slips his tongue inside my mouth and kisses and kisses

and kisses

and kisses me.

He frames my face in his hands and his gaze bores into mine. "I love you. Very much, Charlotte. So much I couldn't let you go. So much I *won't* let you go. I've been in hell without you. You're in my every waking thought and in my fucking dreams. I'll fight to deserve you, to keep you by my side. I'm never making that mistake again, of thinking that I can't keep you. I will. I will always keep you. Do you understand me?" He presses a kiss to my ear and murmurs fiercely, pulling me back and looking deeply into my eyes as he frames my face in his hands, "Do you hear me, baby?"

I peer up at him. "I didn't hear the first part."

A slow-growing smile suddenly deepens into laughter, then he falls sober. He shifts me to my back, his muscles rippling as he goes up on his arms. Looks at me directly, intently, his voice utterly low as he strokes his thumb down my jaw, eyes on mine. "I love you, beautiful."

"How much? Like this?" I move my index finger and thumb as far apart as I can.

Matthew shakes his head.

"No?" I ask, disappointed.

"Immeasurably, baby. I love you immeasurably."

He holds my face in his hands and gently kisses me, kisses me with immeasurable tenderness, immeasurable heat. Immeasurable love.

BACK

Charlotte

On our way back to D.C., we kiss at leisure in the bedroom of Air Force One. I'm on his lap, burning for him.

"I'm thirsty for you, too thirsty to get enough," he growls.

We lose it. He sweeps down and grabs me against him, and I grab him by the shirt and kiss him back, raw and hot this time, out of control, his lips dominating and hungry, mine moving just as fast, an inferno of heat and longing blazing between us.

Matt coaxes my tongue into his mouth, groaning, massaging my butt with his hands.

"You're mine. Say you're mine."

"I'm yours."

"I'm sick of hiding. I understand we need to take it step by step with the public, but Charlotte, I want you in my bed—I want inside you. Two steps into my room, we'll be tearing off our clothes and nothing is going to come between us—nothing."

"That's what I'm afraid of. I need to be sure I can truly be the first lady that the country needs."

"You are not just your job—you are a woman, and you're the woman I need."

He covers my breast with one hand and thrusts his tongue into my mouth, faster, harder, and I'm dying from the way he seems to need me. I grab fistfuls of his hair, lost, moaning and groaning, our hands running over each other, our mouths crazy.

"Soon," I breathe.

He groans. "I'm sick of cold showers."

"I'm sorry. I'm physically in pain."

"Focus on what you're sitting on and you'll realize you're not alone."

I smile, quivering in desire. "Soon."

ADJUSTING

Charlotte

Matthew has flown out for a meeting with the prime minister of Canada, and I spend the next few days adjusting to life in the White House.

I look at the menus on Sunday, and I tell the chef that I really don't think we need to have fancy menus or fancy desserts on a daily basis, that plain apple pie will do.

He created this version of an apple pie that's several layers, has a bit of cheesecake mingled in with the cinnamon apples, and I've never tasted anything so divine in my life.

"I've never gone to a restaurant with food as good as the food you cook, Chef."

"It's our job to keep you well fed and happy—and it's our job to make you and our country look good with all our visiting foreign dignitaries."

We're hosting a state dinner for President Asaf in two months and before he left, Matt said, "Spare no expense."

One of the things I learned upon arrival at the White House was that the first family pays for their personal expenses, including their staff and food. "Matt—I know your family has money, but you'll leave with no money if you—"

He started laughing, then assured me, "Spare no expense. This is the United States of America, and the White House. It's an investment."

"If we stick to a reasonable budget for the state dinner, the State Department will foot the bill," Clarissa assured me when I expressed my concern to her, later.

I occasionally wander around the house with the curator, asking him to teach me about the artwork and the relics. There is so much history here. So much heart and depth. I love it, but I haven't seen Matthew for days.

I've looked at my schedule and had chats with my press secretary, chief of staff, and social director, and I'm tempted to work my schedule around his when he returns, when Clarissa tells me, "The president's chief of staff asked me to adjust your schedule so you could do several events with him."

I blush. Is he as eager about seeing me as I am him? "Absolutely; it's my pleasure."

She and the social director sort of look at each other in mischief. I laugh. "I know what you're thinking."

"We didn't say a word."

"Look, we're both really interested in doing our best here—"

"We're not judging, Miss Wells, on the contrary. You look good together."

I just smile, not knowing what to say. I miss him so much. It's still incredible for me to be here, that we're giving this a shot.

A day before Matt is due to return, I just can't take it a second longer. I head to the West Wing.

"Portia, could you connect me with the president?"

"I ... he's on Air Force One. Let me see if I can get him."

After a moment, I wait for him to take the call.

"Hey." His voice is husky.

"I'm sorry to bother you—are you busy? Oh, I'm sure you are." I laugh and exhale. "I miss you."

"I miss you too."

"Would you have dinner with me in the Old Family Dining Room tomorrow?"

"I'm there," he says without hesitation.

I'm nervous about going through with this. I need that connection. I'm going crazy for it. I want his strength, I want his arms around me, I want *him*. I just want him and I want him to know how much he is wanted by me.

Matt

'm edgy and I can't take the edge off.

We're flying home on Air Force One, D.C. already beneath us.

I've been rehashing a new plan to get the economy rolling again.

"The markets have rallied. The dollar is stronger from the moment you took office," Frederickson, the VP, says, tossing a tennis ball up in the air and catching it.

"Markets merely speculate. We need concrete results, to get our economy running again. Where are we on our education bill?" I ask Dale.

"Should be done by next week."

"I want us to invest in our youth. Education, top level. Next up is healthcare. Women having equal pay—paid maternal leave so they can spend the time they need with their newborns. Too many people who are hurting out there who weren't tended to properly."

"Your call, Mr. President."

"And get me the Speaker of the House. And I want a meeting with the Democratic and Republican leaders—there are ways we can make this work without putting up a thousand and one walls."

Dale nods and leaves, and Frederickson follows to the door, shouting, "Catch!" and sending the ball flying my way.

Jack leaps up before I can grab it, then trots and brings it over.

"Good dog!" Frederickson applauds, impressed.

I pull out my glasses to continue reading and catch Jack sniffing my coffee cup as he sets the ball on my desk. "No more, buddy." I turn the cup and let him lick a drop—and I think of her, with her red hair swinging, bringing me coffee. I think of her spread out beneath me. Moaning. Wanting it.

She wants us to have dinner. I know what she wants. I want it too.

She wanted time, concerned about the media.

I've been patient. But I'm tired of worrying about the media. I'm tired of being unable to take her out in public. I'm fucking tired of hiding the one thing I personally value aside my job and my country. Yeah, I'm looking forward to dinner. The only thing I hunger for is her.

HIM

Charlotte

I hear Marine One long before I see the helicopter descend over the South Lawn of the White House. I want to run to the doors like Jack does when Matt is out and he stays home, but instead I force myself to walk primly down the stairs and outside.

Matt hops off the helicopter and Jack rushes across the lawn, while I wait by the steps, smiling as Jack leaps up to greet me. I pet his head, my eyes firmly locked onto the tall, distinguished man crossing the lawn toward me.

He's wearing his gabardine over his suit, and the wind is blowing through his hair—making love to every inch of him.

His stride is purposeful as he heads forward. Jack waits by my side, tail swishing side to side.

Our eyes meet. I just smile and start heading inside, and two steps inside—a good distance away from the agents milling about—he draws me into his arms and my resolve to wait until after dinner melts a little. He strokes a hand down the back of my head. "I missed you," he breathes in my ear.

It melts a little more.

His strength seeps into my body. It reaches deep inside me, down to the marrow of my bones. If we were alone, I'd pull him somewhere to feel his hands on me. Feel his eyes on me. Feel his skin under my fingers, his tongue moving over mine again.

"So did I."

Jack barks happily. Matt eases back, but not before I get a glimpse of the smoldering heat in his eyes. "Not here," he says.

I inhale for patience.

He grins, seizes my chin, and stares straight into my eyes. "Go to my room." A promise.

My breathing becomes uneven and jittery. "What about dinner?"

"What I want is right here, and I'm not waiting a moment longer to have her. Now let me tend to something and I'll be right there."

I head to my bedroom first and snatch up a gauzy nightie that I bought in Paris, my only purchase there. A white baby doll with a part in the middle and a bow tying it together.

Did I buy it with the hopes he would one day see it?

I told myself it was for me, but now I'm not so sure. I tuck it under my jacket, and I'm aware of Secret Service stationed nearby as I cross to his room. I shut the door, quickly change in his large bathroom, and head straight for the bed because my legs feel liquid and unsteady.

His room is a little bigger than mine and his bed smells like him. I sigh and delight in the scent when I hear the knob turn—and the door shut.

My happy smile over being in his bed fades as my lashes open, and my eyes start to climb up powerful, long legs, narrow hips, and a crisp white shirt, unbuttoned at the top.

He. Is already. HARD.

He's looking at me with incredible amusement, his eyes dancing, his hair spiked up as if he's been very restless. *Restless on his way home.*

"Always full of surprises, aren't you, Charlotte," he says quietly. Taking in my baby doll.

I can't breathe anymore.

I'm enveloped by the power and confidence he oozes, by the penetrating quality of his stare, by the male smile he wears.

Twisting my lips as I sit propped up on my arms, I shyly hold his gaze. "Do you like my welcome home gift?" I motion to the bow tying my baby doll together.

We're both high from missing each other, I think—our adrenaline twisting and tangling invisibly in the room.

He crosses the room, reaching out to take my arm and help me to my feet. One tug and he's flattened me against the flat wall of his chest. Another tug on my loose hair yanks my head back. The gasp that leaves me only serves to part my lips—and he's there. His *lips* are there, brushing mine, ever so exquisitely. His breath trickling warmly into my mouth.

"I like the gift," he says, fingering the bow at the top of my nightie, "though I haven't opened it entirely yet."

He tugs the bow, releasing it. Desire for him thrums in my veins.

"The fact that I'm nearly naked doesn't mean that I'm ready to sleep with you."

He parts the baby doll open. "The fact that I asked you to my room doesn't mean I've been thinking about you."

But I want him to think of me. Because I can't stop thinking about him. I slide my hands down the front of his shirt. "No?" I rock my hips against him.

He tugs the fabric of my nightie off one shoulder. "No." He leans down, lips whisking across the curve of said shoulder.

It's amazing what he does to me.

He touches me and all my senses attune to the spot he's touching.

His scent intoxicates me and his lips are the wickedest thing I've ever encountered. My eyes drift shut, and I angle my head back, gripping his hair. It's slicked back when he's in public, but I love how it gets spiky when he's been raking his fingers through it.

I pull on it and bring his head up and he chuckles softly, grabs my face in one hand, and presses his mouth firmly—firmly, decidedly—on mine.

I'm in a free fall, and his eyes are shining with lust and yearning before he takes my mouth in a harder kiss. Our tongues tangle, his tongue strong, wet, thirsty. I can't stop myself from opening his jacket, feeling his muscles under his shirt. Perfectly delineated.

Every time we kiss feels like the first time, but this time feels like it's the *only* time.

As I unbutton his shirt and see the flag pin on his jacket, I am reminded of what a huge difference he's making, how small I am compared to the millions of people whose lives he's affecting.

"Matt, I may not have foreseen that people could hear …"

"I don't see anyone here but you and me," he rasps, and boy is he really *looking* at me.

I've got so much desire I'm trembling.

He growls as if he's thinking the same thing, lifts me, and his hands are grabbing my ass. My hands instantly curl around his shoulders.

"God, you little sexpot, you hot little thing … I can't get enough of you." He bites and tugs my lip, then fits his mouth perfectly to mine again. He smells delicious. Of cologne and him, and my stomach tumbles with butterflies as he tugs and rips off my thong.

"Matt," I say, startled.

"What?" He grins, pressing me against the wall, bracing me there so he can ease his hand between us to caress my bare sex between our bodies.

I groan, pushing my hips against him. He grabs my breast and squeezes my nipple. He sucks it, making me shiver.

"Oh god."

"I can't do the first lady against the wall, where are my manners?"

"Oh god, just do me." I grab his hair and pull his face to mine, kissing his jaw as he carries me to bed and lays me down on the center, leaning over me.

I shiver beneath his warm hand trailing along my tummy.

His eyes coast over me, taking me in. His lips graze across mine again, warm and silky. I part my lips and he dips his tongue inside. He groans and allows our tongues to play for a while as his hands wander up and down my curves, slowly, in no hurry, as if he can command time to stop for us and we now have all the time in the world.

He eases back to remove his shirt and looks at me.

"God, you belong in my bed. Look at you."

I swallow, part laughing and part groaning.

I'm desperate for Matt, but I'm nervous to have sex with him again. I'm nervous because it means so much, it feels so gargantuan. He knows how I feel about him and I've been waiting for this moment for so many lonely nights, missing him. It's the first time we're together after he's said he loves me.

"I'm nervous," I breathe.

Standing back calmly, he slowly shrugs off his shirt, revealing those glorious muscles of his. "Why are you nervous?"

"It's just that … you're the president. I feel …"

"Don't be nervous. I'm still the same." Shirtless in his slacks, he reaches out to spread my arms up over my head and trace his hands down my sides.

I rock my hips, moaning.

He inhales a long breath, his eyes catching mine. "So beautiful." He grabs the back of my neck and pulls me forward, seeming to lose control, crushing my lips beneath his so hard and with such passion my head is spinning.

I grab him for support and arch up against him, my breasts aching as I rub my fingers along the back of his strong neck.

Matt unbuckles his belt and unzips, then he strips off his pants, and I gasp, his hardness springing free.

As he spreads his large body over me, I groan and reach for him, out of control, and Matt leans his head to my breasts and the hardened tips of my nipples, sticking his tongue out to lave one, then the other, slowly circling his tongue around the peaks. He suctions, slipping his hand between my legs, into my opening. His fingers move inside me, first one, then two, and I arch and jerk from the pleasure.

"What do you want, beautiful?"

"I want you," I pant.

He leans down and sucks on my shoulder, pulling me closer. "I've been dying to get inside you. I can't forget what it feels like to move inside you, have you lose yourself beneath me."

He parts my legs wider open.

"Matt," I say, my tone sober. And his eyes widen in question.

"I stopped using the pill, since we ... well, I went to Europe and ..."

He reaches out to his nightstand, and then rips open a packet with his teeth. "Don't worry. My staff is very adept at making sure their president has all he needs."

He smirks as he rolls on a rubber and I get wetter just watching him. He strokes me between my legs, then sticks his wet finger into his mouth as he grabs his cock with his free hand and teases it along my entry.

We groan together, kissing without restraint as he curls my legs around him, his voice gruffer by the second.

He penetrates me, his erection thicker than ever, pushing me apart. I moan softly and rake my nails along his back as I thrust my hips up for more.

"Take me in, that's right, Charlotte. That's right, take me, beautiful." He starts thrusting in and out with vigor, his muscles rippling beneath my hands, his breaths coming fast and hard as he sets a rhythm.

I cry out, so loud I'm afraid security outside might hear us, but I don't care, and neither does Matt. He releases a gut-deep groan and pulls my hands over my head, fucking me harder and deeper, out of control and as if he wants to bury himself permanently inside of me, as if he wants to meld us into one.

I want him like a physical ache. I can't stop running my hands over his arms, his shoulders, his chest.

He growls, "Come here," and kisses me. Hard and with purpose. He starts slamming me full force—and I relish the taste of him again, the smell of him.

He sucks my breast again, and I take him, meeting every thrust with a rock of my hips in silent plea for more.

He slows the pace and pulls out, then rubs my clit under his thumb. I growl and he pushes his middle finger inside me, watching me. "So snug, and so wet and greedy." He removes his finger, ready to fill me again.

I curl my legs tighter around him and lift my head, and press my mouth to his as he thrusts inside. And then he's everywhere. Thrusting deep, tapping my heart as he withdraws and does it again.

I moan, he groans.

He's the man I love and he's fucking me like he means it, with strong, deliberate strokes that stretch me almost until I can't bear it. I can feel in the way he moves, the way he touches me, bites me, licks me, that I wasn't the only one dying for this.

He gives me a soul-wrecking kiss that makes me soar and I suck his tongue and use my thighs to bring him closer, our breaths exploding out at the same time as we arch to get closer and closer.

He thrusts harder, deeper, our eyes holding, our mouths crushing, our hands touching, our tongues tasting, our breaths barely enough to keep up.

I hear the slick sounds of him entering me, I'm so wet, and he's so thick and hard and moving so fast, our bodies straining to get even closer.

"So good. So damn good I already want to do this again."

"Yes," I rasp.

Vision blurry with need. My mouth roaming his chest and neck and his hard jaw, the stubble there scraping my lips as I kiss him.

I'm shaking, needing, vulnerable, and he is oh so sexy.

I feel overwhelmed when he's inside me, like I'm going to burst from what I'm feeling, connected with him, one with him—this man who's never really given himself to anyone and is hesitant to let someone in. Who makes me want to claim him.

He pushes into me again, and the rumbling sounds leaving his throat tell me he's just as ready to go off as I am. We fuck slower now, but just as passionately.

My body is snug around him and squeezing him, gripping him to keep him inside me. "Let me see you," he says. "Come the fuck apart for me." He looks down at me and kisses me, commanding my lips as he rubs my tongue with his and rubbing my clit with his thumb as he thrusts up deep against my G-spot. "Come."

I start tightening around him, and the moment I begin to thrash, he tightens his muscles and arches back, and he growls in pleasure as he comes with me.

I'm too weak to move for a few minutes. Matt goes to clean off, then comes back and pulls me into his arms.

He nuzzles my neck, and I press as close as I can.

Oh god, I can't get close enough.

I inhale his scent and clench my arms around his neck, hearing him chuckle softly against the top of my hair, his breath tickling me.

We lie there for minutes, naked …

sated …

and tangled with each other and the sheets.

The dusting of hair on Matthew's chest is too tempting for my fingers. "I should probably leave," I whisper against the thick column of his throat as I caress his chest and force myself to stop. "It's one thing for the staff to speculate about us indulging in a quickie, and quite another for us to start pulling all-nighters together."

I reach for my clothes as Matt rolls to his back and links his hands behind his head, a frown on his face.

"Let them. Let the rumors start. We won't confirm anything until we want to."

I hesitate for a moment. Just a moment. Then I shake my head. "It's too soon. I know everyone is hanging on by threads, wanting to see what bills are to be passed in the next few months—those should be the headline news."

His eyes trail over my bare back as I start dressing, silent, still frowning. "I'll give them enough to talk about. I've got more than one bill in the works; I just need to be sure the parties will cooperate. But Charlotte," he adds as I head across the room, raising one eyebrow. "We'll be paying each other a visit every night."

I bite down on my smile, a fuzzy feeling in my stomach. "Yes, President Hamilton." I smirk and quietly open the door, exiting his bedroom and crossing the hall toward mine.

FIRST LADY

Charlotte

'm so wicked. Bagging the president by night and being a devoted first lady by day.

I step out of the Virginia elementary school to a gust of wind and a bevy of reporters, some of whom were actually allowed into the classroom by the school as I read books to the kids, and told them how reading has improved my life dramatically, giving me knowledge of the things I liked and those I wanted to change in the world, too.

A little girl with cute curly pigtails mentioned that she wanted to grow up to be me, and I laughed, but told her I had a better idea—that she would make a far better *her* than she would anyone else.

I can't stop thinking about that as I ride in the back of the state car to the White House.

I ride with Stacey beside me. I love how efficient she is, always whispering into her mic, opening and closing the doors, carving a path for me.

"My life used to be a little bit more normal," I tell her, peering out the window at the White House as the gates open for us. "Have you worked at the White House for long?"

"Four years. I was on the previous first lady's detail."

"What can one expect from the life of a first lady?"

"The reality is a little messier than the cameras show. But …" She pauses.

"Tell me," I prod.

She seems to hesitate, as if wondering whether she's overstepping, but I suspect my eager eyes and smile encourage her to speak freely. "Mrs. Jacobs wasn't as warm with the people as you are."

I take a moment for this.

"You're *one of* the people. They like that. You and President Hamilton. You both are." She nods respectfully, then adds, "So many of us, especially women, dream of fitting in your glass slipper. Having the attention of the young, attractive president."

"Matthew doesn't—" I cut myself off, then say, "So the rumors have started already."

"Everyone's hoping, ever since he named you acting first lady." She laughs, then says, "We respect him. And you. The White House is not only a place of business; we've taken care of whole families for a long time."

Families. The thought sort of pricks me in the heart and makes me wonder what a family with my country's president, the man I love, would be like. "Thank you for telling me this."

She smiles. She's been my shadow, along with other members of the Secret Service, and I'm always humbled and almost uncomfortable by the dedication they show. I've learned they speak in codes, and especially use codes for Matt and me. Stacey's also unmarried at forty-four, eats a high-protein diet, and has eyes for Johnson, another member of my Secret Service team.

The rest of the week I spend making plans with Clarissa. I adore visiting places and having a chance to speak and interact with everyone, but I also notice people look at my detail and me with a bit of reverence. Whenever I mention the president, their eyes go wide and it feels like I just mentioned God.

I want them to know that the president is not only their driven and intelligent leader, but a human being as well—as am I.

If there's one thing I know, it's that the job of the first lady is determined by the first lady herself. I've been thinking of my predecessors, what they're remembered for, and wondering what I will stand for as a first lady.

Jackie Kennedy turned the White House into a showcase of the evolution of America's style and taste. She was a fashion icon, poised and elegant, who was the first to bring a curator into the White House.

Eleanor Roosevelt was a rogue in her time. She spoke about civil rights and women's rights, and to this day she's probably the most powerful first lady to have ever served. At the time, there weren't any female reporters—they were barred from White House press conferences. But Eleanor held her own press conferences, aimed toward female reporters, in turn forcing the media to hire them.

Other first ladies have sat in cabinet meetings. Many of them have been hostesses, planning the state dinners—but most have done so much more. Pushing for schools without drugs. Improvements in healthcare and nutrition.

So I sit down with Clarissa and tell her I want to define the role the way I feel capable of doing—that I want to represent the president with the same vitality he exudes, keep myself busy and active, having a White House presence in as many states as possible, and not only scheduling talks and visits to schools, hospitals, and workplaces, but inviting citizens over to the White House as well.

I've found the time I've been here so exciting—so inspiring. I wish more people had the opportunity to be so close to all this history and the pulsing heart of America.

"I discussed with the president the fact that I want to make this house open to the public. I want to stay in contact with the people. I also plan to ask him permission to personally address some of the letters that arrive at the White House."

Clarissa is nodding rapidly, taking notes. "Also," she says, "they want to know more about you. Your job is unofficial; the press wonders how much influence you have, if you've got the president's ear. They want to know more about their first lady. Lola is setting up some interviews here in the East Wing."

Nerves hit me—but this is an opportunity to shed light on things I care about, not to focus on me. So I agree.

"Excellent!" Clarissa says.

FBI

Matt

The director of the FBI hands the files over.

"Here you go, Mr. President. I was a fan of your father. I, like the rest of the country, suffered a great loss when he was taken from us too soon. I knew you'd want to have this."

"Everything is here?"

"Every single thing, sir."

"I'll read up on it tonight. Expect to hear from me soon."

"Yes, sir, President Hamilton."

WORK

Charlotte

The rest of the week goes by in a frenzy of visits, interviews, and planning the upcoming state dinner. Matt is even more swamped with work than I am, but I can see him make some effort to carve out some time to see me, and it not only touches me, it makes me truly wish for him to know that I support him and what he's doing for our country. That just being close to him and knowing that he wants to be with me as much as I want to be with him is enough.

The bills he's trying to pass are not easy ones—they will mark permanent changes in our education, healthcare, and energy programs. He's got solid backing from the House, but the Senate will be voting soon—and you really never know how it's going to go.

After dinner one day, we took Jack for a walk along the White House gardens.

It was freezing outside, but I was wrapped in a coat and wore a cap, loving to watch Matt's breath mist in the air as we talked about our day. And how he wouldn't stop poking my reddened nose playfully, wearing the most gorgeous smile.

On our way back into the White House, it was eerily quiet. "I'll never stop feeling awed as I walk around this house," I said.

"It's a privilege not to be taken lightly."

"You know how they say if these walls could speak? These walls actually do. Every piece of art on the walls. Every relic."

We continued in silence.

The usual bustle of the day had calmed down, but it was still in the very air. The electric unfolding of history within these walls. There were births and deaths, celebrations and mourning.

We passed the portrait of JFK, glancing downward, humble and charismatic, and the portrait of Matt's dad, in a long red-carpeted hall.

Matt eyed the hall, his gaze warm as he took in my excitement. "Building took seventeen years to complete. Washington conceived the idea of it, but he never had a chance to move in."

I watched him as we walked, wanting more.

"It nearly burned in the War of 1812, when the British invaded the capital. Middle of the night, enemy troops threw javelins on fire through the windows, set the attic on fire, and the flames started burning through the floor, then the main floor crashed into the basement. Look at it now." He winked. "Yeah, that's America. You fall, you rise back up stronger than ever." He chucked my chin.

And I laughed, and blushed all over, and nodded.

"The portrait of Washington in the Oval? The soldiers looted the house, but the first lady at the time, Dolly Madison, cracked the frame and saved it."

"If the house is set on fire, I'm taking your portrait."

"I want one made of you."

"Matthew!"

"I mean it," he said, then he took my hand and led me up-stairs to his bedroom, Jack padding at our feet and dropping to fall asleep by the time we were naked beneath the covers. Matt was drawing me with his fingertips, slowly telling me what part of me he wanted to immortalize in paint.

Matt has been buried under bills and negotiations for the last couple of days. I, too, have stayed busy, but then I wait for night, wondering if Matt will wrap up the day early or not—he's been working so hard that the White House press office is always abuzz with information. Headlines are always pertaining to the White House. Matt is taking the alphabet campaign and absolutely crossing out every … single … word. As promised.

There are presidents and there are presidents—but we haven't had one like this one in a long, long while. And exactly like this one? Not ever.

I've never been so busy in my life either, but as I wait with my muscles sore from the day I ache for him and our time alone. I wonder what he's doing and whether I'll fall asleep before he reaches me, like I have for the past three nights, or if I'll be awake when he walks into my room and takes every single inch of me that craves to be taken again.

Tomorrow we have our first evening out, a fundraiser for Clean Water Across the Nation—with several celebrities in attendance. Though it's been three days since we made love, I've already realized that Matt meant it when he said he'd be paying me a nightly visit. Every morning I've woken up to the feeling of having been spooned at night and the scent of him on my pillow.

Last night, I was taking a walk outside to clear my head when his best friend from Harvard, Beckett, arrived.

"Is the president still in the West Wing at this hour?"

I nodded.

"Wow." He frowned. "He hasn't answered my calls. Any reason he's so hell-bent on getting everything done now?"

"He said he would. He wants to make his first one hundred days groundbreaking and set the tone for the rest of them."

"He's inspired by you," Beckett said, winking and heading over. "I'm going to drag him out of the office, take him out for a run."

"Good. Take Jack with you—he's been restless with the rain and cooped up inside. I don't think he gets a kick out of politics the way Matt does."

His words linger with me.

Do I inspire Matthew, really?

I know that he's driven to succeed, that he inherited a broken kingdom that he must mend, burnt bridges between parties that he has to rebuild, all while navigating the complicated politics of D.C. involving a myriad of players, quite like pieces in a chess game—the lobbyists, the House, the Senate—all while keeping in mind the goals, the will, and the welfare of the people.

When I met his father, President Lawrence Hamilton, I felt so inspired. But nothing in my life has ever inspired me the way watching Matt work does. So I decide that tonight, rather than wait in my room, I'll visit him at the Oval Office when he's back from his run and the halls are quiet.

"What is it?" I ask, alarmed and confused over Matt's expression.

I came to visit him at the Oval. I was barefoot, finding him behind his desk, working behind the light of a lamp. I thought I was being sassy when I headed over to his desk and tried to prop myself up to the desk top. When I did, something loosened from underneath, and Matt caught it in his hand as it started fluttering downward.

It was a scarf. A pink scarf, that seemed to be tucked into some sort of compartment in his dad's desk.

Now I have a sick feeling in my stomach as we both stare at the pink scarf in Matt's hand.

My lips tremble as a bone-chilling shiver travels down my spine.

"This doesn't belong to my mother," Matt says.

I can't even think about it. I'm too shocked about seeing such a flimsy thing in the Oval, and feel sort of like a voyeur, as if Matt and I just caught his father doing something forbidden.

Matt's expression is a mix of rage and disbelief.

"I'm sorry." I reach out and take his hand. "Do you want to …"

"I need some air."

Matt stands and steps out of the room, and after a moment, I hear the agents rushing after him—and I'm alone in this house, with my dreary thoughts and my mind buzzing with worry.

Matt comes back shortly after.

He seems to have cleared his head outside, for he dives straight for the phone.

Matt calls my father over. He was a friend of his father for many years, and I suppose he trusts that whatever he discussed with my dad will never leave the room.

We sit with him in the sitting room adjacent the Oval as Matt asks him questions about his father.

"But you never knew of his interests outside of policy and the White House?"

"I knew—suspected—something changed the year before he was killed. He smiled more, he traveled more. He seemed to get new life injected."

"Could this have anything to do with a woman?"

"Possibly. I don't know for sure. I always assumed it was him realizing that he was close to done serving as president, and he'd be able to make it up to his family now."

"Thank you, Robert."

Matt seems calm, but only someone who knows him— truly knows him—could detect the tension pulsing in his shoulders.

"Charlotte, I'd like to talk to your father alone for a moment."

I smile when I look into his reassuring eyes, nodding quietly as I go and hug my father. "Thank you, Dad." I kiss his cheek and he pats my hand when I rest it on his shoulder, watching me with pride as I leave.

Something about the way Matt asks makes me tingly. I wonder if he's going to tell my dad about us. It seems in character that he'd want to let him know there's something between us before we eventually move forward and tell the word.

Two minutes later, I'm pretty sure that he *did* tell him *something* about us—for when my dad leaves, he's got a spark of mischief in his eye as he waves goodbye.

Matt contacts the FBI next. I'm still rattled by things. As Sigmund Cox arrives to the Oval, Matt asks me to stay. As he hands over the scarf, his roiling bronze eyes meet mine, and they look crisp and metallic, cold as I feel.

I know what this finding means. How disappointing it could be—to imagine that his father possibly had an affair what he was president. Especially considering he neglected his mother and son. For the country, it was one thing, but for another woman?

After explaining to Cox what we found, Matt slides the FBI files across his desk.

"I want the case reopened and I want a special task investigator working twenty-four seven on this. I want real information on this. I want specifics. Details. I also want this to be top secret. Nobody but you, those of us in this room, and the special investigator will know."

GALA

Charlotte

I slept that night in his arms in the Queens' Bedroom, thinking of his father, knowing he was in Matt's thoughts too. "What did you tell my dad when you asked to talk to him alone?" I whispered.

"That I'm in love with you," he said simply.

Now it's past 6 p.m. the next afternoon when I'm told by one of the members of the residence staff that the president sent the gown that hangs in my dressing room.

Jack hurries excitedly into my bedroom as if he plans to report to Matthew what I thought of his gift.

It is breathtaking.

From an up-and-coming American designer who's going to take the world by storm, it is a heavily detailed lace-and-sequin dress with just the right amount of sheerness to give a glimpse of skin on my back and shoulders.

I dress carefully and glance at myself in the mirror to make sure I look about as good as the first lady representing our country should. The gold dress falls to my ankles, sparkling like a jewel, and I let my red hair tumble down my shoulders. I grab a little shawl that matches the dress and step out into the hall.

Matt is standing at the end of the hall, his hands in the pockets of his pants, his jacket raised at his back because of his position as he gazes out the window at the gardens. When faced with the perfection of that tall, black-clad figure, his stance emphasizing the force of his thighs and the slimness of his hips, his pants pressing into his ass because of his hands being jammed into his pockets—

Breathe, Charlotte!

I force my lungs to work in a breath; and as if he senses me, he turns.

A look of surprise flicks across his features, followed by a slow trailing of his eyes down my dress. Jack pads toward him and Matt pets the top of his head as he comes to a perfect sit beside him, and yet his whole undivided attention seems to be on me. His eyes study my face as if memorizing it. As if he'd forgotten it.

I eye him covetously too. Standing there with his dog, he would already kill me. But in a tux? I'm completely gone over this guy. He wears the tux like he wears the presidency. With grace, confidence, and so much ease he seems to have been born destined for both that presidency and that damn onyx-black tuxedo.

He looks devilishly handsome.

His hair is combed back and oh, how I love every chiseled inch of his face. He's the first to move, prying his hands from his pockets, eyes flaring, inhaling visibly—his inhale stretching the fabric of that black tux.

Disbelief and a punch of longing to have all of this man, his love and his name and his babies, hits me as he approaches. I'm gazing at him walk to me down the hall of the White

House residence, both of us ready to attend a social dinner. My first public event with him.

I need a moment, or a thousand moments, to adjust to this new role.

Matt continues advancing—with every step his eyes drinking me in, his lips curling in a seductive, appreciative smile.

"You ready?" He stretches out his hand.

I nod and look at that hand—the hand I've held so many times, and that held me. I slide my fingers down the length of his, and he grips them and leads me down the staircase with him.

I grab my dress and lift it to avoid tripping on the hem as we descend, watching as Jack bounds down and announces with a happy bark to the rest of the Secret Service that we've arrived downstairs.

Matt glances ahead at our waiting detail as we head toward the exit of the North Portico doors.

"It's not my first time with the media. I should know better than to feel exposed."

"Don't be nervous. You'll blow every single person in the room away."

I stop in my tracks, looking at Matt.

Matt, recently showered, absolutely poised and drool-worthy in the tux.

He looks every bit the president. Cool and completely confident.

"You don't look that blown away," I say.

"I'm schooled in the art of controlling my emotions. Trust me. I'm blown away." The heat in his eyes sizzles as he looks at me, and his voice thickens, making my knees wobbly under my dress.

His gaze smolders as he reaches out to tuck my arm into the crook of his and lead me down the White House steps and to the waiting car.

"Behave, Jack," Matt warns with a raising of his brows as Jack sits at the door and watches us leave.

We climb into the presidential state car and head on our way with a line of black cars flanking us front and back.

It feels surreal to be riding in a motorcade with him. The size of the team required to protect him is in the hundreds. Twenty-six cars travel with us, including medical assistance, motorcycles, and press. I know snipers are planted on the route, mailboxes removed to avoid explosives. It's a perfectly orchestrated master symphony of hundreds of players, all circling around the president and his safety.

I'm so aware of the people glancing toward our cars as we pass that it takes me a moment to become aware of Matt watching me.

He looks stunning in that tux and he smells so good, his cologne making me dizzy.

His presence, his nearness, his gaze. I clench my thighs together under my gorgeous, glittering Cinderella dress, wanting him. Wanting him so much, not just physically, but emotionally. I crave our nights alone, talking …

In the White House, there are so many people—butlers, maids, doormen, ushers, plus the West Wing staff—I wonder if I'll ever be able to have the courage to do more than steal in secret into his room. Or let him steal into mine.

I meet his gaze. "It feels completely surreal."

His lips curl, and he looks at me a moment more. "Let's come out as a couple tonight."

The low but firm words trigger a tremor down my spine.

I remember hundreds of nights during the campaign, sleepless, wanting him.

I remember that he won. That I went to Europe. That I'm living in the White House with him, more in love than ever. And that we're taking it slow.

Slow.

And utterly, exquisitely slowly, Matt slips his hand under the fall of my hair and places a kiss on my forehead, then my mouth. It's a soft kiss, fleeting, but it leaves a burning sensation behind when he eases back.

He looks at my kissed lips with a male pride and not one bit of apology. "I'm tired of keeping you in the shadows. I want everyone to know that you're mine. But I know what I'm asking is for you to become even more public, and possibly under scrutiny. I will wait for as long as we need to, but I'm ready to move this forward, Charlotte."

I swallow.

"I want that more than anything," I breathe.

He slips his hand over the curve of my shoulder, touching my bare skin as we ride to the event.

"I just had this hope that … I'd prove myself as a first lady first, before we announced our relationship to the world. I'm not so sure what I want to do anymore." I meet his gaze.

There's something predatory about the way he's looking at me.

"But I've always wanted to just be with you. Without the concerns and the hiding," I admit.

"So. Be with me."

The smoldering flame in his eyes warms me to my core, and I hear myself say, "It seems to me that if we took it slow, there's a better chance for the citizens to adjust to the idea of you having a girlfriend in the White House."

"The speculations are running amok already. Half the country will be worried you distract me—the other half will be thrilled. It doesn't matter. I want you. I want you indefinitely—and eventually, baby"—he takes my chin—"you're going to need to own up to the fact that the man you're in love with is the president, and you helped put me here."

I laugh, and he smiles too.

His hot gaze caresses me and heats me down to the marrow of my bones. "When we can't be together, I miss the way you smell. The way you look. The way you feel." His lips curl, and he cups my face in his warm hands and leans to whisper in my ear, "I'm blown away by you. And so will every person who looks at you tonight. Not that I'm too happy about that."

I'm blushing head to toe, so thoroughly I don't even know what to do with myself. "You're so forward, Mr. President."

He laughs, then releases a deep groan and ducks close to my ear. "Think about what I said. Let's talk about your concerns this weekend."

I swallow again. "That sounds good."

He nods, releasing me only when we are seconds away from arriving at the fundraiser.

The state car comes to a stop, and I feel queasy from the stress of my first public appearance. Matt gets out of the car, and I hear the people waiting outside. Some gasp, others sort of whisper, and then the press just starts to roar.

"PRESIDENT HAMILTON! *MR. PRESIDENT!*"

Matt looks into the car and extends his hand to help me out.

Overwhelming doesn't cover it. I'm not sure if it's because it's our first night out, or if things will always be like this, but I paste a smile on my face even though the strongest urge I have right now is to avoid the cameras. I take his hand for support, slipping my fingers into his as I set my feet on the sidewalk and stand, blinded by the flashes. I slip my arm into the crook of Matt's and feel him tuck it even tighter as he guides me inside.

A line of people eager to greet him instantly forms inside the ballroom.

I stand by his side, meeting friends of his, celebrities.

Hearing them gush over Matt is amusing, and I'm mindblown by how easily he steps into his president role—how easily he owns it.

The way he smiles at the people, sometimes slaps a man's back as they shake hands, shows how accessible he is, how open, human, and honest. Even in a tux, you can't miss the ripple of muscle under his jacket and shirt as he moves, shakes hands, is greeted by everyone in the room. It makes the very tips of my breasts sort of ache against the fabric of my dress. And wearing a dress that *he* sent for me to wear makes me feel so sexy, as if he's claiming me somehow. After the conversation that we had in the car, knowing that he wants to move forward and make this official causes a fire between my legs whenever our eyes meet.

Stifling a hot little shiver, I make my legs move around and mingle, making myself accessible too, trying to tell myself *this is how my mother would do it. This is how Matthew's mother would do it.*

I greet ambassadors, congressmen, senators.

From across the room, Matt watches me, and I can see the admiration in his eyes as I work the room.

At some point during the first hour, I feel him advance, passing me, his shoulder brushing mine, and he tells me, "Look at you work it," his voice rough with desire.

"I know this game's rules," I say flippantly.

He raises his brows. "Do you? Baby, I invented this game." And just as he leaves to greet an incoming crowd, he whispers in my ear, "I'd kiss you right now, but like I've said before, I don't do things half-ass, especially my woman."

And we part again, swallowed by the crowd.

"But my, was I surprised when President Hamilton announced you. You are so, so very young," one of the elderly women, a judge, tells me, eyeing me narrowly.

I swallow nervously, feeling judged. "I *am* young," I say. "But you can't always measure maturity in years. I'm fully devoted to both the president and my role."

I ease away, and only after that do I realize what I said.

I'm fully devoted to the president ...

I wonder if he knows that though I'm doing my best to be grateful and polite, to put myself out there, this is hard for me.

Finding it a little hard to breathe, my dress constricting, I search for him among the crowd. He's still being chased by a dozen people approaching him to say hello.

A yearning for something more normal steals into my mind, and suddenly I fully understand Matthew's own wish for normalcy, growing up the way he did.

I know that whenever I see him for the following four or eight years, this will be the case. Every time we go out in public, this will be the case—he will be the sun all the planets in our universe gravitate around.

And the women?

The women are everywhere.

I watch them throw themselves at him and I get a sinking feeling in the pit of my stomach. It's never-ending. And of course they want him. He is Matthew Hamilton. Not only the hottest bachelor you've ever seen, but the country's most powerful man.

I'm his acting first lady. I'd thought that it was a good idea to let him do his job, and me mine, before anything about our personal relationship came out. Maybe I'm just trying to get used to the cameras, trying to be sure the people will accept me. I would hate to be the intern the president screwed— any number of scenarios could come up, and a part of me has hoped that if I gain their respect as a first lady, they will accept me, no questions asked.

I may be deluding myself.

The press thrives on tiny morsels and tidbits. They can feast on me in a second, and like Matt has said before, people will think what they want to think.

I've wanted them to think he's available.

Now I'm so resentful of the situation.

Feeling my cheeks flush with frustration and a desire to simply breathe, I turn around in search for a safe zone.

Right this second, I can't fake the part with so many eyes on me, while all the female eyes are on *him*. I feel a little bit sick to my stomach wondering if I can really do this—be with someone like him, love someone like him, step up this high to do something of this magnitude.

I head outside, watching Stacey move across the room to where I'm going.

"I just want some air," I explain.

She speaks into her mic and opens the door for me, and I'm grateful that she gives me space as I head down the long terrace, as far as possible, into the bite of the chilling wind.

I'm rattled and need some space. I'm trying to compose myself outside, and my heart nearly flies out of my throat when I hear his deep voice behind me. I hadn't heard him approach. He's stealthy like that; he comes to you unaware and before you know it, he is EVERYWHERE. Freaking *everywhere*. In your dreams, in your every thought, right in front of you, so big and beautiful and brawny and elegant and untouchable.

His voice is low, concerned. "You do realize I've never seen you pissed before."

I swallow.

"I know, I ... I *know* I asked you to go slow. This is all me, feeling jealous, and wondering if I can do this." I inhale and search for words. "It's just hard to share you when we do find time to be together ..." I turn around to face him.

There's a silence. Matt looks at me. "You don't have to. We don't have to complicate this, Charlotte."

I swallow.

"You've been working the room like a pro, and I've never seen anything so beautiful in my life."

I inhale and head forward, then I reach out and brush my fingers across the back of his. "You're worth it. I'd do it a thousand times for you," I say, and I mean it.

I squeeze his fingers, stepping toward the room as he opens the door.

"I do want to come out. Soon. I'm ready. I want you. I want to be with you. I want this. I want everyone to know that I do," I rush out as I let him go.

People watch us walk inside, and my breath catches when Matt—Matthew Hamilton—slips his fingers back into mine.

I almost jerk as a bolt of lightning runs through my body at the gentle but firm grip.

Oh my fucking god.

I jerk my eyes to his, asking silently, *What are you doing?*

And his eyes are twinkling as he looks down at me, as if expecting my shock. And he says, "Dance with me."

"What?" I'm so stunned, everything drowns and fades except the man before me, his eyes dark and coaxing.

A god, really.

My throat feels like I've got a ball of fire in there somewhere as I try to make it work. I notice the daughter of the attorney general, models and actresses, all glancing this way, and I can't help but tease him as I feel that lingering jealousy prick me again. "Are you sure you want to dance with *me*? You have hundreds of admirers hoping for you to ask."

His eyes sparkle with amusement. "I happen to admire only one." His voice dips as he tugs on my hand. Amusement lost to heat—raw heat simmering with fiery passion. "Come here, Charlotte."

I start to shake nervously, but he pulls me to him and onto the dance floor.

I'm panicked, and also overcome with little bubbles of excitement swimming in my veins. We start dancing. Everything that is him envelops me as cameras flash and people watch him move me around the dance floor.

He holds me very close, and protectively. My body comes alive at the touch. Arousal swims in my veins. It's not the appropriate sentiment to feel here, dancing with the president, but I can't help it. I want him close. I want to feel him inside me. I want him to remind me that of all the women fawning over him, I'm the one he loves—but at the same time, I want to pull away, too afraid of what we're doing. Of coming out into the light for everyone to know. To see. That Matt and I …

"This isn't a good idea," I breathe, aware of people watching with awe and excitement.

"I don't care."

"Matt—Mr. President," I protest, hoping that professionalism will change the proprietary look in his eyes. I'm glancing around for an escape route even though I can barely move my legs.

Our bodies brush as we dance, his legs hard and grazing the sides of mine, his biceps bulging around me as the song swarms around us.

He simply smiles.

"You once said you might not mind being by the president's side," he says. My libido goes crazy under that smile. His words husky, seducing me. The proximity of his mouth to my earlobe making my heart go haywire.

"That was before," I whisper worriedly.

He captures my gaze with his powerful one. "Before you fell in love with me, or after?"

We hold each other's gazes as the song finishes.

"Before you did this—everyone is looking," I say, panicked.

"Good."

He's smiling as he dips me backward for the song's finale and crushes his mouth to mine, with a little bit of tongue.

"I cannot believe you did that," I tell him on our way back.

"Can you not?" he asks, laughing softly.

"If I were to go online right now, I bet there are a thousand and one rumors, stories, and the like circulating."

"I am not one bit interested in what they are. Neither should you be." He tugs me forward. "We're adults. You're my first lady. We can be together, Charlotte. We are, and we need to face up to the music, regardless of the tune. We will get through this."

There's a silence. Matt holds my face and pulls it up, smiling. "All they know for a fact is that I kissed you. The message implied is clear—you're mine. I'm dating you, and you're dating me. Which reminds me, I want to take you out. I've been jealous just thinking of you alone with anyone else. I get jealous of every man out there who can be with you, hold your hand and kiss your face. Now it's me ..." He presses his lips to mine.

"You don't have anything to be jealous of," I scoff.

He grabs me by the hips and lifts me to his lap, his eyes blazing with heat and possessiveness.

"Neither do you. I saw you tonight. You were flushed, jealous of the women greeting me."

I bite down on my lip. "You're … their absolute fantasy. Of course I'm jealous. You're their fantasy *and* mine."

He looks at me biting my lip, and I release it. "You seem to be ignorant of the fact that I'm taken. I've been taken for quite some time."

Leaning to smooth his tongue over the lip I bit, Matt slides his hand under the skirt of my dress, touching the inside of my thighs with his fingertips. My breath snags in my throat when he caresses the damp spot in my panties.

His eyes flash when he realizes I'm wet.

"Lift your dress. I want to feel more of you."

I start to lift my dress and part my legs as he presses his lips to mine, opening them so he can rub his tongue over mine as he eases one finger inside me.

"God, you're addictive. Who do you want here, beautiful?" he groans, finding me soaked inside.

I moan into his mouth and link my arms around his neck, thrusting my hips out for his touch.

"You."

"Who does this belong to?" He dips his tongue into my mouth and moves his finger in and out, in and out, driving me crazy. Crazy with jealousy, with desire, with want.

"You."

"That's right." He smothers my moans with his mouth.

A WARNING, PLEASE

Matt

Lola slaps a newspaper on my desk the next morning. The headline reads, ***KISS OF THE AGES: PRESIDENT HAMILTON AND THE FIRST LADY STUN GUESTS WITH A PUBLIC KISS FOR THE HISTORY BOOKS!***

"We need to talk about Charlotte."

"No, we don't."

"We've created a million new jobs with your new clean energy program and it's been overshadowed by your little stunt." She stutters when she realizes what she's said. "Mr. President. Respectfully." She nods. "You could've warned me," she hisses.

"No, Lola, I couldn't." I lean back and link my fingers behind my head. "The fact that our million jobs didn't make the front-page news doesn't diminish the fact that we *are* creating new employment. That number will look like kiddie play in a couple more months. Relax." I lick my thumb and flip through one of the pages on my desk.

She exhales.

"I *will* give you a heads-up," I add, pausing a moment. "I'm going to marry her."

"Excuse me?"

"What I said. Thank you, Lola." I dismiss her.

Our country is broken. Jacobs was a weak president. So many minorities have been ignored. The problem in the Middle East is raging full force.

I have other shit to do than worry about the media.

She's wide-eyed and blanching. "How will I handle the press?"

"They don't need to be handled. I'll take care of it when the time comes. Make some calls. Be sure we get some features on what we're doing. Besides me kissing the first lady." I smirk.

She smirks back, then seems to catch herself and shakes her head. "Mr. President."

And she excuses herself, while I gaze at the headline. There's a photo of Charlotte in my arms, her hands on my shoulders—she was pushing me back but, oh, that mouth was definitely opening beneath mine.

Lola wanted a warning?

I didn't even get one myself.

I want to worship this girl. I wanted to glide my hands all over her body. Hundreds of women were trying to catch my attention, and the only one it lingered on last night was her.

I really hadn't planned to make a scene. Lose my shit. I'm used to being tightly controlled. Blame it on all those expectations. The expectations for me to carry on as a Hamilton, the whole world resting on my shoulders. With her, it feels like she wants me to be nothing more than I am, nothing less. Everybody else is asking questions, what my stance is … not

Charlotte. I know she secretly loves it when I lose control, and I lost it well and good last night.

I went with it. I wanted her mouth—I wanted them all to see her, in my arms. Mine, mine, mine.

This girl has seen me, every side of me, and still she looks at me like a sun.

She's concerned; she wanted me to take it easy. Now I feel like I can do anything but.

My father cast my mother into the shadows, and keeping Charlotte close yet far away ... I cannot do that. I want her up in the limelight, with me. First lady, not feeling like a secret: a true wife. She deserves better than what she thinks she does.

I want more for her.

I want more for myself.

Yeah, I want her more than ever.

Her passion, her kindness, her realness, her ability to laugh ...

Her.

I'm in over my head for this girl. Once I thought I couldn't do both, govern a broken country and have her. But I know now that I will die trying to do both. This is who I am. I'm the president and a man. She's the girl I love and the woman I want to spend my life with.

Really, it can be as simple as that.

I toss aside the newspaper Lola dumped on my desk, then glance at my watch to check for my next meeting just when Portia announces, "Mr. President, Mr. Cox from the Federal Bureau of Investigation here to see you."

I stand and button my jacket as Cox strides inside, extending his hand in greeting over my desk. "Cox," I say, reciprocating. We both take a seat.

"We followed through, checked the scarf for fingerprints and traced the prints to a store in the D.C. area. The owner confirmed that the president's wife was a customer of their store and that President Law frequently ordered them to choose his gifts for her."

"He had this to give to my mother. Jesus." I scrape a hand over my jaw as frustration gnaws me raw.

"We're following every thread no matter how minor," Cox assures me.

I level him a look. "Do that."

WAKE UP
THE PRESIDENT

Charlotte

After *THE* kiss of the decade, we're watching TV the following evening as Matt steps out of the shower, a towel draped over his hips. He looks like God embodied in a damn dark-haired, espresso-eyed, edible human candy bar. I cannot believe he kissed me. With tongue. In front of hundreds of people and, it seems, the whole wide world.

"... stunned when President Hamilton kissed the first lady on the dance floor. White House press has been asking the question on everyone's mind during this morning's press conference. Is President Hamilton dating Miss Charlotte Wells? The official stance of the White House is yes."

It's all over. I got a hundred calls today. Alan called too, his disappointment evident in his voice, considering he once maybe wanted to be the one dating me.

"You're *dating* the president of the United States?"

Kayla: "I could have died when I saw the photo! I'm missing out on so much that's happening! Charlotte! Tell me *everything*!"

And my mother: "I don't know what to say. Your father and I ..." She sounded teary. "You love him?"

"You know the answer to that, Mom. Why else would I be here? I wouldn't ever have dreamed of finding the courage to try on a role this big if it weren't attached to Matthew."

"Then that's all that matters."

They can't get enough of it. Not the public, not our friends and family. Matt says Beckett called and simply said, "You go, sir!"

They absolutely cannot get enough of the story.

Matthew turns off the TV as he hits the bed, where I lie in wait—so ready, so anxious, gravitating toward him as he reaches out with one powerful arm.

I can feel it—the electricity between us, the connection too strong to deny, always there, crackling, whipping around us, tugging us closer and closer yet never close enough.

We make fierce love. He tells me how beautiful I am, how special, how much he wants me. We're sweaty and sated, my body buzzing in the aftermath, when there's a knock on the door.

Matt leaps out of bed and slips into his slacks.

"Mr. President." It's Dale Coin's voice.

Matt swings the door open and I pull the sheets up, mortified and scared to see the grim look on Dale's face.

"There's been a situation. Six of our crew members have been taken hostage in Syria."

From lowered lids, Matt shoots a commanding look at me. "I'll be back."

"Matthew ..." I begin, just not knowing what to say.

His eyes meet mine harshly as he slips on his shirt.

A knife of pain and concern for our people gets trapped in my throat. Matt charges down the hall, and I get dressed quickly and head to my own bedroom, where I pace, pace, pace—and pray.

I see it on the news.

The harsh reality of every catastrophe that happens to the United States of America too close now. So close. So real.

These are our people. My country attacked. My guy.

This being first lady isn't just the interviews, the pretty dresses. It's everything else.

I'm not sure I'm prepared. That the little bubble of a perfect life my parents created for their only daughter prepared me for this—to live this so closely.

It's hard to keep my hope alive when I see the burning American flag on television that the rebel forces in Syria have lit.

The exploded armament trucks that had carried our troops.

I break down and cry, and I eventually fall asleep, only to wake up to my bedroom door being opened.

Matthew's silhouette fills the doorway.

Whatever he's ordered done—is done. I can see it in his eyes.

And a part of me doesn't want to know if it will take more casualties, what the exact situation is.

I'm scared. I'm hurting for our country. I'm hurting for my president.

He starts walking forward, and I stand on wobbly legs, the urge to embrace him and have him embrace me too strong—but the pain feels just as strong.

He tugs on the flimsy ribbon holding my nightgown closed. "Are you okay?" I whisper.

His hand pauses; he looks at me.

"Do you want to talk?" I ask.

"No," he rasps.

I slide my fingers up his jaw, the stubble abrading my fingertips as I rise up on tiptoe and kiss him. No tongue, just a kiss. "I don't know what I can do. The whole country is crying. I feel a pain like I've never experienced, as if the whole world's pain is mine now."

"It is. It's ours." His eyes hold mine. My lungs feel like rocks; no amount of air is able to fill them.

"Let me just ..." I glance down at myself, sure that my eyes are swollen and I look a sight. I want to look pretty; I want him to lose himself in me. I want him to take whatever he needs.

I head to the bathroom. I inhale and put water on my face, brush my hair. Try to look pretty for him. I pry the nightgown off—stripping. Stripping for him.

I step out, and he's gone.

I fasten on a robe and head out of my room. He's sitting in the Oval, his head in his hands, staring blindly down at some papers.

I walk in and he lifts his head, and I open my robe. "If you think I can't handle what you have to give me right now, you're wrong," I say, my voice thick with emotion.

His jaw starts ticking as I shrug my arms from my robe sleeves.

He comes to a stand and I throw the robe at my feet. He catches me when I approach, boosts me up to his desk, spreads my legs open, and licks me.

Right *there.*

I come.

I *come.*

A moan of ecstasy slips past my lips as I jerk beneath his mouth, coming with his mouth pressing tighter and deeper on me, Matt drinking up my orgasm like a starved man.

I sag with a soft cry.

Matt eases himself up and looks down at me, his pupils so dilated I can hardly make out the color of his eyes.

He scoops me up and covers me with my robe.

And steps outside.

"Sir," Secret Service says as he steps forward.

"I've got her," he tells both the agent and the doorman who walks him to his room every day when he also steps up to help. He motions to me to follow.

The staff that we pass on our way there? They smile under their gazes, and too late I worry that this will erupt into a media frenzy.

"My bedroom is that way." I point when we reach the residence.

"We're not going to your bedroom."

The doorman opens the door to Matt's bedroom, and Matt thanks him. "Go to bed, Bill—we're done here."

The door shuts behind us as he drops me down on the bed. I cling and kiss him, burning for him.

He strips quickly and I look at him. All that strength. His muscled arms with silky, dark hairs running along the backs of his forearms. The soft mat of hair on his chest and the line tapering beneath his pants. My gaze following the arrow of hair from his belly button down to the cock beneath.

He crawls on the bed over me, his body hovering over mine, and we're eye to eye.

He trails his tongue along the seam of my lips. I mewl. "Tell me you want it."

His erection is heavy against my abdomen as he grips my hip with one hand and my face with the other. He dips his tongue into my mouth with a slow, wet, powerful flick. "Tell me."

"I want you," I breathe, arching beneath him.

He slides his hand from my face downward.

Down my throat.

Down my cleavage.

Across my belly button.

Down.

To cup my sex.

And penetrate me with two fingers.

His features tighten with raw passion.

A groan vibrates up his chest. A groan just like the one that vibrates up my own chest.

I shudder beneath him.

He watches me for a moment, eyes darkening by the second as he takes his cock and teases my wet entrance with the head. I'm waiting for him, panting. Wanting. He rocks back and then starts filling me, not with a fast thrust, but with a slow, deliberate drive of his hips that makes me aware of every inch of him entering—every inch possessing me.

He fills me—no condom, all bare, just him—as if he doesn't plan to leave an inch of me unclaimed, unfucked, or empty. He fills me as if he's home. He tenses when he's fully inside, and groans when my body clutches him greedily—my channel gripping his hot length, not wanting to let him go.

We're both fighting for control, to take it slow, his body shaking with his need. I rock my hips and he does the same, a low growl rumbling up his chest as he lifts his head from my breasts and kisses me, kisses me as if I'm all there is right now, all he wants.

"You're everything, everything good and pure and right," he rasps into my mouth. He seizes me by the hips and pulls out only to drive in, so deeply I feel him in my heart.

"And you're all I want," I gasp, and he slips his hands under the small of my back and grabs me by the ass, holding me there as he starts pounding me harder. He lowers his head. Forehead hovering above mine. Pounding inside me.

My body starts seizing as I hit the pinnacle. His hard, muscular body moving over me without mercy now. Tears of pleasure burn in my eyes as Matt relentlessly drives in and out, in and out, watching me now—watching me take it, take him, writhe for him, go off for him.

I cry out, a soft yell I fear echoes all over the White House.

I'm lost. I'm his. I don't want to be anywhere else, will never be anyone else's, he's my guy, my commander, my *god.*

As I come, his eyes flash as he looks down at me, every raw emotion written on his face, every feeling he's tried to hide in public is out here in the open for me, every ounce of passion etched across his normally impassive face here for me to see.

I come even harder, if that's possible, my body reverberating top to bottom, side to side, and down to the marrow of my bones.

He reaches his climax right in my depths, and I know it's because my own climax detonated him. His body pulses with his orgasm. I'm still going off in a crazy undulating motion beneath him, but he holds me down by the hips and forces me to take everything. A thousand bursts of color behind my eyelids. I cling to his body and hear him exhale in satisfaction against the top of my head.

We fall still, our breaths echoing in the Lincoln bedroom. I ache because of him and I also ache for more. Even when he's still hard inside me.

A sheen of sweat coats our bodies. Matt's coffee gaze feathers over my naked form.

"I can't get enough of you."

He sounds amazed and a little frustrated as he cradles the back of my head as he lifts me up an inch for his mouth. He pushes his tongue inside until I mewl softly. "Fuck if I'm not ready to take you again," he says, his voice gruff as he slides his large, gentle hand down my abdomen.

He cups me between my thighs and gently feels me.

"How sensitive are you, Charlotte?" he asks, lightly rubbing his index finger along my opening.

I hear a low mewl leave me. I want to lick him up, every inch of him, and I definitely crave to lick every inch of his big presidential cock.

"I want you," I breathe. "Again and again. And I want to …"

I let my eyes fall on his erection and shuffle my body closer. I stare at his cock, the head turgid and swollen, the veins popping up the length. Matt is so swollen he feels heavy in my hand as I reach him. I cup his balls in both my hands, then slide my fingers upward, encircling his width with both my hands as I take him in my mouth.

The taste of the salty drop of pre-cum already on the tip of his cock along my tongue makes me moan deep inside.

A groan rumbles up his throat as he begins to pump into my mouth. His hands are fisted in my hair. He's plunging deeper, filling my mouth with his cock. With every upward thrust groaning my name, *Charlotte.*

Before he starts coming, he pulls me back and dives for my mouth with his hungry one.

His kiss so hard our teeth gnash together, our tongues tangle without holding back.

"More," I moan as we keep kissing and running our hands all over each other's sweat-slicked bodies.

He instantly rolls me to my back, and goes where he wants to go.

The pace is frantic, the bed squeaking, he's fucking me so hard, his eyes watching me as if there is nothing more beautiful, nothing he'd rather see, than me—naked and writhing—in his bed.

He fucks me primally, like he knows he's the most powerful man in the world, and I'm so hot for him I come right away.

I'm loose in bed, languid in his arms, Matt chuckling when I groan as if in pain.

"You okay?" He cups my face and inspects my features, then all of me, sort of in a concerned but admiring way.

"Better than okay. I just bagged the president." I smile, a sad, forlorn, haunted smile, then Matt looks down at me as he pinches my nipple, playfully.

"I just fucked the daylights out of the first lady and I don't intend to let up anytime soon."

Matt brings a Kleenex and wipes me between my legs, and watching him do this makes my heart sort of crumble.

"I'm sorry. I got carried away. I'll be more careful." He cups my face and kisses my forehead, looking into my eyes. "Are we going to be okay?"

I look into his eyes, realizing what he's asking me. If there's a risk of me getting pregnant.

"I think we're okay," I breathe, then nod more firmly. "Yes."

He smiles at that, kisses me on the lips. "You felt incredible," he assures.

When he returns and sits at the side of the bed, he's silent, and although he's leaning forward on his elbows, his broad shoulders tense.

"If you need to go, I don't want to keep you," I whisper.

He drags a hand over his face and glances at me. "Nothing I can do right now. I made the call. I'm meeting in the Situation Room"—he glances at the clock on the nightstand, then shakes his head—"later."

I knee my way on the bed toward him. "Will they be okay?"

He clenches his jaw as I wrap my arms around his shoulders. "I'm betting a rescue team of eight on that." He nods firmly, his eyes glazed, warlike.

"Can I do anything?" I ask.

He kisses me, thoughtful. "Pray."

"I'm sorry this happened."

"There's a price for peace. Always." He looks at me. "But it's worth it." He runs a hand down the back of my head. "Go to sleep, baby."

I lie back down, and he stretches out beside me, a pillow propped behind his back as he pulls me to his side.

My eyes drift shut. No matter what goes on outside this room, in these arms, I feel safer than I ever do anywhere else, and the relaxation seeps into my pores as I drift off and keep my arms around him—as if I, just a small, normal girl, could somehow comfort the most powerful man in the world.

I wake up at 5 a.m. Matt isn't there. I sit up. "Matt?"

I look around the empty bedroom, ease out of bed, and quickly get dressed. I find him in the small family kitchen. "Are you all right?"

He takes my hand and draws me to sit next to him, then he presses his thumb into my palm, quiet. My heart speeds up with a mix of panic and dread. It feels as if my ribs have just collapsed in my chest, crushing my lungs.

"I had an early meeting in the Situation Room."

I know why. It's not easy to make the hard calls. But then our eyes connect again, and a smile tugs his lips. "It's done. The men are free. A couple wounded, but no casualties. The rescue team did an outstanding job."

"Oh, thank god."

"Yeah, thank god."

"And *you*. And *them*."

He rakes a hand through his hair, then pulls me to him, pressing his lips to mine. Pressing them hard.

"Mr. President," a Secret Service agent says. "Marine One's ready, sir."

"Let's go," he tells the agent as he reaches for the suit jacket he has draped behind his chair. "They're flying them in. I'll be there to receive them."

"I have to do a talk at a middle school in New Orleans."

He nods. "I'll see you this weekend."

He's flying to Fort Lee.

I watch out the window as several marine helicopters depart at the same time. Only one carries Matt.

HOME

Matt

I spend two days with our men and their families. I engaged in a meeting with some of my generals, and requested several new and detailed plans for the handling of the Middle East crisis.

It's late evening when I climb into the state car along with Wilson, who joins me in the back as we head to Marine One to return to D.C.

"She's home?" I ask Wilson.

It's pretty convenient that my agents have constant contact with her.

I'm eager to see her. I shed more than my clothes when I'm with her. I shed every preconceived notion of who I should be. My last name, the presidency, everything is gone—only I remain. A man, flesh and blood, not perfect, but trying his damn best to be, and a man who wants her. Bad.

"Yes, sir." Even Wilson sounds amused.

Shit, I'm too old for this.

My heart is pounding like a wild thing and I'm drumming my fingers on our way there.

Just remembering the way she gave herself to me, open to whatever I needed, so sweet and vulnerable, makes me thirstier, hungrier.

I reach the White House and Jack is barking at the top of his lungs. "Go find her," I say.

And I follow him as he dashes up the steps and stops at her room, wagging his tail.

"Good boy." I pat the back of his head, then I twist the knob, telling him under my breath, "Stay," and walk inside.

She's reading on the bed. Looking up to see me, her eyes widening, her mouth parting in a tiny *O*.

I clench my hands. The need to protect her burns me on the inside. To rid the world of every evil, every injustice, everything that could hurt her or anyone like her.

I'm wired, have had little sleep, and am instantly hard. I should step away, chill with a glass of wine. Fucking unwind. But I couldn't move away if threatened with a bullet to the head.

She uncurls that sweet body and comes to her feet, setting her book down.

I head over to where she stands at the foot of the bed and pull her to me, lowering my head. A graze first, my lips on hers. It turns hungry. One second, two, and my hands are diving into her hair, grabbing her to me.

"You seem happy to see me."

"You know damn well that I am," I growl, feeling possessive, smiling at how pleased she seems.

She smiles happily and nibbles on my lips, and I groan and nibble harder, faster. She's so sweet; she is sweet inside and out, and I've developed a sweet tooth of the kind I've never had.

I want to marry this girl. I want to marry her now.

We kiss. I'm getting into the taste of her, the feel of her, the freedom of her mouth, her wandering hands, melding the taste of espresso in my mouth with the mint in hers.

I push her down on the bench at the foot of the bed and then crouch before her, parting her ties and pushing her lacy pajamas up to her hips. She's bare underneath the silk, her pussy pink and wet. My cock pulses relentlessly against my zipper. I suck her clit into my mouth and slide my fingers into her sweet wet sex, one first, then another, then one more, stretching her. Rubbing her G-spot. Watching her arch her back and make those noises deep from within her throat that I can't get enough of.

I'm thick to the point of pain.

I strip her of her clothes, and then I strip too. I kiss her, slow and thorough, sticking my tongue inside. She starts coming when I drive inside her. I stop kissing her for a moment—watching her come. Just like that, all over my cock. I take her mouth and kiss her quiet. She moans and gurgles during orgasm, tilting her hips up against mine.

I hold her down and ram as hard as I can, barking as I release, pushing us hard until it's over.

"You missed me," she says, smiling, her face reddened with exertion, a sheen of sweat coating her skin.

I smile back, then look down at her, staying inside her for a while.

"Yeah." I brush my knuckles down her cheek.

She's the kind of woman you keep and cherish, the one you want to enjoy a full, complete life with. But she hasn't been hardened by the political life that women like my mother have. Charlotte is soft, soft and sweet, everything that politics is not. I don't want it to touch her. I get off on the idea that somewhere in the world, people harden and push so that others can keep their innocence. She was one of those others. But that changed the night our men were taken. I can see the tiny shadows in her eyes. It kills me that they're there, but along with those is the steely look of a woman, of a woman coming into her own.

And much like the sweet, fiery girl … this woman? This woman is mine.

AMERICA

Charlotte

No matter how much I love the White House, there is something about going out and interacting with America itself. I know I'm not the only one who gets inspired by this closer view of our country; Matthew does as well.

He's intelligent at reviewing the changes, but the ideas for changes—the realizations of what this country really needs—sometimes don't come at you in the Oval. They come at you in the street, while shaking a veteran's hand and thanking him for his service, looking into a little boy's eyes and realizing all he wants is a family.

Matthew Hamilton is the president of the United States—and now is the time he's putting his ideas into action.

Now is the time when I realize that I can make a difference, through him, through the White House, if I am only brave enough to step out of my comfort zone and make real changes. Even small ones. The tiniest change is still change, the ripples from it sometimes farther and wider than you'd ever think.

I notice even our presence anywhere inspires people—gives people hope. The hopeless are hopeless no more. We stand for something. We stand proudly for that something.

We've been touring the country, me on a mission to speak to women and children while Matt takes on several projects, evaluates the proposed bills, and puts the pedal to the metal on all the changes he wants to take place during his first four years.

I'm not used to this lifestyle, to having so many people tend to me—assistants, makeup artists, the Secret Service. Sworn to secrecy, they'd give their lives for us. I'm humbled by their service. I'm also not used to all the attention and the frequent invitations from fans and supporters, or the requests from charities who clamor for Matt's endorsement or mine.

I've scrambled to keep up. I'm in California now, the land of the stars and the paparazzi, and things have been getting hectic. Matt said he'd join me after accepting an invitation to NASA.

Several of his managers and chiefs, along with Alison and me, have just finished a shoot promoting clean energy when he arrives on Air Force One from his NASA tour. I ask my detail to drive me to the airport to greet him, and I watch him descend from the plane in a black suit and a crimson tie, surprised when he pulls me close to him and flat-out kisses me on the mouth.

The press has a field day with it:

Hamilton Holds Nothing Back from the First Lady

That night, after he went to dine with a list of influential Hollywood figures, the latest headline caught our attention in Matt's suite:

Psychic Communicates with Ex-President Hamilton. "Matt Will Exact Vengeance!"

"Sounds like him, doesn't he?" Dale Coin says—almost as if he believes this psychic could truly impact Matt's own memory of his father.

Matt smiles wryly and lets the newspaper fall back with the others, but when he looks out the window, his eyes have darkened.

"Not vengeance. Justice."

My eyes widen when I see the shadows in his gaze.

The press has been all over the Middle East conflict—Matt has been talking to the generals, executing several covert operations to clear our men out of there. Aside from that, everyone is still hung up on us dating. And his kisses, and the fact that he takes my hand to help me out of the car and doesn't necessarily let go. The fact that he puts his hand on the small of my back when leading us somewhere.

All of it has been photographed and recorded, to my continued blushing about the celebrity of our now open relationship.

A reporter observes, "It does seem that the president appreciates having Miss Wells around, as we can see in this short video, where not only the public seemed enchanted by Miss Wells and her cute little purple dress at the state dinner held for President Asaf, but the president himself didn't look at anything else for a brief but very obvious moment. What we all want to know is how this is going to play out and whether our president's head will be in the right place."

He powers off the TV, leaning back and looking at me with a silent, dark expression as our staff leaves us alone for the night.

Matthew booked only one suite for us—another fact that was recorded.

I swallow and look out, remembering all the people that have been gathering around him, how much they crave just a glimpse of their president.

"I don't want to distract you. The media seems more hung up on *us* than what you're doing. I don't know that I like that."

"They focus on what gives them ratings. So be it." He looks at me as if he thinks I'm the cause of their ratings—not him, the most coveted bachelor shamelessly chasing after me—and glances at the eagle pin I'm wearing on the right side of my dress. I know he loves it when I wear it. His voice lowers a decibel. "Every presidency has had its defining moments. We don't know what they will be for us. Battling ISIS. Nuclear war. Cyber war." He tells me, "Do you know what the problem is with the past decades of elections, and why the candidates' views shift so dramatically, their promises unkept, after they take office?"

"What?"

"The day you're sworn in, you become privy to confidential information—everything you need to know to run the country. Information that's sensitive, powerful, from espionage, delicate treaties, foreign relations. Some of this knowledge crushes the candidate's dreams of what he wished to accomplish. People get disappointed, and the country continues carrying the weight of decisions made even decades ago, three presidents past."

I'm transfixed, wanting to know more.

"Every president leaves the office looking aged far more years than those he served. It's the hardest office in the land. I swore I'd never walk in. Every time my dad and I flew back on Marine One, onto the lawns of the White House, and he would tell me, 'We're home,' I'd say, 'Home to jail.' And he'd say, 'Yes, son.'"

"What did you find, Matt?"

"Nothing without loopholes. Treaties not to our benefit. Dangers lurking that we must tread carefully around. This is why I'm here, Charlotte. I knew this wouldn't be simple. But I'm sick and tired of watching the train wreck and doing nothing to stop it. I know what it takes to run the country—it takes your very soul, and tough calls that might not always be the right ones. But we deserve someone willing to make them and back them up, make us thrive again, even if he has to sacrifice everything to do so."

"But your father sacrificed his life," I say miserably.

He rubs the back of his neck, then drops his hand with a sigh as he tugs his tie a bit loose. "I'm not sure he was killed because of the presidency."

"What do you mean?"

"Cox and I suspect it was something personal, more than his policies."

A thousand—no, a million—knots wind up in my stomach. "Matthew, please don't put yourself in danger. You're the commander in chief; you can't be opening a can of worms, like my dad once said."

"I will take care of myself. And Charlotte," he specifies, his eyes darkening as he shifts forward to brush his thumb along my jawline, until he uses it to tilt my head back by the chin. "I will take care of *you*. Do you hear me?" He holds my gaze with steely determination. "You and this country. Go to sleep now."

He kicks off his shoes and throws his tie off as I take off my clothes and slide into bed in my lingerie, under the sheets.

"I bet you joined me here because you missed me."

"Not one bit," he says too easily, grabbing some papers and bringing them to the chair by the bed.

"Not a little bit?" I put three centimeters between my fingers.

He narrows his eyes, then from his seat, leans forward and squishes my fingers. "Maybe that."

"You're a dick."

He scowls. "Hush, you don't talk to your president like that." He slips his glasses on and starts thumbing through the papers.

"I just did, Mr. President. Sir."

He laughs, sets the papers on his lap, and reaches out and strokes my hair. "Go to sleep. I've got to read up on something."

I lie down, Matt, with those sexy glasses, reading but sporadically glancing up to check on me, as if it gives him peace to watch me sleep. The monsters lurking in the shadows can't get close to me, not with him here.

"Do you remember the boy we visited when campaigning?" he asks.

"Of course. They named him after you!"

"I followed up on him. I invited him to the White House. He and his parents will be gracing us with their company next month."

"You kept your promise."

"Of course I kept my promise."

I squeal and I leap out of bed to throw myself at him, tackle-hugging him and raining kisses on his face. "You're the best!"

But the best is truly Matt's low, quiet laughter as I pry off his glasses and shower him with my appreciation. He tugs the papers I just sat on and sets them aside, letting me rain kisses all over him.

Getting instantly hard.

"Now *that* missed me at least," I whisper in his ear.

His voice is gruff as he cups my face gently in both hands, and his eyes are hot and liquid as they coast over my face. "You know I missed you, girl. You know I miss you." He lifts my hand and laces our fingers, running his thumb along mine, and then he lifts my fourth finger to his mouth and wraps his lips around it, licking it clean.

"What are you doing?" I gasp, suddenly more aroused than ever.

"Hmm. You taste good." He smirks, letting go of my hand and grabbing a fistful of hair as he crushes my mouth beneath his.

Once back in the White House, Matt schedules a few press conferences during the week. I steal into a couple just to hear him.

I love Lola introducing him. "Ladies and gentlemen, the President of the United States …"

I love how the room shifts and reenergizes when he enters. How everyone seems to feel more important, wants to do more, *be* more in his presence; the man has red, white, and blue running in his veins. American royalty: the country's new commander in chief. The press can't get enough of him.

He speaks to the reporters casually, as if they're longtime friends, as if he's used to speaking to them, which is quite true.

I'm actually sorry that Clarissa told me I needed to look at some crucial issues about the upcoming state dinner this morning, causing me to miss the last press conference.

HEADLINES

Matt

"Make no mistake about it. Right and left need to be working together. There needs to be an understanding and full cooperation to move forward. Globalization is a must not only for society, but for our industry, for our trade, for our personal growth, for our mental understanding. We're working on eliminating the fragmenting of our society. Right and left wings against each other ... those burnt bridges we've encountered? They must be rebuilt. The misinformation that helped lead to those breaking points must be addressed. The White House will have more open communication—online, via letters, and through appointments with the president. New knowledge about our policies, our passed bills, and our plans will be at your fingertips. We're opening up more than we ever have with a new portal, and ... ladies and gentlemen ... the portal will go live tonight."

I stop there, letting the press corps take notes before I proceed, changing my tone to a more personal one.

"I'm sure you're all wondering why I'm telling you this, since Lola would have done just as good a job as I did, or even better." I smirk, then pause.

"Starting today, I too will share something important to me," I admit, cocking my head from one side of the room to the other, meeting their gazes. "The most important thing that has happened to me next to the death of my father, and being elected your president."

Heads rise from their scribbles.

I know they can tell I'm talking about more than policy now.

I know these reporters, and they know me.

Some of them I grew up with. Some of them were with me in college. Some, even, I've known since my father was here.

Oh yes, they know me.

"I'm sure it may not be a surprise," I say, clearly and succinctly, meeting their eyes as candidly as I can. "I am in love with the first lady of the United States. At the moment, a dozen vans from District florists are pulling up at the White House, and the staffers are helping me fill up her room. I'm going to ask her to marry me. Today." I smile and lean closer to the microphone. "If you have any extra time, say a little prayer that she agrees."

"Go get her, Mr. President!" someone yells.

"I will." I grin.

I show them the ring from my pocket. "My father's mother had two large diamond earrings, which she gave to my father. The first diamond, he gave to my mother. The other to me. I want it on her finger. I've measured and calculated, and I think I've got the size right." The thought that I may not makes me frown as I look at the ring, then I shake my head as I tuck it away. "And don't think I'm asking her because Jacobs said I needed a first lady—though it's true I like the outfits she wears."

The correspondents laugh.

I chuckle too, and lean into the mic again.

"I think she is marvelous. She is untouched by politics, unmarred and untainted. She is absolutely, brilliantly humble. Honest, hardworking. And it would be my honor that she accept to be my wife. Now if you'll excuse me, I have a country to govern and a woman to woo."

"Which is the most difficult, President Hamilton?"

"The latter, for sure." I grin again, then nod. "Good day, ladies and gentlemen."

"When's the wedding?"

"As soon as possible. Today if I have my way."

ROSE GARDEN

Charlotte

The White House smells of roses. In fact, the East Wing of the White House where I usually work is *filled* with them. We got back a week ago and I don't think I've ever watched so many staffers, one after the other, pile into the room with more and more flowers.

"What is this? Is there a state dinner somebody forgot to tell me about?" I ask, panicked.

Clarissa's eyes go to the door, and Matt is there, lounging casually, looking at me.

I gulp.

Clarissa scurries out of the room, along with the rest of the staffers.

Intense emotion forces its way into his eyes. "Did you like my welcome home gift?"

"I didn't leave home. I mean, I did, but I got home a week ago."

"That's right. You're home for good. At least until my term is over. You're home with me."

He starts walking.

"Don't, Matt." I don't know what's happening, but I'm not sure I've ever seen that particularly fierce look in his eyes before.

"Then come here." He pulls me close. "I love you. I love you and I want to marry you." He inhales, kissing my jaw.

He slips something into his mouth and then takes my hand, lifts my finger to his mouth, and works a ring onto my finger with his tongue.

I gasp, my heart hammering. He licks the finger base to tip.

"Hmm. You taste good."

"Matthew ... the country—"

"They're all holding their breaths, waiting to know if you said yes."

"What? You're crazy!"

"For you."

I stare at him, stunned.

"They know, Charlotte; they've known for a long time how I feel about you. It's nothing I'm ashamed of, nothing I can hide anymore—nor do I want you to." He slips his hand over mine, and we watch our fingers link together. Mine and his.

"You are the man of my dreams, Matthew Hamilton," I blurt out, still sort of reeling. A tear escapes.

"No more tears, not for me."

"I'm just happy. I'm so happy. Did you mean it when you said everyone was waiting?"

"Everyone. It's probably on TV by now."

"What?" I turn on the TV.

"Our President Hamilton is proposing to the first lady and we're waiting with bated breath to hear!"

Placards say *I'LL MARRY YOU, HAMMY!*

Others plead *SAY YES!*

I start to cry. All this time, I worried that I might not be good enough for him, that the public might not like the idea of me—and Matt just put all that to rest. Matt made them want me by his side merely because he told them truthfully that he wanted me there.

I cry because of the way they love him, because he has never really feared being himself with them, letting them see all of him, that he is not just the president but also human and a man, and I'm inspired again, and so in love I cannot stand it.

"Don't just stand here! Don't leave them all like that! They're practically not breathing."

"Baby, *I'm* practically not breathing."

I look at him. "Summon Lola and tell her—do something—tell her to tell the press corps I said YES! How can I not say yes? Are you crazy?"

"I think we've already established that I am."

Alison and Lola appear at the door. Suddenly everyone's eyes are on me. I'm especially aware of Matt watching me, as if my reaction is crucial to solving some worldly problem.

I'm perplexed, once again wishing I knew what he was thinking as he turns back to Lola and Alison and smiles. "Look at the ring on Charlotte's finger."

Lola's eyes widen in excitement.

Matt grins. "Take a shot, spread it out wide. It'll speak more than a thousand words."

"Charlotte!" Alison cries, and I walk over and we hug each other.

"Okay. Picture." Alison realizes Matt—President Hamilton—is waiting and quickly steps back and takes an engagement shot of the two of us.

"Lola is going to be so busy," I tell Matt, canting my head to meet his gaze.

"She's always busy."

"And you?" I can only imagine how hounded he's going to be after this.

"I know someone who's going to be even busier." He flashes his wickedest smile at me as he crosses the room and lifts the phone. "Portia. Get the team ready. We have a wedding to plan."

I duck my head as I try to wipe the lingering tears from the corners of my eyes. For sure my makeup is ruined. For sure you can even tell in the picture Alison took. But

...

I wanted to make a difference, to find out my calling, to have a man to love. This is it. Unbelievably, this is it. A normal girl, with the most extraordinary love from the most extraordinary man.

I call my parents first. My mother is sort of speechless, and my dad takes the phone from her and tells me he'd talked to Matt before he proposed, but he hadn't told my mother, that she's shocked but they're thrilled with the news and that they look forward to the wedding.

Then I call Kayla.

"I've been trying to contact you!"

"I was on the line with my mom and dad."

"Charlotte, oh my god!" she says.

"I know, I *know*!" I say, giddy, looking at my engagement ring. It's a pear-shaped diamond, with two trapezoid emeralds flanking its sides, and it's so stunning I can barely look at it without feeling myself go breathless.

"You're marrying the president of the United States," she declares.

"Yes," I say.

"You're marrying the fucking *president of the United States*," she repeats, disbelieving.

"I'm already his first lady; don't act so shocked," I say, laughing.

"He's like … the most coveted bachelor in the land! Hammy! Hammy is marrying you, and you're marrying Hammy!"

"Kayla," I groan. "Make sense for a minute. You can't be all awestruck when you stand by me at the altar as my maid of honor."

"Your what?"

"You heard me." I laugh. "It's going to be a speedy wedding. When Matt told reporters he wanted to marry me 'today' he wasn't exactly joking."

"So when is it?"

"As soon as we can. It'll take me at least a month to get everything ready, but—"

"A month. Oh my god!" she cries. "I'm in." Her voice breaks. "Charlotte, I'm so happy for you. I always thought Sam would propose first and that you'd be sort of heartbroken

COMMANDER IN CHIEF | 149

because you still hadn't found a guy of your own. Now look at you!"

We laugh, and we reminisce about the days when we were younger, and both promised that we'd always be friends, even if one of us got married and moved across the continent, or became a philanthropist recluse.

After we hang up, I take calls from Alan and Mark, both of whom sound sort of mind-blown and a little sore about it, and then from twelve more friends, a mix of ex-coworkers from Women of the World and old Georgetown friends.

The news travels fast—especially considering it's on every website. Clarissa shows me a few of the headlines, sounding as ecstatic as the rest of the White House is, and I've been hugging the staff members—many who have become warm, gentle presences in my life.

Wedding at the White House!
Say Hello to the First Family
While America continues rising as the undisputed superpower of the world, President Hamilton falls (in love, that is)
Hammy finally to get wed—to his FLOTUS!
Condolences to the women out there: The most coveted bachelor in the world, our very own President Hamilton, is to be a bachelor no more.

In the meantime, Lola is busy fielding the White House press corps, all of whom want to know more details about the wedding.

Within a matter of hours, the excitement in D.C. is palpable in the air, as palpable as the incoming spring. After Grover

Cleveland's long-ago White House wedding in 1886, there's finally another presidential wedding taking place—and even the international press is reporting on the news.

We've been receiving calls nonstop.

"*Vogue* wants to feature you and the president on the cover of their April issue."

"Vera Wang wants to design your wedding dress."

"The designer of the yellow outfit you wore on the *Today Show*? He called to say he sold out of the outfit and got orders from Bergdorf and Neiman Marcus. He wants to send more designs and is sending a huge congratulations on the wedding."

"That's great!" I say.

"Charlotte, the chef wants to know if you'd like a tasting menu prepared this Sunday so you and the president can start looking at dishes—"

Matt

I'm a happy man when I walk into the Oval Office to find one of the White House staffers leaving a pile of letters on my desk. "Oh, I'm sorry, Mr. President," she says, about to leave. She pauses. "I'm one of those who read the letters and help select the ones we will place on your desk."

I absently nod. "Thank you."

"Sir, I also read some of the letters for your father. I've been working here for a long time."

I skim through the envelopes.

"You get some hate mail," she says.

I keep flipping through the envelopes as I laugh. "Yeah, I don't doubt it."

"He got more. Sometimes from the same guy."

I frown. Raise my head. "And you know this how …?"

"Just the postage, the way the letters were made. Looked like the same guy. He sent you one. It's not hate mail, just a magazine cut-out of an eye."

"Where does all the correspondence go?"

"I'm not sure."

"Do me a favor. Talk to Cox at the FBI about this. I'll have him contact you."

"Yes, sir."

Dale Coin walks in as she heads out. "A bit like a needle in a haystack, no?"

"Yeah, well, haystack's all we've got now."

PLANNING

Charlotte

Work doesn't stop. In the midst of the wedding preparations, little Matt is coming to the White House.

I've been excited about his visit. You just never know when you will meet someone who's going to touch your life. In ways you'll never forget, I suppose sometimes good, and sometimes bad. Even the most fleeting encounter can leave the most lasting mark. And since that day Matthew visited Children's National on Michigan Northwest, where the boy was being treated, and met with young Matt Brems, the seven-year-old boy has held a special place in my heart. Not only because he's the son of one of the women that I worked with at Women of the World. The boy is simply a fighter, living with an aggressive type of leukemia that he's fighting to conquer, his dream of visiting the White House becoming a reality today.

"Matt Brems is here, Mr. President."

"MATT!" the boy cries from the door of the Oval Office.

"Mr. President!" his mother chides the boy, horrified. "Mr. President, thank you for having us."

"Hey, tiger." Matt approaches and lifts his hand for a high-five.

I greet the boy's father and hug his mother, Catherine. "How is he doing?"

"He's a fighter."

The boy looks around, smoothing a hand over his tie, his awe of the Oval etched on his face. "I want to be president one day."

Matt motions for his chair.

The boy approaches with mounting disbelief.

Matt sits him down. Our eyes connect over his parents' heads—and I know what he's thinking. That we may have one of these, one day.

"Are you getting married?" the boy asks, surprising us.

"Yes." I add, "Do you want to come to the wedding?"

"YES!" He giggles happily. "But Sara will be mad she couldn't come too."

"Who is Sara?"

"A girl at the hospital."

"I suppose we should invite all of the children—they'll be our special guests."

I glance at Matt, and he stares back at me with this half smile that makes me blush and a look in his eyes that says *go for it, baby; it's your only wedding.*

I'm grateful when Matt turns to the boy, giving me a moment to recapture my first lady role.

"Do you think your friends would want to come?" Matt asks the boy.

"Definitely!"

"Can we count on you to deliver the good news?"

"Yes!"

The boy hops off the chair and walks with his chest expanded, as if he just grew a couple of sizes because of the task ahead.

Before they leave, Matt sits across the coffee table from his parents and tells them, "I want you to check all options. I would like to personally support his treatment. I'll also be starting a special fund in his name."

"Thank you." His mother starts crying.

When they leave, my eyes sting too. "Here we are with so much power but no ability to help him."

A melancholy frown flits across his features. "We do what we can."

Our eyes connect once again, and my heart somersaults in my chest. The vitality he radiates pulls at me, but the way his steady gaze bores into mine with silent expectation holds me in place.

"Were you thinking what I'm thinking?" I ask.

"We will have one of these in the White House."

I nod.

Standing less than a foot away, he glances down at me, his gaze admiring as a corner of his lips hikes up. "You'll make a great mother."

"You'll be the best dad."

He runs his knuckles down my cheek, and sparks ignite all over my body. "I look forward to making you my wife soon."

During the day, I don't see Matt much. He's been working nonstop and traveling occasionally too. He wants us to escape to Camp David for a few days after the wedding—a place where there will be no press, just us, and I'm looking forward to the peace and quiet.

Thoughts of our nights together keep filtering into my mind as I plan the wedding and make tour stops around D.C. and Virginia, visiting children and speaking to them about their futures—and how our future as a nation depends on them.

We've been running together on the White House grounds every morning when he's in D.C., though. Having dinner together, then spending the night closeted in his room.

Every time I see him step across the threshold of his bedroom, my heart grows giddy and I'm breathing faster. I know it's because we're in love, but it's also from the fact that we have never been openly dating each other until now, and I cannot get enough of him.

He cannot seem to get enough of me either.

It's as if his masculinity has grown tenfold, his testosterone at an all-time high. We have sex multiple times a night. Shower sex, sleepy sex, morning sex. I sometimes watch him get dressed with a look of disbelief, wondering if he's truly my fiancé. Sometimes, when I'm the one in a hurry to get dressed, I catch him standing in his towel, watching me dress with the look of a man who admires his woman, who wants his woman, who plans to keep enjoying his woman anytime he wants.

Most especially, with the look of a man who respects his woman.

I could not be any luckier.

He leaves for Africa for five days, and I take advantage of those days to plan something special for him. I've been trying to think of something to give him as a wedding gift. But what can you give the man who has it all?

"Alison, I want to get something special for the groom, a wedding present. He once told me he wanted a portrait of me. Would you photograph me? I want it to be a small picture, maybe five by eight, and I want to wear my hair down, my shoulders bare, and maybe just something sleek and a little sheer around my torso. And I want to be wearing his father's pin."

Alison's eyes grow wide at my description. "I just fanned myself on his behalf. Whoa."

I laugh. "I want it to look intimate. This isn't for display; it's only for him to have."

"I'm your girl then. Where do you want to do the shoot?"

"I was thinking at my apartment. It's leased for another month. I want it to be in simple surroundings—because I'll always be the girl he met."

Alison is thrilled at the prospect, so a day before he's scheduled to arrive, after the Secret Service give us the green light, we head to my old apartment. I pull up a chair to the small window. There's hardly a view outside, but I like the window in the background, with a regular view ... of a regular life.

I know Matt has always craved normalcy, regardless of the fact that he's the least normal man of all. Maybe that's why he craves it.

I wear my hair down, keep my shoulders bare, and wrap a gauzy shawl around my front, secured by his father's pin, making sure the fabric covers the dusky pink of my nipples.

"Perfect—now look at me as if I were him," Alison says.

My mind instantly gets transported to Matt—his arms, his voice when he's holding me, Matt asking me to be his wife—when there's a knock on the door, and Stacey peers inside.

"Charlotte. The president is on his way up."

"What?" My eyes widen, and Stacey nods.

"He must have finished early," I breathe, hurrying to remove the shawl and slipping back into the elegant day dress I was wearing while Alison hides her stuff.

"Did you get the shot?"

"I got like four great ones," she says, tucking everything into her duffel just in time for there to be a knock on the door.

Alison slings the bag over her shoulder and shoots me a look. "Enjoy, First Lady."

"Oh, I will," I assure her.

I hear her greet, "Mr. President."

"Alison." His tone sounds amused.

When he steps inside and looks at me, I want to cry because I missed him so much.

"Hey," I say.

"Heard you were here—decided to stop by."

"How was Africa?"

"Eye-opening." He looks at me like a thirsty man in need of water.

Matt looks gorgeous even after a full day of travel as he drapes his jacket over the back of a chair, removes his tie, and opens the top two buttons of his white dress shirt, his eyes fixed ravenously on me as he does.

My body responds to his presence instantly. I want to give him something. I want to give this man everything.

"Come here," I whisper, but instead of waiting for him to move, I cover the distance between us.

I lower myself to my knees and reach up to his belt. I unbuckle him, hear the rasping sound of his zipper as I lower it. All the while my head is angled back so that my eyes can remain on his beautiful espresso ones.

I drop my gaze and pull him out, his erection thick already, a pulse beating there. Feeling a hot clench between my legs, I lean my head forward and kiss the crown. He groans and curls his hands around the back of my head, holding me there with a little pressure, silently asking me to take in more. I do.

I curl my fingers tight around the base. It throbs against my palm, hard and thick, velvety. My lashes flutter upward and I meet his gaze as I use both hands and my mouth to pull him inside my mouth. Matt watches me, jaw flexing, a glitter of pure lust and hunger in his eyes.

I draw his cock deep between my lips, and he thrusts. In. I groan, and the salty drop of liquid on his cock makes me want more. I want everything from this man.

With a low, sexy groan, he pulls out, holding my hair, his voice causing ripples down my body. "Look at me."

I raise my eyes again and suck him back in, twirling my tongue around the head and his length, admiring the hard muscles of his abdomen and chest, the fierce angle of his jaw.

I pull him deeper into my mouth, licking him slowly, and never once do I stop looking into his gorgeous face as I do this. It's the best part.

I grip the base of him and suck him deep, our eyes still connected.

Another deep sound rumbles up his chest as he touches the back of my throat, and I swallow, unable to stop making a noise of pleasure too. God, I love him so much, I want him so much.

I ache between my thighs, but I love touching him, having him between my lips, pleasuring him. I run one of my hands up his hard thighs and his abs, and he smiles a little.

"You're going to make me lose it," he rasps, moving his fingers in my hair, his fingertips caressing my scalp.

I pull back, easing back on his cock so I can whisper, "Lose it."

He laughs a little, shakes his head, then narrows his eyes as I take him in again, and he's hard and he looks like he's doing everything possible not to lose it—so he can make it last.

He grips my hair in a fist and begins to thrust rhythmically. God, I'm the one losing it so bad. I sink him in deeper, watching him, stroking my hand along his ab muscles, unsure of whether he's the one setting the rhythm as he drives into my mouth or if it's my head, moving frantically up and down.

He lets a low sound loose and grabs the back of my head a bit firmer, and I'm so hot I feel myself shiver as Matt feeds himself into my mouth, not once taking his eyes off me, not even when he finally lets himself go, his eyes flashing with passion as he comes with a soft growl, driving in as deep as he can so that I'll get to drink every last drop in him.

He zips up when we're done, grinning. "Your turn." He grabs me by the hips and lifts me to his shoulders, carrying me to my bedroom.

I squeak, laughing, my arms going around his neck. "This is supposed to be about you."

"Oh, don't worry, it's about me." He smirks as he drops me on the bed and slowly starts pulling down the zipper on the side of my dress.

When we're done, we lie in my bed for hours, naked and spent. It's nighttime already, and I've been wanting to hear all about Africa, but I sense he's tired, his voice groggy, his expression thoughtful. He seems to be keener to talk about me and what I've been up to.

"What else but planning your wedding?" I frown. "It's not easy to plan a thousand-guest wedding in a month."

He smiles, running his hand over the back of my head, looking at me with that quiet possessiveness I've come to know so well.

"The team wants to know if we'll agree to have the wedding televised." I study his chiseled features. "What do you think?"

"I'm all right either way." His eyebrows furrow thoughtfully. "We can't hold a secret wedding—now that we've come out. I have no problem coming full out if that's what you want to do."

"I don't know. I know you like your privacy, but these four years, they don't come with that. Everyone is so excited." I shrug. "There's no reason why only the bad things need to make the news—we can put a good thing on the news too."

"Then let's go for it," he says easily.

"And the vows? Will we write our own?"

"No," he says. "The traditional vows say everything I want to say, and whatever more there is, I'd like them to be ours." He cups my face and rolls over on top of me, looking into my eyes. "If I want to say more, I'll tell it to you. In private. I might let the public enjoy you a little bit, but you're mine. Just mine."

He kisses me, and before we leave, we make love one more time.

I thought we were heading to the White House, and I'm surprised when the state car stops at a five-star steak restaurant, very well known in D.C.

Wilson tells Matt, "Everything is ready, sir."

And suddenly Matt is pulling me out of the car and into the restaurant.

A restaurant that seems to have been fully vacated for us to have dinner in private.

"What is this?" I ask, eyes wide as I look at Matthew.

"I can't marry you without an official first date. Now can I?" He pulls out a chair at a table by the window with a small candle flickering at its center, and I sit down and watch in awe as he takes the seat across from mine.

"I haven't even eaten and this is already the best date I've ever had in my life."

He rewards me with a delicious laugh.

And I remember the wink of a young man teasing a little girl, so many years ago.

"You do like every man's attention on you, don't you," he teases me.

"Not every man's, just the ones who capture mine," I joke.

"I'd better be the only one now," he says.

I smile, glancing at the engagement ring on my finger.

I slide my hand over the table, seizing his. "I love you," I say, breathless and swooning inside.

He places a kiss on the back of my hand. "I love you too, baby."

I move the index finger and thumb of my free hand an inch apart over the table. "This much?"

"Not that much."

"Matthew!" I chide, pulling my hand free with a playful scowl.

Soon, several waiters approach us with a bottle of their best wine.

"Mr. President, First Lady. An honor to serve you tonight."

While the waiter uncorks the wine, Matt looks at the menu. "Bring us all of the house specialties. Bring us each a different plate so we can taste them all."

"Absolutely, Mr. President."

We drink a light red wine, and once the plates are on the table, he looks at me, his espresso eyes piercing intuitively into mine. "How's your lemon sole?" he asks as we dig in.

"Oh, so good." And it really is.

He reaches out with his fork and steals a little piece from my plate, slipping it into his mouth. "Hmm, that *is* good."

I pick up a piece of cut steak from his plate and speak through the corner of my mouth as I savor. "That's good too."

He pushes his plate in my direction, takes mine, and brings it over to his side. I actually have no problem with that.

"I always seem to like what you're eating better than what I'm eating," I say, digging into his rib eye.

"You're a classic case of grass-is-greener-on-the-other-side, Miss Wells."

"Says the guy devouring my lemon sole."

"Pretty good. Do you want to try the chocolate mousse cake?"

"I would, but we'll need an ambulance at the ready outside."

He summons one of the staff, and a waitress hurries over. "One chocolate mousse cake, one homemade cheesecake. And an ambulance." He grins and winks exaggeratedly at me.

The waitress smiles dotingly and flushes. "Yes, sir."

We finish our desserts, and Matt leaves a huge tip and tells the staff he'll take care of the bill from his office.

"Do I need a stretcher to bring you out?" he asks me. His eyes are brilliant with mischief, his smile amused.

"No. I can walk. Barely," I add, loving how his arm still comes around me.

"Thank you, Matt," I breathe, going up on tiptoes and kissing his jaw.

The following week, we're getting dozens of confirmations from the foreign dignitaries who plan to attend the wedding as they receive our invitations.

Press conferences are the thing of the day, though Matt doesn't attend them all. Lola has been delivering the news as it comes—the press wants every detail, down to what gifts we're receiving, and since Matt has no intention of warring with the press over details, neither do I. I'm simply happy the country is getting swept up on cloud nine, right along with me.

A PRESIDENTIAL WEDDING

Charlotte

The gifts start arriving the week before the wedding, vetted by the Secret Service before they reach Matt's and my sight. The President of China sends an American flag sculpture, cast in bronze. The Prime Minister of Canada sends a pair of swans that will find a home in the south fountain of the White House. The President of Mexico asked for special permission to send a mariachi band to sing to us on the evening of our wedding. Soon the rooms of the White House are piling up with gifts from all over the world.

And I'll never forget this day.

Today, the Senate passed Matt's first bill for education.

The White House is buzzing at full capacity as everyone gets ready for the event.

I get my makeup done early, and everyone has been very stern with Matt, telling him that he needs to keep out of the Queens' Bedroom—that he can't see me until I head to the altar.

The day begins with a parade down Pennsylvania Avenue that the citizens are welcome to attend. They pile down the streets to a twenty-one-gun salute while workers set up a line of tall white tents along the Rose Garden.

Banquet tables with grand arrangements of baby's breath and peonies line the tents, their scent, along with the scent of the roses, filling the air.

I wear a dress with a plunging back, a long train, and a veil made of the most exquisite lace.

Matt and I settled, along with the chef, on a four-course meal with wine pairings, including crab and Bibb salad with pear and goat cheese, butternut squash soup, roast lamb with rosemary vegetables and poached Maine lobster, and my favorite dessert of the White House, the chef's special apple pie cheesecake. All served on silver-rimmed plates that look gorgeous over the ivory silk tablecloths and with the gilded silver chairs.

Among our wedding guests are twenty-one presidents and their first ladies, two prime ministers, NBA players, Hollywood directors, actors and singers, Nobel prize winners, all of the children of the Children's National hospital, and our families and friends.

But with my groom in the vicinity, even all of them combined play a second fiddle to him—the POTUS, in a sharp black tux, wearing one of his most charming, disarming smiles as he watches me walk down the long red carpet in the gorgeous White House Rose Garden with a train of white ruffles trailing behind me, finally making me his. Finally his in every sense of the word.

Matt looks stunning with his bow tie and crisp white shirt, the small flag pin of the United States pinned to his jacket.

Hot.

Powerful.

And mine.

With the backdrop of the gardens behind him and the thousands of white roses up the trellis behind the makeshift altar, I cannot believe that today America's prince, who now so easily wears the king's crown, is marrying *me*.

Today he'll be taking his second oath of the year—the two most important of his life, in the same year.

The best thing of all, as I walk down the aisle, is the smile on his face. It's a subtle smile, not overtly wide, but combined with the quiet, intense, brilliant look in his eyes as he watches me approach, along with the chorus music, it makes a knot form in my throat as my dad walks me down the long red-carpeted aisle.

My dad is clenching his jaw really tight and his eyes are a little red, and I can't imagine what my father is feeling to see his only daughter get married ... to *this* man.

"You take care of her, Matthew," my father murmurs as he hands me over, and Matthew assures him, "I will, sir."

His fingers slide over to grip mine and he locks eyes with me as he leads me up the two steps to the altar to stand before the priest.

Beneath the flowing skirts of my dress, my thighs feel flowy, like I'm made of air.

I know that we're being televised and I keep wanting to restrain myself from getting overly emotional, but my eyes keep stinging, simply being aware of his powerful presence beside mine.

When we face each other to deliver our vows, I'm sure my throat has caught fire and there's no chance of swallowing at all.

His voice, so firm and commanding but with an edge of huskiness to it, kills me most of all.

"I, Matthew, take you, Charlotte, for my lawfully wedded wife, to have and to hold from this day forward, for better, for worse, for richer, for poorer, in sickness and health, until death do us part."

My voice comes out steady but soft. "I, Charlotte, take you, Matthew, for my lawfully wedded husband, to have and to hold from this day forward, for better, for worse, for richer, for poorer, in sickness and health, until death do us part."

The ceremony continues, and I memorize the way Matt stands there. He's not one bit emotional. He simply looks certain. So certain of becoming my husband, making me his wife.

"I now pronounce you man and wife. You may kiss the bride, sir," the priest says.

Matthew raises his brows at me as if saying *you're done for, now*, and he tugs me closer, the sparkle in his eyes a full-on blaze as his gaze falls to my mouth.

He rubs my lower lip with his thumb, and he keeps his thumb beneath my lip as he frames my face in both hands and sets the most delicious, the most tender, and the most firm and confident kiss ever on my lips.

"Ladies and gentlemen. The President of the United States, and the First Lady!"

Beckett slaps Matt's back and I embrace Kayla as cheers erupt. Then Matt leads us down the aisle, and I'm laughing because of the crowd and cheers and the camera flashes, so wild and blinding, and I love that I feel his smile against the back of my hand as he kisses my knuckles.

FOR LUCK

Matt

"Long life, President Hamilton!"

I pull her to the dance floor, and I want to devour this girl. I want to run my mouth all over that sweet, smiling face, kiss the lips she's been gnawing nervously all day, slowly unbutton the buttons on the back of her dress and have my way with her.

I feel invincible, like I can do it all, have it all.

And as I twirl her and hear her laugh, then hear her sigh when I pull her back up against my chest, I know for certain—I want for nothing more.

I used to argue with my father, those last few years.

"Why would you marry a woman if you weren't going to pay attention to her?"

"One day you'll meet a woman, Matthew, that you'll have to make yours."

"I'm not that selfish."

Well, Father, turns out I am. But I'm determined to make her happy. I won't do what he did.

Once our dance is finished, she dances with her father, and as I pull my mother to the dance floor, I'm sure she's struggling with the same thoughts I am. That he should have been here. That he'd have been as proud as Charlotte's father looks tonight.

"I'm finding his killer," I tell her.

"Matt, don't. It's pointless."

"It's not pointless," I counter.

"Matthew, please …"

"Hey," I stop her. "This is the United States of America. You don't kill a man and get your happily ever after. Not here."

"Oh, Matthew," she says, forlorn. She glances at Charlotte. "Enjoy your bride. She loves you."

"And I love her. I'll do right by her."

She purses her lips, fearful, worried. "You're not your father. You may have chased the same dream, but you're all of our better assets, all of our virtues combined."

I laugh and kiss her cheek. "Thanks, Mother."

"May I have the next dance?" my grandfather asks.

I smile at him and hand my mother over. "Thanks, Grandfather."

"Congratulations, boy. She brings freshness to the house. I see what you've seen in her now."

I glance at her, and she's dancing with the children from the Children's National hospital. She's laughing as little Matthew Brems tries to twirl her around like I did, and I feel my lips curve into a smile. I plunge my hands into my pockets and watch her—I've never derived so much pleasure in watching anything in my life.

She makes me want to be the best man I can be. There aren't that many people who do that for you. She also makes me want to drop to my knees and worship the living daylights out of her.

I see her keep stepping on the train of her gown, then excuse herself from the dance floor and whisper something to Stacey, who ushers her into the house.

"We never thought we'd see the day, Hamilton."

"Hey, he's your fucking president now."

"Come on, he's still Hamilton."

I just smile. "Hey," I greet Lucas and Oliver, old friends of mine. "Good of you to come."

"Some speculated that it would be difficult to take *People*'s Sexiest Man Alive seriously for president. Look at you now."

I smile dryly as they motion to their table, and I take a seat and sip from my glass when one of the ushers approaches—and a vision in blue with red hair tumbling down her back follows. She's wearing a traveling outfit, blue skirt and a matching cropped jacket that accentuates her waist, that skirt letting me look at those lovely legs of hers.

I slowly come to my feet, the blood pooling instantly to my groin.

Our eyes meet. Her blue eyes are wide in happiness and awe, vulnerable. I want to grab her to me.

"Charlotte," I say, introducing her, adding, "Harvard friends, Lucas and Oliver."

"Nice to meet you," she greets them, then heads over to another table to hug my mother and grandfather. She comes back, taking a place to my right. Our eyes meeting yet again as I set my hand on the small of her back and guide her to sit.

"Remember that teacher at Harvard, that cute little thing who did a double take when you came into class that first day? She wouldn't look Matt in the eye without getting flustered," Lucas says.

"You passed with an *A* for good looks," Oliver adds.

I lean back and partly listen to the conversation. Nothing I haven't heard. My college friends get hung up on college days, as if those were the best days of their lives. I find I like my life just fine now, and I'm more interested in her reactions, her laugh.

I've never seen this girl so happy. God, she looks gorgeous.

I shift, my groin aching.

Nothing stands between us anymore. I won't let my fears of not being able to be both a good commander in chief and the man she wants stop me. I'm sure as hell going to do everything in my power to excel at both.

I only hope I can calm myself enough tonight to give her the time she needs to enjoy the wedding, before I take her to Camp David and get a little peace and quiet for us both.

I eye her in that sexy-as-hell blue dress that accentuates her curves, and it only heightens the need I have to see her naked body—to claim my *wife.*

I set my drink aside and my gaze pins her down. "Excuse us, we have a few heads of state I need to look for."

"Nice to meet you." She's laughing as she says goodbye, and she tugs at my sleeve. "Matt, wait. I think the kids are waiting for me to finish dancing with them."

I'm stopped by the President of Mexico as she goes to say goodbye to the kids.

"*Hermosa, la primera dama,*" the president says. "Beautiful, the first lady. Congratulations."

"Thank you for coming, sharing the joy." I grin, and we begin discussing the longstanding treaty between our countries when I watch her approach the group. Little Matt Brems steps up with his hand outstretched and pointing back to the dance floor.

She accepts. I plunge my hands into my pockets as she takes him to the dance floor, her hair falling over her back, and the cameras are flashing like crazy. When the dance is done, she bows her head, and then she retrieves something from nearby. She kneels before the boy and gives him the gift, and the boy just stares at it, then at her in full wonder, and she glances at me with a smile.

I smile in return, knowing what it is. Then I flash on an image of a younger version of me, with her kneeling before him ... our child. I clench my hands, a fierce want hitting me.

I shake it off, smiling at her, and continue talking to the President of Mexico, telling myself now isn't the time. But thinking of the years ahead, I don't know when that will be.

"I gave little Matt the photograph of his visit to the White House, the one with you in it that I asked you to sign," Charlotte says, back at my side.

"I know."

"For luck."

"You're gorgeous. I'm looking forward to whisking you out of here."

CAMP DAVID

Charlotte

Marine One takes us to Camp David, where we attack each other the moment we walk into the Aspen Lodge. Matt crushes me between his body and the door, his tongue plunging relentlessly, his hand fisting my hair, pulling me back so his mouth can roam down my throat, ravenous and damp as he reaches between our bodies to pull up my skirt and lift me.

I let him hold me up by the ass, then brace me against the door as he lowers himself between my legs. I feel his mouth wander down my abdomen and between my thighs, the stubble of the day on his jaw rasping the sensitive skin there as he pulls my panties aside and gives me a long, wet lick.

I groan and grab his thick, silky hair, groaning yet again when he repeats the motion with his tongue—a long, delicious lick, covering my opening and caressing my folds.

He inserts his thumb and looks up at me, his hair mussed, his eyes glistening, his lips wet.

"Please don't let me come without you," I beg.

He licks me again, a low growl leaving his chest. "What do you want?"

"I want you naked," I breathe, and before I know it, he's setting me on my feet and standing back, looking at me as his fingers begin working on his shirt.

I reach behind me and undo the buttons at my back, panting as he shrugs off his shirt and unbuckles and unzips.

Him naked.

There's something about him naked.

Primal and powerful.

In his element as man.

It turns me on.

He is mine.

Just mine, mask off, tie off, suit off, all the power of the executive branch off. Just his muscles. His lips. His words.

I'm married to the president. I don't care that he's president.

But who he is.

I'm married to my childhood crush, the man I love.

It makes me quiver. He does.

He's the only one I'd ever want to spend forever with.

And the girl in me still marvels that from his pick of women, he picked me. Loved me. *Saw* me.

Sees me now, as he stands before me, all lean muscle and man, watching me shed my blue form-fitting travel outfit.

He's breathing hard, his gaze raking me.

I take a step and he grabs me, gathering my hair above my head in one fist. He leans his lips to my ear. "I fucking love the hell out of you," he whispers, touching my breast with one hand, caressing the taut peak.

"I love you so much. I want you inside me as soon as possible."

He kisses me. I sort of lose all my thoughts, reaching between us to touch him—hard and pulsing. I groan when he scoops me up, carries me into a large bedroom with a king bed, and throws me on the mattress. He falls on top of me and ducks his head to my breasts, and Matthew's mouth becomes the center of my galaxy. I can't get enough. I groan as he licks and sucks hungrily, taking his time to enjoy me, taste me, tantalize me, his mouth often coming back to mine, gentle but fierce.

"What does my wife want?"

"God, you know what," I say.

He rewards me with a kiss. I never thought a man would kiss me with this passion, would want me with this passion, would love me with this passion—I never thought, when I once told him innocently that I wouldn't mind being by the president's side, that I'd actually end up by his side. That he'd be the man I would not only be with for his first term, and maybe second, but for the rest of his life and mine.

And I think this is why we're kissing like this—because we're not the president and the first lady when we're together. Because him proposing, him marrying me, has nothing to do with the circumstances that he's currently the commander in chief and I'm his first lady. It's despite that.

He asked me because he wants forever with me—and the thought of forever with him makes me the happiest woman alive.

It doesn't matter that our forever will grace the history books. It's *our* history, his and mine.

Matt sets his forehead on mine and looks intently into my eyes.

"Are you on the pill, baby?" he asks thickly and when I motion 'yes' with my head (having started when Matt asked the White House doctor to prescribe me), he kisses me deep, opening me up so he can enter me.

I groan. He lets go a rumble that tells me right off the bat that he loves the feel of me—the feel of us without anything in between. And god, I feel *full*—full and ready to splinter into a million delicious particles from the pleasure of feeling Matt—long, thick, hard Matt—driving inside me like he belongs here.

He *does*.

He folds my right leg over his shoulder, opening me up even more. I can feel the ripple of muscle from his shoulder and arm under my calf, and he thrusts, and suddenly he's even deeper—deeper than ever.

A whimper of pleasure leaves me, and his mouth is there to eat it up. "How deep do you want me?" he asks, pulling my other leg over his shoulder too.

I'm nearly at the peak already.

"Oh god, Matthew," I pant.

Keeping my legs draped over his shoulders, he drives in deeper.

"Like that," he rasps.

He fills me as if he doesn't plan to leave. As if he belongs inside me. As if my body was made to fit every inch of his. He groans when he's fully embedded, and I clench my legs around his shoulders, wanting more, wanting everything, my muscles gripping his hot length every time he drives in and even more so when he's pulling out.

"How right you squeeze me," he purrs, licking my lips. "Make room for me, Mrs. Hamilton. Take all of me."

"Yes," I pant. "I'm all yours."

I cry out in pleasure and Matt watches me, making me come, letting me come, watching me with desirous eyes and a wolfish smile on his face—as if he couldn't relish anything more than having me lose control.

He comes with me with a roar, his mouth capturing mine for a wild kiss as we come together.

For the next minute, we lie tangled, our bodies naked and damp from making love. Matt goes to the restroom and returns with a tissue, running it between my legs. He cleans me, disposes of the tissue, then comes back to bed and looks at me as he stretches out beside me. There's no hiding the blatant heat in his gaze as he takes me in. He curls his palm around the back of my head, pressing his forehead to mine.

"Can you take me again?" he asks, his voice gruff as he nuzzles my face with his and caresses my side.

He finds the tight pearl of my clit and starts rubbing as he kisses me.

"Can you take more, Charlotte?" he asks, switching his fingers on my clit from his index finger to his thumb—his index finger penetrating me.

I arch up and catch my lower lip to stop a sound of pleasure from leaving me. His scent drugs me, makes me dizzy with want. His finger exits and he rubs my clit again, getting my juices all over me. I start thrusting my hips up to his hand, desperate for more. He eases his finger back in, then out, once again rubbing my clit. I'm thrashing, tossing my head, fisting the sheets at my side, undone by the way he touches me.

"I want you," I breathe.

He doesn't make me wait for long.

He groans and squeezes my breasts, licking the tips, sucking them. I arch up to his hot mouth and clutch him by the back of the head, fistfuls of his hair between my fingers as I press him to my mouth and Matt fills me again, as deep as he can go, deep enough that I feel my soul leave me as I shatter for him.

The living room has a fireplace, and in the middle of the night, Matt gets it going.

Soon there's a warm fire crackling.

He smiles and strokes his hand down my back, exhaling contentedly as we lie on the couch after another round of delicious sexual intercourse.

"So many nights I wished I could … feel you hold my hand"—I lift his hand and set my own against it—"and look at you without fear of everyone seeing what was written in my eyes."

He holds me by the back of the head, his cock stiffening beneath my lap at my words, kissing me with his long, wet, roving tongue.

"Now … you're my husband."

He looks at me. "I love you."

He takes my hand and licks my ring finger, from root to tip. *Mmm.* This man is going to be the death of me. I remember him doing that the day he told me little Matt was visiting the White House, and suddenly … *light bulb* moment!

"This is how you measured my ring? With your mouth? Mr. President, I'm shocked!"

He smirks. "You will be pleased to know there are other things I can do with my mouth." He expertly eases me out of his white button-down shirt (which I slipped into to lounge around in) and nibbles on my bare shoulder.

"Oh, I bet. You're very adept during press conferences."

"My mouth is even more adept at finding warm, sweet locations to suck and taste." He slips one hand under the blanket and caresses the skin of my stomach, then tugs the blanket downward and ducks his head to kiss one of my nipples.

I giggle.

He lifts his head. "You're cute." He smiles, his eyes so gorgeous I have trouble breathing.

"I wonder what the country would think of your fetish with the letter *C*," I tease.

"That I'm commander in chief. And am allowed to enjoy any *fetish*," he says thickly, "that involves my *wife*."

I grin. "Your father, if he could see you now. His only son, the president, and doing a damn fine job."

"He'd be just as happy knowing I'm settling down."

"With me?"

"No, with Jack." Matt just grins and runs his thumb along my jaw. "With you," he says, his voice raspy now.

"You think so?"

"I know so."

"He'd approve of me? Good pedigree? Daughter of a senator?"

"My father had great respect for your family—but you charmed him. And there's no word for what you did to me."

"I'll have you know, I'm just getting started charming you, Mr. President."

"Are you now?" He smiles, then frowns as he looks at me. "Did you tell whatshisname you're taken?"

"He doesn't need to be told. He knows all bets are off. He didn't stand a chance against you ever since I started campaigning for you. Nobody does—*did*. Even before." I raise a brow. "Did you tell all your groupie fangirls? Even the staffers have a crush on you the size no other president has ever enjoyed."

"I'm taken. I've got a ring right here to prove it." He taps his wedding ring with his thumb.

"So I heard through the grapevine …" I begin.

"You have some big ears, don't you?"

I nod with a kittenish smile and swipe my tongue out to lick the top of his chest. "I've got a very warm tongue, too."

"Hmm. Give me more of that tongue. Lower."

"So I heard … Matt, are you listening?" I say, as I lick the center of his chest.

"What?" He laughs, obviously distracted.

"I heard … the bill passed. Education."

"God. Yes." He squeezes his eyes shut, throwing his head over the back of the couch. "I'm so fucking relieved. For a moment there, I thought we'd miss by a vote."

"Matt, I'm so proud of you," I say.

He looks at me, smiling, stroking his hand down my hair. "Healthcare is next."

It's surreal that the next morning, I wake up in Camp David—a married woman. I am married. From now on, people will address me as Mrs. Hamilton.

Matthew didn't seem to get excited by the idea of a paparazzi circus if we headed anywhere else, and so Camp David it was. I'm so glad this was his choice. It's absolutely quiet. Peaceful.

It's so early the sun is barely rising. I can tell from the parting in the curtains that it's close to dawn. I glance at the ring on my hand, identical to the thicker, larger ring on his hand, and drink in the man sleeping next to me, cuddling closer to his warm, hard chest to catch some more z's. There's nowhere I'd rather be.

We wake up at 9 a.m. and have morning sex, then we do a breakfast cookout on the terrace. It's relaxing. It's the first time I've ever been alone with Matt Hamilton without sneaking or hiding. We are alone—truly alone (I suppose we've reached the point where the Secret Service and Matt's shadow don't count, especially when they've been doing their best to give us our privacy and stay on hand, but out of sight)—and this feeling of privacy is a nice change from the limelight of the White House.

We turn on the television as we wash plates, only to see pictures of us on every channel. We decide not to watch.

So we head out and explore the wilderness. Matt tells me about how he would golf with his father, and enjoy just wading through the trees that surround the cottage with Loki, one of his pets then.

It's almost 1 p.m. by the time we get back to the lodge, and I've never felt happier or more at peace than I do now.

We walk into the living room, then the bedroom, and Matthew heads into the shower, turning on the water. He gazes at me expectantly, his eyebrows rising a millimeter.

"Oh!" I gasp. "You want me to ... you expect me to ..."

Ever so slowly, he nods as he starts unbuckling and unzipping, the corners of his mouth lifting a tiny fraction. "I do."

It's the hottest shower sex ever. He makes love to me against the shower wall, then he pulls out and finishes off, his semen raining on my abdomen, his eyes on me, and it is the hottest thing I've ever seen. Hottest sex of my life. With the hottest man on the planet.

We laugh the rest of the afternoon, and make love in the kitchen, and talk policy and politics, and we even call the White House to check up on Jack, and ask them to bring him to us at Camp David by car.

He arrives hours later, bounding happily to the cottage when he sees Matt at the door, and we spend the next day walking the wilderness, with Jack barking, dashing, and wagging his tail.

After a glorious Saturday evening, going out about the camp—relishing the fact that Camp David is paparazzi proof, because of it being a military base—and then curling up in bed to make slow, foreplay-laden love, it's Sunday afternoon, and we're back on Marine One heading home, Jack peering out of the windows.

I look at the wedding and engagement rings glinting on my finger with a smile on my lips and then study Matt's thoughtful profile as he gazes out the window. I can tell his mind is already drifting back to work.

I'm sad to let the calm of Camp David go. But as we approach the District, I look at the Washington and Jefferson monuments as we get ready to descend over the South Lawn of the White House and feel a sense of peace and amazement seeing the city from this vantage point. I absorb the lights streaking over columned walls, and I know that this is where Matthew needs to be. This is where he belongs. Where *we* belong. No matter how much we sometimes wished to freeze inside a simple, normal moment forever.

LIFE

Charlotte

"This girl in the photograph," my husband says as he stares at his gift, tapping a finger to the glass, raising an eyebrow. "I want her. Always."

"I'll let her know," I croak, breathless at the look in his eyes.

He sets it aside and strides to me, in a towel, ready for bed. "I'm assuming she intended to give me a hard-on, what with the come-hither look."

I laugh. "Not a come-hither look! Alison told me to think about you and I just did …"

"That's the expression on your face when you think of me?" he asks, leaning forward.

I nod breathlessly as he cups my face.

"Think of me now," he commands, his voice husky, watching me.

I scan his face. "I can't. I'm too busy looking at you."

"Close your eyes then, and think of me."

I close my eyes, giggling, feeling his eyes on me.

Then I picture him, standing there watching me, in that towel, hot as hell. I picture the expression on his face when I gave him the portrait Alison made for me, in elegant black and white, with a sleek gold frame. I picture the way his eyes drank me up, almost as if I were alive in the picture and he expected me to leap out of the frame and make a grab for him.

I start to breathe heavily, and then I feel the ghost of his touch, his knuckles running down my cheek. My lungs strain for more air as his hand drops a little more, to caress the skin revealed by my own towel.

"You're exquisite," he says, breathing against my lips as he seizes the back of my head, and his kiss is so deep, my toes curl and all the atoms in my body seem to shudder.

"Do you want me again?" I breathe. We just had shower sex again. We're like honeymooners; it doesn't matter that we're back in the White House. I'm thirsty for him, and him for me.

"Yes," he says, tugging my towel loose. I swoon a little when he releases his own towel and draws me into his arms, skin to skin, mouths meshing, his hands stroking down my damp skin.

The next day, after I hurried to get dressed and then watched Matt put on his suit and cufflinks to head to the Oval with Freddy, his escort, who was waiting at our door, I find, in my desk in the East Wing, a Post-it with his handwriting.

Mrs. Hamilton—
I love you.

P.S. Nice skirt.

I smile. I find it funny, because I told him that I would love to answer some of the mail that the White House receives daily. It was just days ago, in Camp David, and I find myself remembering as if I were back in his arms, right *there.*

"Matt, you know all of the letters that arrive at the White House daily?"

"Hmm." He's falling asleep, my head on his folded arm, resting right on his biceps.

"You get a few on your desk every day. To answer," I specify.

"Uhmm." He nods, ducking and tucking his nose to my nose, scenting me.

"Would it be possible for me to answer a few too?"

He smiles against my throat, and I hurry on. "I don't have to, only if you agree."

"You like your letters, don't you," he says, stroking a fingertip along my abdomen.

"Well, I suppose I do," I say, smiling in the dark.

"I'll write you my answer then."

I scowl. "What? You're going to write me a letter?" I ask, dumbfounded. How complicated does he want this to be?

Then I realize he's writing with his fingertip, on my skin. Tingles race along my body as I glance down and watch, rapt, as his finger forms the letter,

Y

My core clenches, god he's so sexy, I can't stay still. I suppress the urge to squirm as his long finger draws, slowly, the letter,

E

And then, exquisitely slowly, around my belly button, the letter,

S.

He's still smiling but looking down at me now, his eyes glimmering. "Content, wife?" he husks out.

I purse my lips and then press them to his, where I murmur, "Yes," before he bites my lower lip, then draws it slowly into his mouth, and that's about all the business talk of the night.

Now I see his note, right atop a pile of letters. He knows I love my letters—and I find that Matt's note is only the first out of dozens of letters that will now be left on my desk.

I store it in my drawer, still getting a shock whenever my eyes land on my hand and I see the glinting engagement and wedding rings on my finger.

Matt

You're telling me it's a dead end?"

It's me and Cox again at the Oval.

"Looks like it, Mr. President."

Cox motions to the images of the letters, each photographed in a ziplock bag, on my desk. "We've run the letters similar to the one sent to you, all those we could find dating back to your father, and all the prints match White House staff. *One* shows a print from an external." Cox pulls out an image of a large, balding man. "We sent a team. The guy worked at the Post Office in Milwaukee around the times the letters were dated. He doesn't remember a thing."

I rub my thumb restlessly over my lower lip. "Any other leads?"

"Negative, sir."

"Let's keep digging."

"Yes, sir."

He exits, and for a second, I grind my molars and glance at the photograph of my father on my desk as I pull out the files and get prepped for my meeting with the Attorney General.

THE UNEXPECTED

Charlotte

A week after our return from Camp David, I slip on my bra and feel a little bloated as I step into my skirt.

Last week when I realized I was late, I attributed it to the huge life changes of the past few months, plus the fact that the pill could be making everything screwy, but now I'm concerned.

I'm just not that irregular. I never have been.

I can't stop thinking about it as I do an interview in one of the White House rooms. The moment we're done, I call up my press secretary. Lola is thirty-five, young and feisty, and I've developed a good friendship with her. Although I may be closer to Alison, as she's new to the White House like me, Lola is a bit savvier on secrecy and I really need this to be between us. She meets me in the Yellow Oval, where I've been pacing nonstop.

"I need a favor."

"Anything."

"I need Kayla to come visit me. And to find a way to discreetly bring me a pregnancy test."

"That's not necessary. I'll set you up."

"Thank you, Lola."

It doesn't take her long. Less than an hour later, she returns with an unlabeled plastic bag in hand. "Okay, I was careful with who I asked. I ordered several brands, too." She hands them over, smiling. "I'm nervous and excited for you."

"I'm nervous and excited too."

She leaves, and I rush down the hall to the Queens' Bedroom and go through the whole procedure. Four times. Each of those times, it's positive.

I'm pregnant with Matthew Hamilton's baby.

I look at the tests in bewilderment, amazement, excitement, and fear. Complete, paralyzing fear.

Shock slaps me.

I'm confused, wandering restlessly down the halls as I wait for him to wrap up in the West Wing for the day. I call Portia and ask her when I can see the president. He's in a cabinet meeting, but she assures me she'll let me know when he's done and fit me in before he meets with his national security advisor.

Forty-eight minutes later, I walk into the Oval, and Matt is looking down at some papers, his glasses perched on that elegant nose of his, one of his hands gripping his hair as if he's frustrated. Some bill not quite there yet, I suppose.

"Matthew?"

I breathe in shallow, quick gasps and place my hand on my stomach as he raises his head, concern etched on his face.

"I'm pregnant." My voice is quiet, worried, but it lands like a gigantic weight in the room.

Matt slowly pries his glasses off to look at me, raising an eyebrow. His face set, thoughtful, strong and unreadable. There's a glimmer of hope in his eyes—hope and something raw and primal.

"I'm pregnant. I'm trying to stay calm and not freak out," I admit, my voice trailing to a whisper.

His eyes flash as if he's fighting some unnamable emotion; he lowers his head for a long, eternal minute.

And then he sets his glasses aside and kicks his chair back, crosses the room, grabs me by the chin so my eyes are level with his, and reaches out and puts his hand on my stomach, lowering his head, his chest expanding as he inhales and sets his forehead on mine.

"Say it. *Again*," he growls.

Ten minutes later, I'm looking at a hand resting against my belly as we lie on his bed. My heart is racing and practically about to jump out of my body.

He hasn't really said anything. He simply opened the door to the Oval, jerked his head in the direction of the hall, and I followed.

I followed down the hall, and up the stairs to the residence—and to his room, where he shut the door with a soft click.

I lie down in his bed, watching him kick off his shoes and come to sit beside me, his hand pulling my shirt up and resting on my stomach—his eyes as firmly fastened to me as his hand is.

I start to speak. "I know this is crazy but I ..." My voice breaks then, because the hand starts to gently rub against my belly. A soothing motion that just makes me exhale and melt farther into the bed pillows.

His skin tan and smooth, his hand contrasts with the milky white skin of my stomach as it rises and falls with each breath I take.

I look at that hand and feel waves of emotion crash against me. Excitement, fear, amazement …

His head is now bent down to my stomach. He hasn't said anything yet. I am practically bursting with nerves.

"Matt … please say something," I beg softly.

I didn't know how he would react, and I even considered showing him the "positive" marking on the first pregnancy test I took. Never mind the three subsequent positives I got after that. But I didn't. I just spoke the words.

God. He was just sworn into office, is just laying down his plans to create real change in the country. A baby is the last thing he needs right now … it would overwhelm him and stress him beyond belief.

But now, there is no avoiding it, and my heart is clenching as I look at this man, his soft, dark hair hovering over my stomach, his hand soothing my belly.

I realize he may be disappointed. Or maybe contemplating how to handle this. The press conferences we need to hold, how to tell his mother …

Then I feel his eyes on me.

His eyes are impossibly dark, as if he's fighting some emotion he doesn't want to feel or acknowledge. "I don't even know where to begin …" His voice thickens, but his expression tells me what he doesn't speak in words.

He cups my face in both of his hands and kisses me fiercely, telling me everything I need to know.

Suddenly, as he sucks on my tongue with so much thirst that my toes curl, I really want to cry.

Because I didn't plan for this baby. Neither did he.

But I want it. I want him to want it too.

When he draws back, he glances down at me proprietarily, his eyes lit up like firebrands, his expression so harsh with emotion and yet so tender. "I love you," he says quietly, cupping my face in one warm hand. "You know that."

His lips kiss my forehead as he whispers, "God, I really don't want to fuck up now."

He pulls back to bend over my stomach again, and I see the look of amazement in his eyes as he kisses right below my belly button. He rubs his cheek against that same spot and our eyes lock.

We're having a baby.

Holy shit.

A million realizations start to rush into my head.

I have this man's baby inside of me. We're going to be a family. I'm going to make him a father. I'm going to be a mom!

Holy crap!

Are we ready?

I look at him and he sees the worry in my eyes and shakes his head, signaling me not to worry.

I nod my head and whisper, "What if we're not ready?"

He looks at me and comes up to a full sit beside me, taking me into his arms.

He rubs my back with his big, warm hands, and I let myself be supported by him completely.

"I'm scared," I breathe.

I love him so much I feel like my heart will break with the magnitude. I feel tears well up in my eyes as I think of all he is and all he has done. He is more than I ever wished for, more than I ever dreamed of, and I cry silent tears, thanking the world and the universe for giving me such a man.

"I love you, Charlotte," he says against my ear. He turns my head to look into my eyes. "I'm not going to lie, I'm scared too. I don't want to leave this child fatherless. Worse, I don't want to be my father—not to you, not to this child."

I see the fear in his eyes when he says that, and I am reminded of his life growing up in the White House.

"I know you didn't want a family while in the White House. I feel awful that you'll be burdened—"

"It's no burden. I want this baby as much as I want you." He looks at me, then swallows. "Holy shit." He chuckles.

He frames my face in his hands and looks into my eyes.

"I want it. I'm going to be here for you, and for this baby." He sounds as determined as a warlord. "Jesus, beautiful. Come here."

I push my fears aside as he pulls my face in closer to his and kisses me with a tenderness so beautiful and loving, I don't know whether to smile or cry.

I guess people weren't kidding when they say pregnancy hormones make you very emotional …

I laugh a little at that and he smiles back to me.

"Charlotte … I am incredibly turned on by the idea of you carrying my child … *our* child … inside you."

His eyes hold mine as he says, firmly, "This is perfect. The timing. The woman. The baby … Please, I don't want you worrying," he warns, shooting me a stern look.

I nod, my fears assuaged as I look into his eyes and realize he is completely right. I have never been more in love. More committed to someone as I am to him.

I know he will try to make this work, somehow.

I realize I not only want to be his wife, I want to be his children's mother, and I want him to be the father of my children. I want to have a family with this man. I want this baby more than anything and as I look at him gazing at my belly again, I know this is perfect, and that we'll be okay.

It's my turn now as I take his face in my hands and tell him, "Matthew Hamilton, I am so in love with you, I don't know what to do with myself anymore."

He smirks and kisses my lips. "You're going to pamper yourself senseless, because I want nothing but the best for my baby and its gorgeous mother."

I laugh and then groan. "Gorgeous? If I'm like my mother, I'm going to be a sight for the time of my pregnancy."

He shakes his head, then his gaze travels down to my stomach again and he growls, "You're going to look incredibly sexy, not to mention completely desirable. I won't be able to keep my hands off you ..." He trails his tongue from my navel to my panty line, and all of a sudden things take a very different turn.

I play along with his game and give an exaggerated sigh. "I don't know, Matt ... I think you'll want me to sleep in *my* room instead of with you because I'll take up too much bed space and might not be too attractive."

He looks up from where he was licking, to my dismay, but the look on his face makes me laugh because this man is completely serious. "The day I'm not attracted to you, I'll be dead," he says, as he unbuttons my pants.

"What are you doing?" I exclaim, excitement building both in my heart and somewhere else. I feign concern and say, "Are we having sex?"

"You can't be serious! We're having tons of sex," he asserts, kissing along my stomach. "I'm not the kind of man"—he kisses again—"to deny himself his woman." Another kiss. "I think it's arousing as hell that you're carrying my child and it makes me want to give you all kinds of pleasure."

"Really?" I say. My heart practically combusted hearing his words.

"Yes ... starting right now."

I feel him pulling down my pants, and along with them my panties.

My breath catches in my throat. "Matt ..."

"*Shhh* ... let me," he says.

I gulp and nod, unable to produce any words as his warm tongue slowly licks along my inner thighs.

"Don't you have work to do?" I peep.

"I'll go back to work as soon as you come. On my tongue, baby," he croons, a low command, licking his warm tongue around and inside me.

He's back in the Oval in twelve minutes flat.

I'm just that easy.

Or maybe the POTUS is just that good.

He calls the White House physician to come look at me, and he declares both mother and baby to be healthy and the delivery date to be early December. Now I'm visiting with his mother in the Red Room.

"When Matt called to tell me the news, I couldn't believe I'd be a grandmother so soon," she tells me, her expression animated, her eyes shining as she passes me a cup of tea and sits across the coffee table from me.

"Thank you, Mrs. Hamilton."

"Eleanor, please. Have you decided when you'll announce to the world?"

I shake my head. "We haven't discussed it. I suppose we can't keep it to ourselves for very long." I smile, spreading a hand over my jacket, right over the baby.

Her eyes cloud over, and she pauses midway to taking a sip of her tea. She sets her cup on the table, her expression sober, and almost surreally understanding.

"I know this lifestyle can be harsh, especially with a baby on the way. You feel watched, vulnerable, and like you don't have the right anyone else does to make a mistake. It gets easier, but never too easy." She smiles encouragingly, then says, "I could hear the concern in my son's voice when he told me he was going to be a father. You know he worries he'll do the same things *his* father did, make the same mistakes ..."

She trails off, then continues.

"He is a great man, like his father—ambitious, determined, noble. He will stand by you—he won't ever want to be the one to hurt you, or abandon you or this baby."

She becomes misty-eyed and presses her lips as if trying to get a grip, then stands and comes over to take a seat next to me. She takes my hands in hers, squeezing. "Welcome to the family to both this little baby ... and you, Charlotte. I haven't had the opportunity to say ... welcome."

STATE DINNER

Charlotte

Galas are now my life. The gowns, the accessories. I'm swathed in fine fabrics and in Matt's arms.

"She went from private citizen to public figure and she's handled it with grace and style. I'm proud of her," Matthew was quoted staying.

And about my pregnancy rumors, addressing them eight weeks after we found out: "That's right. I'm going to be a father in six months' time. I'm kindly requesting to the most shameless of you"—he addressed the press with a warning look and a smirk—"to take it easy on my wife."

"President Hamilton, is it a boy or a girl?"

"We don't know yet."

"Will you want to?"

"That would be a *yes*." He grinned.

I restore the tulip beds, and add ducks to accompany the swans in the south fountain.

I'm mistress of the White House.

I plan events where artists dazzle audiences, arranged in our guests' honor. Arrange for a famous singer to perform the national anthem when someone important comes to visit.

I give talks in middle and elementary schools and invite schools to organize field trips to the White House, where I plan state dinners for the children (which are really lunches), complete with healthy foods.

My weekends I dedicate to the planning of these events, including those held for foreign heads of state.

I try to juggle it all, paying utmost attention to every detail of the state dinners we will be hosting, the next to be President Kebchov's dinner this weekend. From the linens, to the plates, to the flowers, to the food, to the table arrangement and the entertainment. I want everyone who steps through our doors to be swept away by the elegance and glamor of the White House.

There is a history in every wall, every artifact, a story in every room. Reading about them, knowing Abe Lincoln walked through these halls, JFK and Jackie made love in the same rooms Matthew Hamilton and I do, it's humbling. So humbling, it's been hard to believe that I—just a girl, one who had no interest in politics to begin with but was too enraptured by a man to stay away—could deserve it.

But I'm here nonetheless, and I am here to serve, and I want to make a difference.

I want to own up to my childhood dream and take this opportunity to make it a reality. I want to touch lives in the way that Matthew and his father touched mine, the day they came to dinner at my home and treated me as if I had something good to offer. We all do; sometimes we just need someone to tell us.

So I try to keep my schedule heavy on the days Matt is traveling, and lighter when he is home. And sometimes when we both get home after an exhausting trip, we just make love and stay awake all night, talking about our days apart—and I tell Matt how the things we're doing not only touch others, they touch me too.

The hustle and bustle of the White House is up a notch on the day we host President Kebchov's state dinner.

The U.S. – Russia relationship has been strained for years.

Kebchov is the one you want to intimidate. You want him well aware of the power of the United States and its leader.

We don't live in this world all alone. We have neighbors and allies. Enemies, too.

I've planned the perfect dinner—all American courses, including Maine lobster and Idaho potatoes.

Matt and I receive President Kebchov and his wife at the door, the sentinel guards standing by as he and his wife exit the car.

"President Kebchov." Matt shakes his hand.

"Kev is good," he says with a thick accent.

His wife is clad in gold, with glittering jewels on her wrist and neck.

I chose simplicity for this event. My gown is the color of emeralds. I'm wearing a small pair of emerald studs Matt gave me to match it and no necklace, because my gown is strapless and I like the way my bare shoulders look. I know Matt likes it too.

"My first lady, Charlotte." Matt introduces me to them, and I shake the president's hand as he, too, introduces his wife, and she goes on to press a kiss to Matt's cheek.

"If you'll allow us the honor ..." Matt motions us into the White House, where the four of us walk inside to a thousand camera flashes.

The artists entertaining tonight in the East Room are acrobats from Cirque du Soleil, who prepared a special performance just for the occasion.

President Kev is amused, and keeps saying *AHHH!* whenever the acrobats in their colorful leotards perform gravity-defying feats.

Matt squeezes my thigh, shooting an approving glance my way that tells me he's happy with the evening so far.

After dinner, the men are in deep discussions that Matt suggests taking to his office, and I remain with the first lady.

"Your husband. He's very young and virile. *Da*?" Katarina says.

"Yes." I smile, and she shoots a covetous glance his way and drinks from her glass of wine.

"He's also incredibly loving to me," I say, and her eyes widen as if she didn't expect this from me.

"I like you!" she declares. "Not as much as I like your husband, but ..." She grins, and we end up laughing and discussing her duties as a first lady in her country, and the troubles she believes her people face.

"My husband has been very angry at the United States for a long time." She eyes me. "We haven't had the same ... agenda, shall we say."

"No two countries ever do. That's what compromises are for."

She scowls delicately. "Yes, but my husband is not good at compromising."

"My husband is great at what he does. I'm sure they'll come to an understanding. May I show you around?" I offer.

We watch as the men head to the West Wing, and I lead her around the White House, telling her stories about our ancestors, funny or interesting tidbits about things that happened in each room.

"How lovely, your passion," she says.

I only smile.

"You are to have a baby, yes?"

"I'm due December."

"We never had children. Kev said it was too much, to have brats and be in charge of Russia."

She sounds forlorn. "I'm sorry to hear that. I'm sure Matthew has his concerns, but I do believe it's possible to both have a family and be commander in chief."

"Ah, youth."

"Maybe it is youth, or maybe simply determination."

"Is your husband not concerned he'll leave his child fatherless? Like his father?"

I raise my brow. "No. We trust the Secret Service to keep him safe."

"But they couldn't keep your beloved President Law safe." She eyes me. "It would be a shame to lose such a perfect example of masculinity to a mistake."

I manage to keep my expression neutral, my gaze direct. "Thank you for your concern, but my husband and his administration are stronger than ever and will continue to be," I say, my tone no-nonsense.

Katarina leaves early, and her husband remains with mine—I'm not sure where, but somewhere in the White House, probably the Oval, where all the big stuff is discussed.

I'm exhausted, so I hit the bed in the Queens' Bedroom, unsure of when Matt will be done.

I keep replaying my conversation with Katarina as I drift off to sleep.

I have a nightmare. It's dark and I'm aware that I'm dreaming, but everything feels too real to be a dream. The fear pulses through me, the regret, and the confusion.

Carlisle is bloodied, and I look and follow the trail of blood to Matt. He's lying down, not breathing, his hand holding a small one, and it's me, lying in that same pool of blood, his father's pin bloodied on my lapel.

I sit up in bed with a gasp, then glance around as the world spins. My throat constricted, my heart beating, I'm dizzy. I scramble out of bed in search of the bathroom and realize I'm not in my apartment. I'm in the Queens' Bedroom. In the White House. I inhale, then grab a robe and step outside. My agent Stacey stands up at attention.

"Everything all right?"

"Yes, just getting some water, thank you."

I head to the kitchen and notice Wilson down the hall— and my eyes instantly jerk to the side to see Matt seated in the yellow sitting area.

"You're back," I gasp.

"Got in a while ago."

"How did it go?"

"Not as well as I wanted, but better than I expected." He scrapes his hand over his jaw and looks at me, then at Wilson, and Wilson scats.

The fear of my nightmare wanes with his presence.

I'm aching, his piercing coffee eyes, his infectious smile, his husky voice, and the way I want to be with him greater than my fear.

His low, sexy voice is like a blanket around me. "How are you? Are you uncomfortable?"

"I don't have time to be uncomfortable." I smile.

I head over to him and he draws me to sit on his thigh. "You outdid yourself tonight." He cups my abdomen. Kisses it. "You look tired." He peers at my face, his gaze too penetrating. Too knowing.

"A little. I think it went well. The Kebchovs were definitely impressed. The first lady was impressed by *you*, but I'm getting used to that."

He frowns and strokes a hand over my hair, and I angle my head into the touch, stroking my hand up his chest. There's a nearly imperceptible darkening in his eyes, a hunger lurking all of a sudden in his irises.

"Let's get you to bed."

"Are you coming with me?"

He doesn't answer, simply leads me there.

Once in bed, he strips me, and then strips himself. I cuddle into his chest, in his arms, Matt sitting with his back propped against the headrest. "Rest, Matt," I groan, kissing his pec, caressing the dusting of hair on his chest.

"I will. I'm just thinking." He kisses my forehead.

I reach up to press his face against mine, stroking his hair, until I feel him turn his head into my hair and close his eyes, able to catch a few hours of sleep before the hum of the early-morning White House begins, and it's a full day for the both of us again.

During the week, I have another group of important visitors at the White House. Kids from a local art school arrive, and I've set up small tables in the East Room so we can all do a White House-themed project.

One of the six-year-old girls calls me to her table and asks, "Like this?"

I reach over and adjust the paper so I can see it. Just then, she lifts the brush and smears paint on my cheek, and I laugh when I see Matt stop at the door—the room falling silent for a second, followed by a round of gasps from the little kids.

"Children—" I straighten up, still laughing as I grab a napkin and start to wipe my cheek—"we have a special visitor. It's the president!"

And how I love the expressions on their faces as Matt leans forward into the mic at the podium at the end of the room. "Whoever painted the first lady," he says, winking, "good job."

I laugh and he walks over, leans over to the little girl, and assures her, "She looks even more beautiful than she did this morning." He takes the napkin from me and wipes off the paint, smiling.

We look at each other over the children. Both of us thinking there will be one of ours here before we know it.

CROWDS

Matt

"My intention to pass a carbon tax for all carbon emissions is unwavering. The very air we breathe has been polluted for years. That's not happening anymore."

"Mr. President." Coin is at the door, interrupting my session with one of my advisors. "There's been an incident."

He leads me to the adjoining room and turns on the TV.

I watch Charlotte walk out of the Virginia elementary school to a crowd of reporters and fans, the Secret Service struggling to keep the area secure.

A little boy tries to break through the security line. He's pushed back, falls, and the line breaks, the crowd engulfing Charlotte.

I see her duck protectively over the little boy that fell, while Stacey fights to open up room to pull her out of there.

"Where is she now?" My tone sounds menacing, even to me.

I lost my father—in the blink of a second.

I see the pool of blood. Hear the damn phone call. See the damn news all over again. Feel the damn *loss*.

"On her way, sir," Wilson tells me after checking into his speaker.

"I want to see her when she gets in."

I head back to the Oval and stare down at my desk, clenching my hands together as I try to breathe. I'll lose my shit if I ever lose her. I'll lose my shit if anything happens to her or our children. I spot the FBI file for my father. A reminder of how justice hasn't been served to one out of hundreds of thousands of evildoers in this country. I grab the file and toss it into my drawer, the frustration of Charlotte being careless suddenly getting to me too fucking much.

Charlotte

W
ell, *that* wasn't supposed to happen.

I'm still in shock over the number of people coming to my visits. It seems the crowds only keep growing, their obsession with me nearly rivaling their obsession with Matt.

"Charlotte, please, a picture with me!"

"Charlotte, would you please intercede for my boy, he was suspended—"

"Charlotte, do you know what you'll be having?"

I'm heading back to the White House, and a doctor is tending to some scrapes on my arm in the back of the state car. I caused them myself. Well, maybe. A little boy—he couldn't have been more than four—was getting trampled as he tried to reach me, and I threw myself forward to try to protect him.

I've already been scolded by Stacey and the rest of my detail, the men shooting each other concerned looks, and I've already heard them speaking into their mics. Explaining what happened to the president.

The fact that this has already reached Matt's ear and possibly worried him makes me feel worse about it all.

I'm exhausted when we get back to the White House. I reach my room and remove my pumps, exchanging them for a pair of pretty ballerina flats, and the floor is quiet—except for the staff. I find myself heading to the West Wing.

I just have to see him. I crave him like air. He's the anchor that holds me down in this new and frightening, exhilarating experience, and he's the reason I want to do better than well. He's the reason I even have this opportunity in the first place.

I also want him to know I'm fine.

Dale Coin intercepts me on the way to the Oval Office entrance.

"Charlotte. I want to touch on the fact that the president is taking no prisoners during this administration—"

"Coin." The word is bit out from the door.

The command makes Dale stop speaking—both our eyes flying to Matt, standing at the door of the Oval.

My heart stops when I notice the steely admonishment in his eyes that he sends his chief of staff's way, as if he has no right to talk to me like that.

I think my knees are knocking together, or maybe it's my heart.

I've never seen Matthew angry. Not really angry. Not like this.

Dale nods at him and whispers to me apologetically, "The president has enemies. All focused on finding his weakness."

Matt's vexation is so evident, I can feel it like a tumultuous ripple in the air, though he fights to keep it under control as he waits until Dale Coin moves away from me.

I glance at Matt. Stare at his tie and the thick column of his throat as I walk inside. I close the door behind me as Matt rounds his desk, then leans forward, his arms braced on the desktop as his eyes meet mine disparagingly and he slowly rips out the words, "You're my first lady. You cannot act like you're a normal twenty-three-year-old out there. You can't risk your safety. You will NOT risk your safety. Do you understand me, Charlotte?"

His stare drills into me, and we stare at each other across the ringing silence.

"Matt, he was getting crushed. He was just a boy trying to give me a drawing he made for me."

He grits his jaw so tight, I can see a muscle flexing angrily in the back, his glare burning through me. "You want to make your mark and I'm proud of you for that," he growls, clearly struggling for control. "But for all that's holy, baby, do not ever—*ever*—put yourself in danger again. Do you fucking *hear* me?"

His voice is deathly low, deathly quiet.

Suddenly angry and frustrated, because I *know* Matt doesn't seriously want me to stand by and watch a boy come to harm, I spin around, open the door, and start heading down the hall, wordless.

Wanting to cry for some reason.

Matt catches up with me, taking my arm and leading me up the stairs and to the residence.

He releases me in my bedroom, exasperated, his frustration evident on his face.

"What the hell was that?" he growls.

"I'm sorry I scared you!" I yell. "I was scared too! I didn't want to make a scene in the Oval—that's like sacred space. But all the attention was on me, Matt, everybody trying to save *me*—nobody thinking of the little boy." My voice breaks and my lips begin to quiver. I purse them.

His eyes darken as he looks at me. He works the back muscle of his jaw like there's no tomorrow.

Matt looks clearly tortured, torn between wanting to hug me and shake some sense into me. "You did a brave thing, Charlotte, but for the love of god," he rips the last word out, trying to sound patient but failing as he takes my shoulder in his hand, squeezing, "think of what could have happened to *you*. You're over four months pregnant and you're pushing yourself too much—too fucking much. I don't like it."

"I'm just keeping busy, Matt! Trying to do my part the best I can. I like what I do, and with the baby on the way I'm trying to do as much as possible before it's born. You've been so busy, and I don't like it when I start to miss you ..."

I drop my gaze to his throat, my voice quieting over my confession.

"I keep waiting at night to see if you come to bed and I always fall asleep before you do. I want to make a difference, and there are so many things that I don't have time for them all, but sometimes instead of thinking of that I'm thinking of *you* and when I'll be with you ..."

"Go on," he says, thickly, squeezing my shoulder.

I swallow. "I won't. I've said enough."

Silence.

His tone turns gruff with emotion as he tugs me closer. "For what it's worth, you're doing an incredible job out there. I'm proud of you." He runs his knuckles down my cheek, his expression so intense, I'm weak-kneed. "I'm so damn proud of you."

He grabs the back of my head, pressing his forehead to mine.

"I think of when I'll be done so I can come and lie next to you. And by the time I get there you're asleep. I sit on the chair in my room, just like the one you have here in yours, and I watch you, and I watch you dream—not always good dreams, sometimes you're restless, and I do this ..." he strokes my hair, "and you settle down. And I don't want to catch some sleep because those hours are the only hours when the demands aren't pressing on me, and the few hours I have you to myself, and I don't want to miss any of it. Not a second."

I grab him by the tie and kiss him. He grabs the back of my head again and takes control of the kiss, deepening it.

"I love you," he husks out, taking me by the back of the neck as his eyes blaze down on me. "You can't pull a stunt like that again. Not ever, not even when we're out of here—do you hear me? You're every fucking thing to me. You don't need to keep exposing yourself like that—understand me?"

"It's just that I miss you. Doing things that make a difference is all that can fill some of the void of missing you. Sometimes being here, with all these amazing people, I feel alone." I drop my head. "I can't explain it. I don't want to feel it."

I squeeze my eyes closed and cover my mouth. *God, I can't believe I just said that.*

Here I am, being selfish. I want him all to myself. He's the fucking president. What do I think I'm doing?

He looks slapped.

Oh god.

I probably sound like his mother did when his father was busy, and I never want to sound like that.

How could I be so selfish and say that aloud? This man is giving his all to his country, his whole life.

"I didn't know you felt like this," he says. His voice is gruff and low.

I turn away, but he stops me, raising his voice. "Don't pull away from me. Jesus!" He lifts my chin and turns me to meet his eyes, and his fingertip sears my skin. His touch sears my heart. "I'll do better."

"No, you're already doing so much. I'm sorry I said that. I want *us*, now and in the future," I admit.

Regret and frustration swim like dark shadows in his eyes. "You're my future."

I place my hand over the one holding my chin, my palm against his knuckles. "Let's not fight."

He clenches his jaw again. "You're not alone. Ever. Do you hear me?" he says sternly. "You have me."

I nod, and he places his hand on my stomach, drawing me with his other arm to his chest. His voice becomes gruffer and his eyes darker when he notices the scrape on my arm. "Has this been looked at?"

"Yes, it's got ointment—I just didn't want a Band-Aid. It's fine."

Matt just stares at me beneath drawn eyebrows.

"It's fine," I groan, pulling free.

He continues to stare, stroking his thumb down my face. "I'm going to get back to work, and you're going to put a Band-Aid on that—and tonight I'm going to take you out for a walk and dinner somewhere."

"It's such a hassle to move the team of hundreds so you can take me out to dinner. We could have dinner here outside. Like a picnic."

A glint of light touches his eyes. "You, worrying about everyone." He shakes his head. "Worry about yourself and our child." He pecks my lips. "It's a date tonight. Wife."

We end up having a picnic in the most secluded area of the gardens, under the trees. I had the chef make sandwiches for us, and vegetable chips—healthy leader, healthy lifestyle—and we then lie down and look at the stars, our bodies sort of naturally fitting together, our hands slowly roaming, our lips slowly finding each other's.

"I want you to take it easy, Charlotte," he says, nibbling on my lower lip.

I kiss him back. "I can't take it easy. I'm starting the Kids for the Future campaign to inspire children to step outside the box and use their talents."

He eases back, frowning, his eyes stern under drawn brows. "You control your schedule. Pace yourself."

I don't know how he does it. Even when it's thick with arousal, he still manages to make his voice sound commanding.

"I'd hate to cancel."

"*I'll* cancel," he says.

I laugh, loving how protective he is, especially now with me expecting. "By order of the president?" I tease.

And when he only stares at me with an unreadable and unrelenting expression, I simply kiss him, swooning when he firms the kiss and massages my tongue with his. Breathless, I slide my hands up his hard chest and feel his hand curving around my stomach, then around the small of my back, easing me to his lap.

My breath hitches as he guides my legs to straddle him and whispers, "Come here, beautiful." I close my eyes, arching wantonly.

"Matt." A plea.

"You want me, my love," he says against my ear.

"So much."

He moves his fingertips over the sides of my rib cage and into the front of my waistband. I inhale a shaky breath.

"Close your eyes," he coaxes. "Let go of everything but this moment. Me. You. This." He dips his fingers between my legs, where I'm wet and aching, and with his other hand, he draws me to him by the back of the head, kissing me senseless as he then swiftly unbuckles and unzips and lowers me down on him.

CHANGE OF PLANS

Charlotte

"Is he alone?"

"Yes, but …" Portia trails off as I walk in.

"I was ready to leave for my Kids for the Future campaign when Clarissa told me you gave her the order to pause until I looked at the schedule again," I tell him.

He's in the middle of picking up a call and says something unintelligible into the receiver.

Pressing my lips into a thin line, I spin around to leave.

"Stay," he tells me as I cross the room for the door.

I inhale and turn around, staying in place, the presidential seal right beneath my feet.

His brow furrows as he listens on the phone.

Moving forward, I place my palms on his desk and lean forward. Scowling. I've been working on this event for weeks; I told him that yesterday. Does he not trust that I'll be careful? He's being so frustrating!

I wait for a moment. He's still absorbed in his phone call, so I walk around the desk and then plant myself between him and the damn desk, hands on my hips as I give him my fiercest scowl.

A tug plays at the corners of his lips all of a sudden. He reaches out to pop a button of my shirt loose. I catch my breath, his eyes flaring.

"Absolutely, I concur that won't be a problem at all," he says into the phone.

He tugs me to his desk and props me up with one arm, parting my legs so he can slip his fingers under my skirt and pull down my panties.

My voice is hoarse. "Don't."

Enough for him to hear, but not the other person on the line.

I catch my lower lip between my teeth, breathing heavily as he strokes his index finger along my opening. He's talking about some bill as he trails one finger over my sex, then eases it inside. I'm so wet that it slips right in. I moan and arch back.

He loosens my shirt until it parts. "Then we need to get on it, don't we?" he says, looking at me meaningfully as he brushes my shirt aside, then tugs the fabric of my bra beneath the swell of my breast. My nipple is puckered, so hard even the air brushing across the peak hurts.

I gasp as he leans over and blows on it. Pleasure races down my nerves. He bites down on me, and I bite back a cry and fist my hands in his hair, grabbing him for dear life.

"Good. I expect that on my desk tomorrow."

He stands as he hangs up, grabs me by the waist and leads me across the Oval to the adjacent sitting room, and kicks the door shut behind us and ushers me down on the couch, settling on top of me. Pulling my skirt up to my waist, I fumble with his zipper while he pulls my panties aside and then slips his finger back inside.

I pant. The fingers of his free hand trail down my temple.

My cheeks warm with eagerness.

"Lick off the taste of you," he commands, raising his hand from between my thighs to tease my lips open.

I do.

He frees himself—then he's inside. Deep inside, where I want him. Need him.

He starts to thrust, groaning as I do.

He trails wet kisses along my neck, fastening his mouth over my nipple, then stroking his hand along my small, rounded belly. The shadows of the trees outside the window fall over us, but I'm unable to focus on any one thing but him.

I tilt my hips upward, hungry for him—always hungry for him.

"Oh god," I groan.

"Quieter, baby," he hushes, tender as he plunges his tongue into my mouth, and he thrusts harder until he drives home, taking us where we need to go.

Afterward, I sit up and rearrange my clothes, and watch him for a minute. His hair rumpled by me, his mouth pink, and looking a little bit possessive, he's the sexiest thing I've ever seen. But I don't want him to know this.

"I'm still irritated," I mumble.

He stands and zips up. Then he takes my chin and leans over, kissing me, voice husky. "So am I. I know you know better, Charlotte."

I groan, pushing at him as I straighten. Matt's eyes drink me in as he's straightening his tie and securing his cuff links, while I feel like I just got high on a drug called President Hamilton.

"I'm not canceling," I warn him.

"I don't want you to cancel," he firmly retorts. "I want you to take it easier on yourself. Pace yourself. I warned you last night. I'm not fucking kidding about you or our child. You have years to champion your cause."

"Matthew ... the doctor said that I should continue with life as normal."

"And there lies the caveat. *You* don't live a normal life, Charlotte."

He swings open the door of the Oval, striding to his desk, grabbing his glasses and slipping them on, his forehead scrunched as he settles back in his chair.

He scrapes his thumb across his chin, thoughtful, as he starts reading papers again.

"Matt?" I demand.

He lifts his head.

"I promise. Nothing matters to me more than you and this baby," I assure him.

He nods curtly, voice calm. "Good. We're clear then," he says easily, back to work.

I just stare.

He looks up. "I lost my father too damn soon. I'm not going to lose you to exhaustion—or our child to extensive touring. It's not worth it. Nothing is."

My anger melts a little; I can't seem to be able to get angry for long.

I know he's frustrated the FBI hasn't found any new leads into his father's case. It's an old case. What Matthew wants is near impossible. But he's been pressing the Bureau to be better, do more, enhance their strategies, their intelligence, and their teams—he's even strategized to get an increase of funding to both the FBI and CIA, to ensure the United States have the highest degree of competence when in search of justice.

The impossible for him does not exist.

And yet, chaos is the evildoer's best friend, after all. And yesterday I leapt right into it without thinking—stirring Matthew's frustrations anew.

I smile as I watch him read the thick document in his hand. "I love you and those silly glasses," I admit.

My smile fades a little when he looks at me. He gives me a smile.

And he pulls his glasses to the bridge of his nose and eyes me across the room. "Don't try to sweet-talk your way into working yourself to the bone. That won't work with me."

"I didn't think it would," I lie, taking myself to the door. "I know what works." I mouth, *Oral.*

And I see the most adorable smile touch his lips before he leans back in his chair, looks at me soberly, and purrs, teasing me, "That's right."

I laugh as I leave, heading straight to Clarissa.

"Did you give the president a piece of your mind?" Clarissa asks with a twinkle in her eye.

"Oh, definitely." *More like a little piece of pregnant mama booty.* I head to my desk and look over the schedule. "Do you agree with him that this is a hectic schedule?"

"I told you from the moment we drafted it that we couldn't reasonably cover all these schools in such a short amount of time."

"Why didn't you *insist?*" I groan. "We need to redo it."

"Because I knew *he'd* set his foot down," she admits, still seemingly amused.

I sigh and look over everything, exhausted just thinking about moving all the visits around.

"What if I recruited a group of passionate women to help me cover all these areas—spread our Kids for the Future message?" I ask.

Clarissa loves the idea so much that by that evening, we've got a new plan hashed out, and meetings set up with women like me who want the kids to have the best opportunities, the best futures, the best self-esteem, and the best chances at achieving their dreams one day.

I'm beat that night when I feel the mattress of his bed shift, and his body spoon me from behind. I sigh contentedly as he buries his nose in my neck, planting a kiss there.

"Guess what? I won't bribe you with oral after all," I breathe sleepily.

"You may most definitely *try*." His chuckle is warm as he nuzzles my throat.

I smile. "I had a great idea today and found a way to have it all without ... what did you say? 'Working myself to the bone'?" I frown and flip around, shooting him a black stare as he props himself on his elbows above me.

Even in the shadows, I can make out the amusement on his face, his chest bare, gloriously bare and muscular as he leans above me. "That's right," he says.

His eyes. I swear they're like the best coffee you will ever have.

"I appreciate you taking my concerns seriously," he says as he brushes back a strand of hair behind my forehead. "What's mine is mine. And I want my girl to be safe, always." He eases down my body, his eyes on mine looking wolfish and proprietary as he places a kiss on my belly. "And our little one, too."

I squeeze my eyes shut, his tender kiss spreading warmth all over my body.

"Are you ready to find out the sex on Friday?" I reach out to stroke my fingers through his thick sable hair, then against the stubble on his jaw, feeling it rasp over my skin.

"I'm ready for it to be born already." He grins against me.

I run my fingers over his scalp as he nuzzles my pregnant belly. "I can't decide what I think it is," I say thoughtfully.

"It doesn't matter what you think, it is what it is," he says, quite practically, as he comes back up, propping himself on a pillow and drawing me to his side.

I laugh. "True."

"I've moved things around so I can be there with you to receive the news," he says, his voice husky now as he pulls my chin up and kisses me.

"Thank you."

"I wouldn't miss it. Not if I can help it."

Friday, we're stepping out of the car after my checkup with the gynecologist. Matt is fixing his tie after the full-blown kiss I gave him in the car on our way here. I'm just so happy. Blown away. The baby looks well. I have a picture in my clutch purse—several pictures, in fact—and we could see its perfect body, its eyes, and its face. And its sex.

When the doctor confirmed what it was, he told us with a grin, and Matt and I just looked at each other—all of it so real, now that we can give the baby a name.

The reporters at the White House are restless, having heard of my appointment and been given permission to wait for our return on the steps.

"President Hamilton, do you know what you're having?"

He draws me to his chest as we both face the reporters, and they all calm down. He says just three words.

"It's a boy."

"It's a boy!" they return happily.

"Quick picture, Mr. President!"

I hear the echoes of other reporters who second the thought.

"All right—take a few shots, and then I trust you'll let us get back to our jobs."

They start snapping pictures in excitement, and we pose at the entrance of the White House, Matt's hand on the small of my back, his eyes drifting down to meet mine as we smile at each other. I think we're both still replaying the news in our minds—me bewildered and enchanted that I'm having a little boy, my little Matthew Junior—when Matt, back to being businesslike, tells them, "All right, have a good day, everyone," and ushers me inside.

He pats my bum as we head down the halls. "Have a good day, wife."

"I will. I have a baby room to decorate. You go get it, husband."

He winks, his smile dazzling as he starts walking away to the West Wing.

INVITES

Charlotte

Weeks and months fly by as I prepare the baby's room and continue with my Kids for the Future campaign while Matt continues meeting with heads of state, signing treaties, tweaking trade agreements, and more.

One of the schools I'm visiting on my new, less hectic schedule inquired whether the president could make a speech for the high school students, and I was thrilled when he said yes.

Everywhere he speaks, Matt draws crowds. You'd think it was due to the mythical importance of his father's legacy and his family's name, but I know that it is not. People like to feel close to him. Hear him speak. All around America, there are proud people—proud to be American.

Today, I admit I get a little giddy watching him speak again.

"It's easy to believe that we aren't capable of living up to our potential. I never believed I would—or even cared to try to. After the loss of my father, I continued to be reminded of all that the world lost, and I felt a sense of powerlessness. I wasn't powerless. I had in my power to give you the one thing he most wanted to give. Me. Never underestimate the power of your own worth."

Once he closes, the claps and cheers are so deafening, they follow us out.

He rides with me back home, Wilson and Stacey accompanying us, both of them grinning ear to ear, not even bothering to hide their satisfaction.

Our economy is growing by leaps and bounds, our exports have increased by twenty percent, and there are new jobs being offered every day. Aside from that, Matt is a champion of consumer rights, minority rights, gay rights, women's rights, and controlling nuclear proliferation, and advocates embracing the diversity our country has thrived on and welcomed for generations.

He speaks to reporters like they're his best friends, stops to greet all men and women, and the message is always clear—in whatever he does. YOU can make a difference. YOU can create new jobs too. YOU can be innovative, different, free. YOU can be yourself.

Governing is not easy. Sometimes it feels as if ages ago, Matt and I were idealists. But sometimes, like for the past year, it feels like we were the realists.

Months go by fast, between governing and the social scene that comes with the White House. I'm close to full term now—my body so very curvy, and somehow very arousing to my husband, and even to me. It feels so sensitive—his touch always electric on my skin. Tonight we were invited to the Washington, D.C., premiere of a movie one of his friends produced, and I'm wondering how I'll manage to wear heels. Maybe ballerina flats and an empire gown would work.

"Look stunning," Lola advised.

"You mean sometimes I don't?" I arched a teasing brow.

"Haha. Truly, Charlotte. People are obsessed with you, and Matthew Hamilton's devotion to you. Millions of women in the world dream of fitting in your glass slipper.

The hot president, his hands gliding over your body as you dance, his worshipful eyes only on you, the most desirable world leader with his clear adoration of you. Politics are dynamic and young—a symbol of the revitalization in our country. Look daring, edgy."

"I'm nearly nine months pregnant," I say.

"Exactly! And you're still standing."

"Lola, you kill me," I laugh.

But I definitely pulled out a lovely chiffon empire-cut gown in a light pink color, which I'm wearing with my hair back in an elegant waterfall look.

It's classy, but edgy for a pregnant woman, I suppose.

Matt zips up the dress for me and as I stare at myself in the mirror, he remains behind me, drinking me in. His voice appreciative, his smile wolfish. "You're so gorgeous, sometimes it's too distracting," he chides, turning my face and placing a soft kiss on my lips.

"You have no idea the amount of cells that become inactive in women's brains when you walk by," I say.

He lets go a surprised laugh, and I laugh too, grabbing my little purse as he escorts me out.

There's a party after the movie, and Matt and I decide to hit it for an hour, have a little fun.

During the night, as I meet the lead actors and Matt talks with his producer friend, I notice the women approaching him and I find it very interesting to watch them fawn, even knowing that he's married. He's cordial and polite, of course, he's a Hamilton, but the ease with which he'd been standing is gone and he seems to close himself off from any flirtation. He's so loyal, and I adore him for that.

I'm surprised the women continue to persist, though, too excited and infatuated to notice that he's definitely not interested.

I think it's more than his beauty they're drawn to. More than his power.

I think it's his humanity that calls them. The fact that he never puts on a show or acts as if he's perfect; instead he's always acted as if he's *not* perfect but attempts to be. As if he knows that all of his imperfections—his amusing and heart-warming overprotectiveness and even his fear of not being both the best husband and father along with the best president—make him real, that all of our imperfections make us real and relatable because not one of us is perfect, not even a president. We simply want the one who will give us his unfailing best. Like he has.

I find myself blatantly staring and when I realize it, I quickly chide myself in silence and turn away. When I turn back, our eyes lock—and his eyes drift over my empire-cut gown, to my abdomen, where I carry his son. I'm due in mere weeks. And like I've noticed these past months, when he looks at me—at what I hold in me—there ... I see it. A flash so quick and bright, it nearly blinds me.

He seems to push it down, under control, but I saw it. All the love, all the desire, all the craving that could ever be in a man is in him. For me. For us.

"The president never fails to make heads turn," Alison says beside me as we mingle with the crowd, her camera always at the ready for her to snap the next shot.

It's true people stare. Although I know people love him for more than his face, because despite the fact that he grew up with everything, he lacks pretention. His parents reared him to be a normal guy, with chores, discipline, and an attitude that was honest and never self-serving. In fact he never liked people doing special things for him, such as not allow him to pay for things; he always paid his way, even when they insisted they wanted to do the gesture for him. Fairness was ingrained with him, or maybe it's just part of who he is.

The man is unforgettable and he knows it.

And now he's the president, my husband, soon to be my baby's daddy.

I frown when I notice Wilson approach him as discreetly as possible, which, considering how much attention Matt draws, is not very discreet, and Matt ducks his head to him. He nods and then lifts his eyes, his gaze instantly landing on me because he's been keeping tabs on me all night.

Something in his expression alarms me. I pick up my skirts and start walking across the room as he motions me to the door.

"Something wrong?"

"We need to go," he says.

He escorts me to the door, his hand on the small of my back as we climb into the state car.

I know whatever has happened is big; otherwise we wouldn't have left. Something needs his attention ASAP.

"We've been attacked in the Middle East."

I gasp. Then I set my hand on my stomach when a contraction hits. I've been feeling them on and off, and was told it was normal—the body preparing.

"What is it?" He looks at me in concern.

I meet his gaze, unsure. "Hopefully … practice." But Murphy's Law says it won't be.

YOU LOVE ME

Charlotte

He's making me time them on our way to the White House, and the contractions are coming regularly, every four minutes.

"Can you wait for me?" Matt asks when we reach the White House and he sits me on the nearest couch.

"I'll try," I promise.

"Wait for me," he says. His tone is firm and sounds like an order to the universe, part command, part request to me as he glances at my stomach.

I can see the tearing need inside him to be in two places at once, a need that is impossible for him to fulfill, even as the most powerful man in the land.

His jaw flexes in the fiercest way. "I hate doing this to you." He leans over and he cups my face. "I love you."

I nod, wanting to appease him. "Every time you hold me close, every time you look at me, I'm reminded of how much you love me. When you do this …" I lift his hand and kiss the back of it, the way he sometimes grazes his lips over my knuckles. "That's all I need. Just knowing it's there, that you're there and you're what's best for our country and what's best for me."

I suck in a harsh breath as a contraction hits, and I try not to cringe.

Matt notices. "Another?"

"It's okay. Go."

He hesitates.

"*Go.*"

He mutters a curse.

And then he spins around and heads away.

"Call her mother," he orders Stacey.

"Yes, sir."

I don't tell him my mom is in the Caribbean with my dad and she can't get here to support me no matter how fast she'd want to.

The pain comes and goes in waves, but the concern about what's happening to our people feels even worse.

I feel like I just swallowed glass, the dread of all that could happen plaguing me as I try to calm down and keep my baby inside me a little longer.

TRAGEDY

Matt

One floor below the Oval Office is the Situation Room. Manned 24/7, this is the place where you figure out and tackle the important things. The White House *brain.*

Where I've talked through the videoconference system to other heads of state. And ordered covert operations, among other highly classified endeavors.

I walk in with Dale Coin and Arturo Villegas, my chief security advisor.

Before the inauguration, the CIA director briefed me on all the covert operations the U.S. was engaged in against foreign enemies. Those had all been personally authorized by my predecessor, Jacobs, and would cease if I gave the word. If I remained silent, the operations would continue.

It's one thing to be a candidate; another, the president.

Some of those operations were highly dangerous, with little benefit to the United States. But we have allies, too, which was something to consider.

Still, when you command the most powerful army in the world, you cannot treat it as a game. Every move of our operatives needs to be planned, strategized, then recorded and analyzed. And no matter what information we have, there are always too many variations of an outcome. No matter how well briefed an incoming president, nothing prepares you to send your men and women to war.

Priorities shift. Gaining more access to intelligence causes your views to shift dramatically as well.

I only hope I made the right calls.

I know as sure as *fuck* I'm making the right one now.

The generals are already seated. I take my seat, lean back, and let the wall before me light up with visuals. The Middle East has been a hot button since long before I took office. Dictators, armed rebels, fucking ISIS.

"In position," General Quincy says.

They all look at me. The silence is deafening.

One second, two seconds.

"Open fire."

I'M HERE

Charlotte

I feel another contraction hit and pain ricochets through my body, burning through even my deepest muscles.

I groan and clutch the edge of the table nearest to me.

I feel the baby move inside me and I stop in place, pressing my legs together against his movements.

Holy shit, this baby means business.

We just walked into the National Naval Medical Center. I asked my team to bring me, and we left a message for Matt. Now I'm rushed in by my security guards, and people gasp when they see me enter the hospital alone.

Without Matt.

Without the president.

"Mrs. Hamilton! Goodness me," exclaims a nurse as she sees me waddling in, clutching my huge stomach, discomfort and fear written all over my face.

Fear that is multiplied, seeing as I need to deliver this baby while my husband tries to solve a national security crisis.

I shudder and try to push those thoughts away as another contraction comes. I moan and feel a puddle of water at my feet.

"Let's get the first lady a wheelchair! NOW!"

"Page Dr. Conwell!"

I feel my body being guided into a wheelchair and before I know it, I am in a hospital bed.

I feel needles pricking my skin, see monitors arranged all around me and doctors rushing in. It seems everyone wants to help deliver the president's baby.

My legs are propped up and a cloth is draped over them, for modesty. But honestly, at this moment, I couldn't give a damn about modesty; I want this baby out and in my arms.

I hear some murmurs and the deep, soothing voice of a doctor addresses me: "Mrs. Hamilton, it seems the baby has shifted in your belly and we are going to have to perform a C-section."

"Is the baby okay?!"

"Yes, ma'am. Don't worry, we have everything under control. I will do everything I can to deliver this baby as quickly and safely as possible."

I feel my heart sink in my chest, weighted down by uncontrollable fear.

I gulp back the scream welling in my chest and squeeze my eyes shut.

Get your shit together, Mommy, I tell myself. *You got this.*

"Okay, Charlotte, here we go. You shouldn't feel a thing, maybe some slight pressure ..." I hear the doctor's words in the distance, but I am somewhere else.

If Matt can't be here with me, I am going to him.

With my eyes still shut, I think of Matt ... his hands wrapped around my waist as he hugs me from behind and meets my eyes in the mirror while I get dressed.

His deep voice gently singing into my belly early in the morning.

His mouth planting soft kisses on my forehead as he says good night.

How his fingers feel against my skin when he rubs my back.

How when he's half asleep, he pulls me closer to him, subconsciously using his body to shield me against anything and everything.

How he nuzzles his head in my neck after we make love, his soft hair gently tickling my cheek as he sinks his nose and inhales my scent before releasing a sound of pure male satisfaction before falling asleep.

I feel tears well up again, and I miss him more than ever before. I want more than anything to have him here, his eyes looking into mine, holding my hand, telling me everything will be okay, telling me I am doing great.

I hear monitors beeping. I turn to the side and see Stacey is beside me, holding my hand.

I asked her to come in before the C-section began, because she is the closest friend I have in the White House. I consider her like family.

She looks at me with her sweet and strong blue eyes, gently nodding to me, squeezing my hand in comfort and encouragement. I smile back at her, feeling so much love and gratitude toward her it gets stuck in my throat and I can't do anything other than tell her with my eyes how grateful I am for all she does for me.

I turn back to look at the ceiling.

I focus on my breathing. *Inhale ... and exhale ...*

In a few minutes I'll finally be able to see and hold my little baby ... the one I've helped and seen grow inside me ... the one who dances in my belly when he hears my or Matt's voice ... the one who kicks when he's (or I am) hungry ...

And then I hear a sound. A baby's cry.

I start to cry, tears pouring out of my eyes of their own will.

"Congratulations, Mrs. Hamilton."

I hear applause erupt around the room as I see a little bundle of white blankets approach me.

I reach out my arms instinctively, wanting nothing more than to hold him.

The nurse gently places him in my arms and I am met with the most beautiful, innocent, chubby pink face I have ever seen.

Long, spiky eyelashes and brilliant gray eyes stare back at me and I have never felt happier, more complete, more blessed than I do now.

I feel so filled with love, I feel my heart cracking into pieces in my chest.

I see myself in him. I see Matthew in him. I see the beginnings of a family.

All too soon the nurses have to take him away to have his vitals checked and make sure everything is healthy.

I ache for him, and more than ever I ache for Matt.

I close my eyes for a second and feel myself drifting off into sleep, exhausted by everything that has happened in the last twenty-four hours.

I fight to open my eyes, but they keep fluttering closed.

Far off in the distance, I hear a voice I could not mistake for anyone else's. Deep, commanding, overwhelmingly male, demanding: "Where is she?"

I hear shuffling and the sounds of shiny black shoes belonging to ten Secret Service agents running along the marble floors of the hospital.

"I need to see her now!"

"Mr. President—" I hear a voice respond.

I hear the door open and shut and I feel his presence fill the room. I whisper his name.

"Mr. President, congratulations ..."

I instantly feel his hands reach for me, cupping my face, enveloping it in warmth.

His thumb catches a tear falling from the edge of my eyelashes as I sob, "Matt ..."

I open my eyes and see him gazing back at me, his eyes brilliant and deep, tender and soothing. "I'm here, baby."

JUNIOR

Charlotte

Eighteen minutes after he walked into the hospital, Matthew Hamilton holds his firstborn son.

I've never been so proud to be his first lady.

He caresses my cheek, pride shining in his eyes. "Thank you."

"You're welcome," I say, smiling weakly.

"He looks like you, Mr. President," I hear.

He winks at me, his arms all for his son, his eyes all for me—staying on mine for a long time, like mine stay on his. Then he looks down at our son, his eyes raking him up and down, glimmering with happiness after I know the night he faced was probably the darkest night of all. "He's perfect, baby," he says, then presses a kiss to my forehead.

He leaves his lips there for long, delicious seconds, as if he wants to brand that kiss on me. I feel his love for me down to the marrow of my bones.

When he eases back to smile at me, his tortured eyes show me the pain he's witnessed, the darkness that will always stay. It sends my pulse spinning, a need to comfort him hitting me with such force, it's overwhelming.

I reach out to hold the back of his head, trying to cradle him even though I'm in bed and weak, and he's the one standing, the one holding it together—like he always is.

Once in my private room, with my parents, Matt's mother, his grandfather, and Matt, I watch his address to the nation from his desk in the Oval on TV, one that was aired while I was delivering.

He's wearing a somber black tie and black suit, and he looks directly at the camera as he speaks. "As of twenty-two hundred hours, we engaged in air combat over the hostile region of Islar. The mission was successful. We have confirmation that the five terrorists behind the attack have perished."

Silence.

"These are sad times for us as a country, every time one of us dies to ensure that here, we can keep on living our lives to their fullest. We need to honor those sacrifices, ensure that we continue prospering as we have until now, not only financially, but as human beings. Now more than ever we need to stand together. We need to fight the fights that matter. For freedom, for security, for our loved ones. We're a kaleidoscope, all different, but what unites us is our love of this country. Our pride in being American. American we were born. American we will die."

There were two American casualties. The media called it a victory, but Matt and I know better. No one wins in a war. But you protect your own. We don't have only one son; the citizens of the United States are our family.

Two days later, I'm allowed back home, and Matt and I have to plan a whole process of introducing the baby to Jack.

Down the hall from our bedroom, I decorated the baby's room by having the walls painted with pastel-colored forests and installing a white crib with a baby-blue coverlet. So many baby toys have arrived since the announcement of him being a boy, we've donated at least two-thirds of them to charities. This is one privileged little boy, and I've been amazed by the love our baby has been getting from America.

For the first few weeks until he sleeps through the night, though, I settle him with me in the Queens' Bedroom across the hall from Matt, where I have a crib set up and a rocking chair, and I wait in the rocking chair with the baby blinking up at the ceiling in wonder as Matt brings Jack to the door.

"Come here, boy," he says, striding across the room.

Jack drops to his haunches, warily crawling across the room to where Matt now stands before me.

"It's Matthew Junior," I say, shifting slightly forward to let Jack sniff him.

The baby makes a soft, happy gurgling sound and Jack's tail starts wagging, and I glance up at Matt, and as my hot husband smiles a quiet *I told you so*, I sigh in relief. I was mildly concerned Jack would be a danger to Matthew Jr.

But I'm already realizing he'll be our son's mischief buddy for sure.

Ooops.

MEDAL OF HONOR

Charlotte

"Ladies and gentlemen, the President of the United States, Matthew Hamilton, accompanied by the Medal of Honor recipient, Sergeant Swan."

After what happened the day Matthew Jr. was born, a hero emerged. Sergeant Swan is visiting the White House today, where he'll receive the highest recognition, the Medal of Honor.

He proved his courage in the Middle East when his unit was ambushed, braving enemy fire and ignoring injuries as he tended to wounded comrades.

I know that nothing weighs more heavily on Matt's shoulders than sending our men and women into danger, and he told me that being a man who always admired those who served in the military, and having failed to do so himself, this is the greatest honor he's ever been bestowed, next to being president—to be able to award this medal to those who serve, and serve so well.

I watch from the chairs lining the room as both men walk up to the podium, Matt sharp in a blue suit, the sergeant in his uniform, as Matthew addresses the audience.

"Courage is not a virtue we are born with. It is a virtue we exercise—a choice that we make. Courage is when our men and women selflessly volunteer to defend our country, and keep us safe." He keeps it short. Simple. As he removes the medal from the box, he walks up to the sergeant.

Once the medal hangs firmly around the soldier's neck, Matt puts out his hand.

Applause echoes around the room.

The soldier is emotional, lips pursed tightly as he fights his emotions.

Matt slaps his back and shakes his hand, and I hear him tell the man, personally, not for the cameras, "Thank you for your service. We sleep at night thanks to our men and women, our armed forces out there defending and protecting our nation."

"Thank you, Mr. President," the soldier croaks out as he faces the spectators again with red eyes.

DANCING ON THE BALCONY

Charlotte

It's day thirty-nine postpartum with mere hours to hit the exact forty-day mark, and he waits for me on the balcony of the second floor while I finish feeding Matty. I find him leaning on the railing, thoughtful as I step outside.

When he turns to watch me approach, a heady mix of lust and love envelops me.

Matt smiles. He slips an arm around my waist and draws me close. The gardens are quiet outside, and he begins to move with me. I shut my eyes. He sets his forehead on mine.

We start swaying to some sort of music in our heads, the music outside the White House, in the silent gardens, the D.C. streets, the rustle of our clothes as we move.

I open my eyes and find myself staring at a swirl of dark as he holds me to him, one of my hands within his, and we're moving all this time, getting closer, turning around on the Truman Balcony, and then he lowers his head, and the next second his lips are slanting over mine. Slowly, tenderly, he takes my lips as if I'm precious—as if I'm the most precious thing this man has.

I open to him.

He probes lightly, leisurely, without any hurry at all, his tongue rubbing over mine, caressing me. His hands go to the back of my head, gently stroking down my hair.

We're still dancing.

But now we're kissing as well, and my body reacts in the usual way. I'm breathing hard, completely enveloped by his warmth, his strength, his scent.

He whispers in my ear, "I miss my girl."

"She misses you."

His eyes sparkle. "You're tempting like you have no idea."

"I should go sleep."

He looks wolfish, catching my wrist and pinioning me in place. "Not happening." He smiles, laughing. "Come here."

His coaxing look weakens me head to toe. A slow fire between my legs starts building into an inferno of heat. My heart's beating too fast in my chest as Matt reels me toward his six-feet-plus frame.

He raises my hand and presses my fingertips to his lips. When he slips his tongue out to lick my fingertips, I gasp. He eases back and our gazes lock.

He says, "Day thirty-nine," with a curl of his lips.

I nod, breathless. Wondering if he's thinking what I'm thinking.

My hands go to his shirt, fisting the fabric. I meant to stop him. Didn't I? We still have one more day to go. But all I know is his mouth is on mine again, and it tastes divine, and I want more of it, and my fingers are clenching his shirt tightly and I can't breathe. His hands slide down my sides, cup my ass, and pull me toward him. Closer.

The ache between my legs intensifies as his cock bites into my abdomen. He's so hard, his kiss warm and sensual as he drags his lips to my ear, where he whispers, "Sleep with me tonight."

I press back against the railing, watching the moonlight play across his gorgeous face. "But it's day thirty-nine, and Matthew Junior—"

"Matthew has a nanny—I would rather he stay with the nanny tonight so I can spend some quality time with my wife."

I swallow, knowing already that I cannot wait a second longer. "I'll think about it for a few minutes," I lie, sliding my hands up the flat wall of his chest, going up on tiptoe, my voice husky. "In the meantime, I'll have a little more of this." I kiss him.

Quick as a devil, hot as sin, he moves me around and sways me against him in some dark, forbidden tango.

He grabs me like I'm the sexiest thing ever.

I moan and edge back to the railing, leaning on it as I fumble with my skirt, pulling it up as much as possible so he can wedge himself between my legs.

He fills the space between my thighs and he looks at me reverently as he smooths my hair behind my forehead, and he ducks his head so that his teeth graze my skin. He nips the curve of my neck and shoulder. Waves of pleasure rush down my spine, and before I realize it, I'm pulling him closer and rubbing up against his flat chest.

"Matt …"

"Yeah."

I can't speak, can't think as his lips flutter over my skin, his groan warm over my throat.

"God, I want you. I miss you. I miss the scent of your skin, the sounds you make." He catches my skin between his teeth and tugs gently. I gasp, and he releases me. His tongue flicks out, circling a slow, wet path to ease the sting. He slides his hand between our bodies, caressing me between my legs.

I'm trembling as I lean on the balustrade, then I boost myself up and curl my arms and legs around him and whisper in his ear, "I love you."

He lifts me higher. My legs tighten around his hips, my arms around his neck as he kisses me fiercely and crosses the balcony to the door.

We're in his bedroom faster than I imagined possible.

Desire crackles in our kiss as he shuts the door behind us. My fingers wind into his hair as he lays me down on his bed, our kiss heated but tender. Our breathing is uneven, mine quick and shallow, his deep and harsh. He drops to his knees on the bed and lifts my skirt, grabbing the hem and raising it to my hips. I groan as he presses his mouth on my abdomen.

And then his tongue.

So delicious.

So hot. So quick. So expert as he kisses my navel, then kisses the scar of my C-section.

He works his lips up my tummy and toward my breasts, and he cups them under my blouse and gently caresses. He flicks his thumb around the peak, then eases my top upward and sucks it until I groan. "I can't wait, Charlotte. I'm starving for you."

I rip open his shirt in my urgency. He runs his hands up and down the sides of my body. We both bare each other as quickly as we can. By the time he's got me stripped, I've shoved his pants down his legs and he's kicking them off and stretching on top of me.

He's so beautiful. His muscles smooth and hard, perfectly delineated. I remembered how gorgeous he was, but I suspect he's been working out a bit more than he had been—sexual frustration, maybe. The thought makes me melt. He really looks a bit thicker and more muscular, and I let my fingers enjoy his hard work. I lean over and kiss his nipple, my fingers brushing over the dusting of hair on his chest.

I'm rewarded by a low, pained sound. "Lick it harder," he says. Voice rough and raw.

"Matt," I moan.

He releases a smile as he looks down at me, eating me up with his eyes, caressing me everywhere. He tells me I'm gorgeous as he moves his finger inside me. "Do you have any idea what you do to me, Charlotte?" He seizes the base of his cock and leads it to my seam. *There.*

Right

At

My

Opening.

My breath goes. I fist the sheets beneath me. And my eyes roll into the back of my head at the sheer pleasure of feeling my husband drive inside me again. Inch by inch. Slow. With so much care, I can feel his body vibrate.

We're heart to heart, skin to skin, heat to heat.

He palms the side of my face, looking into my eyes. I mewl softly, tilting my hips to encourage him to move. But still he doesn't, just looks at my whole face, our breathing ragged as he allows me to adjust to the feel of him again.

I bite my lip breathlessly. "Please," I beg.

"I love you," he gruffs out, brushing his thumb along my lower lip, leaning over to flick his tongue out and soothe the skin I just bit.

He starts moving—slowly, exquisitely slowly. His body powerful and in control, making love to mine. He makes love to me as if I'm a virgin, as if it's my first time and he wants me to never forget it.

And in this moment, all my world is him as I undulate beneath him, relishing the closeness, his nearness, *him*. He is the most powerful man in the world. He is determined and strong and ambitious, he is noble and honest, and he is also true and unwavering—not once does his desire waver; on the contrary, even with a remaining one-month bump that I hope to be able to run off once I resume exercise, I have never felt so sexy to him, so precious, or so loved.

And on this day, the mystery of our love grows, and I realize that it keeps changing, evolving, deepening with every experience we share, every kiss not given and every kiss given, every whisper and every word unsaid. I have never in my life felt the kind of love I feel for him—and as his hands caress me tenderly, the tension in his body evident as he tries to be gentle but hinting at his simmering desire, the deep words of love he whispers in my ear, *beautiful* and *perfect* and *his*, I know he feels it too. And I know that this feeling is probably as mysterious to him as it is to me, and just as wondrous.

GROWING

Charlotte

Matt Jr. is growing so fast, he's walking already—and absolutely has the run of the household, with everyone *ooh*ing and *aah*ing over our charming boy.

I grow too, right along with him.

I grow fully into the role of first lady.

Of mother.

Of wife.

Of hostess.

Of mistress of the White House.

Of champion of children.

Of the president's lover.

One year turns into two, the years consisting of diapers and cradles and children's toys, of red carpets and trumpets blaring as we receive foreign dignitaries at the White House, of black-tie events that embody the might and majesty of the United States.

Foreign leaders receive a royal welcome with the state arrival ceremony, flourishes and flags, sentinels and orchestras. The press corps waits on standby for these events, eager for a video chat. The chef plans the perfect meals, down to the perfect artistic design to present each dish.

We have stage performances. Andrea Bocelli, and the ballet. We celebrate wins from our teams, and decorate every Christmas with a gigantic tree with knitted ornaments (Matty proof).

More than that, the White House is the center where a dozen new treaties have been made. Where several natural disasters have been handled. Where big decisions and changes have begun. The White House is more than just the pomp and the politics, and more than the playground for our son.

It doesn't belong to the president, this house; it belongs to the people.

This is where their futures begin.

"Hey." A slow curve twists the corner of Matt's lips when he spots Jack and me. He loosens the top two buttons of his shirt and rolls his shirtsleeves to his elbows. His groan of satisfaction at having a moment's relaxation after a full day of work makes my nipples bead.

He drops beside me. "How was your day?"

"Good." I inch a little closer even as he ducks his head—meeting me halfway for a short, light kiss.

"What are you two up to?" he asks, frowning at Jack and me playfully even as Jack scoots over to join the coddling, pressing his muzzle into Matt's free hand.

"We're enjoying the quiet. While your son sleeps."

"How is my legacy?"

"Growing. My hips are permanently skewed outward from carrying him."

He laughs.

"Come here, boy." He strokes Jack behind the ear. "He's wearing you down, isn't he?" he asks Jack.

Jack licks Matt's palm and makes a happy groaning sound, and Matt leaves his hand there, stroking him as he leans his head to look at me.

"You look tired."

"I *am* tired. But now that you're here, I'm getting a second wind. Tell me about your day."

He groans. "I'd rather not wear you down even more. Tell me about yours."

"Matty tried to mount one of the ducks in the pond, and he would've completely fallen in if Jack hadn't stuck in his muzzle."

"Really?" He arches an eyebrow at Jack, who's just looking up adoringly at Matt with a gaze that begs his master to keep rubbing his ear. "Good boy," he says, reaching with his free hand to stroke his thumb down my face. "You think we should get rid of the ducks, then?"

"Oh no. It's like baby TV. Matty could watch them for hours."

Matt laughs, his laugh making me laugh too.

Whereas we used to love to talk about politics—it was something that joined us—now we're so immersed in it that we love talking about other things. Matt loves talking about normal things—I see him crave it, the normalcy he's never had. But he was meant for greater things; normalcy is a luxury we don't have. Sometimes, though, we make it for ourselves.

And in those moments he's just Matt, my husband, the father of my son, and the guy I love.

I lie on his chest and his voice is in my ear while we both pet Jack. "They have a lead."

I nearly jump out of my skin. Not because of the words, because we've had leads before, but because of the true hope in Matt's voice. "What? When? Who?" I demand.

"Patience, grasshopper," he says, a smile touching his eyes before the somberness returns. "If all goes well, we'll know soon enough."

"Oh, Matt, I hope this is it," I say, wrapping my arms around him, pressing a kiss to his neck.

I know how much he's been looking forward to this, how every dead end has only doubled his resolution to keep his promise to his father.

Later that weekend, I have my first official outing, and we're heading to a summit. Matthew proposed a carbon tax for all carbon-emitting industries that have been polluting the very air we breathe for years. He says that their continuing to do so is not an option.

He's been discussing policy to me and in the meantime, I let my fingers wander along his abs, sliding along his hard stomach, to the thatch of hair underneath his belly button.

"With India, however …" He trails off and one of his eyebrows rises ever so slowly as he glances down at me in total interest.

I inch a bit closer and lean my head as I unzip him. He's heavy and thick as I take him out. I curl my hands around the base of his shaft and lick the wetness at the tip, peering up to see him shut his eyes. I lick him more, and he exhales and opens his eyes, staring at me with an expression that is hot—completely raw—and the next instant his large hand is engulfing the back of my head, exerting pressure and urging me back down

FBI NEWS

Charlotte

"**M**r. President, the head of the FBI, Mr. Cox, wants to see you ASAP. They found him."

Matt's gaze falls on Dale Coin like an axe, demanding more.

"He's got a presentation for you," Coin adds.

A mix of dread, fear, sorrow, and hope knot inside me as I realize what this means. "Oh my god," I breathe. Coin is talking about President Law's shooter.

Matt's eyes change; they fill with a fierce sparkling.

"Let's go." On his feet, he marches down the hall with Dale and three other men, who are updating him on what's going on.

He pauses midway to the stairs, then cuts the distance back to me. He looks down at me, reading in my eyes how important it is to me. To the whole country. What it will mean to have justice shine.

"Come with me," he says.

I exhale and nod in excitement, stepping beside him as we head to the Situation Room.

Everyone watches as we enter. Matt's gone from staring at the room to now staring at me in a completely intense manner. He stops only when everyone begins to greet him. He greets them back and tells me to sit down.

They lower the lights—and then they're out.

The wall before us flashes, and an image of a man with a beard and light blond hair appears.

"His name is Rupert Larson," Cox says.

Matt clenches his jaw. "Go on."

The pain in my heart becomes a sick and fiery gnawing as I listen intently.

Matt stands and gets himself coffee, then he looks at the image, frowning very hard.

"Age fifty-three now. Wanted for rape charges and drug abuse. Grew up in the system."

The muscle in the back of Matt's jaw flexes relentlessly as sends me a look that tells me we need to fix that system.

"Last seen in Georgia."

The images begin flicking on the wall, revealing the man with several different hairstyles and hair colors. We watch, silent. Sometimes Matt's roiling dark eyes meet mine, and they look crisp and metallic, as cold as I feel.

"Suffers from paranoia and delusions. Apparently he had some beef with President Law. At first addressed letters to him commending him on what a fine job he was doing. He claimed to be able to see the future—his murder. The letters stopped for years. We found one unsent letter detailing exactly how he would die. Three gunshots. He could only get two in before Secret Service caught him. He's been running ever since."

Cox eyes him as Matt drains his coffee cup. He's in control, but under the façade, I can feel the turmoil around him. He gives Cox a bleak, thick look, a look that could cause a lesser man to run and head for cover.

"How can we be sure it's him?" he asks. Voice cold.

"The second unsent letter. A written confession—more like a gloating documentary. Signed."

The torment that flashes for a fraction of a second in Matt's eyes stabs me in the chest.

This is his dad's killer. The man who took Lawrence Hamilton's life and who's been free for all these years. I get mad just thinking about it. As mad as I know Matt is, deep inside. His voice shows no evidence of that torment, or that anger, though, even with that lethal glimmer in his eyes. His face is a mask of stone as he meets Cox dead in the eye.

"You know what to do."

He leads me out of the Situation Room with a hand pressed to the small of my back, and when we're finally in his bedroom, I wrap my arms around him in impulse—feeling him pull me to him just as fiercely.

"Think they'll get him?" I whisper.

"They better," he hisses, his eyes fully open to me now, his face etched in pain. I grab his face as he grabs mine, kissing each other as if our lives depend on it, his kiss tasting of pain and hope, sorrow and fulfillment.

One hour after Matt was briefed, every law enforcement agent in the country has now been informed of the case—and everyone has a face, a photo, and a name of the suspect. He's earned himself a top spot in the country's most-wanted list and is considered extremely volatile and dangerous.

Matt meets with his mother, and they talk for over an hour. He had the FBI retrieve the scarf from the evidence files, and he gives it to her. She cries for a long time after.

It's 2 a.m. by the time we retire for bed, Matty already asleep, and Jack, though he likes sleeping by Matty's door to guard him, seems to sense something's up. He pads into our room as we're stripping for bed, and leaps onto bed with us and barks for Matt's attention.

I pull up the covers and slip into my side, and I stroke Jack's ears as he lies down as Matt approaches. Matt drops his lean, muscular naked body on his side of the bed and strokes his hand down Jack's muzzle, then moves his hand to cover mine. I raise my eyes to his, and he looks at me, and I feel the look everywhere. It says all the things he is not saying.

"I'm sorry," I breathe, uncurling my other hand to reveal that I'm holding his father's pin. I just haven't been able to stop holding it all day.

"I'm sorry too," he rasps. That's all he says.

I slip my hands around his neck, pressing a kiss to his throat as we cuddle, Jack settling with a long sigh in between our legs.

Five hours later, Matt is awakened to the news that Larson's been captured.

The criminal's face is on the front page of every newspaper across the country. America rejoices. Though it only reopens the wound, for the memory becomes fresh for Matthew and his mother. I head with him and little Matt to the cemetery, three dozen white roses in our hands that we set on President Law Hamilton's grave.

"Rest in peace, Dad," Matt says, leaving his roses after I set down mine. He raps his knuckles to the headstone, and a tear slips out of the corner of my eye.

Matt Jr. steps up, setting his right in between ours. "West in peace, Gwandpapa."

He raps his knuckles like his dad did, and I part laugh, part sob.

Matt smiles over Matty's action, his eyes full of love for his son as he rumples his hair, scoops him up, and we head back to the motorcade. Matt quiet but at peace. The only one who can't hold back the tears for my husband is me.

IMMEASURABLY

Charlotte

This fall, the primaries for the main parties have begun with much pomp, and I've watched on television, curious about which final contenders among the multiple options will win the nomination this time. I know that Matthew's grandfather came to have a chat with him about him running as a Democrat or Republican this time around.

"I respectfully declined," he told the press when rumors of the meeting started making the rounds.

I wonder today when he'll announce his intention to run for reelection.

"Why do they all want to be Dad?"

"Hmm?"

I glance at Matthew Jr., the most adorable two-year-old you could ever know, with a head of dark hair, a toothy grin, and a Dennis-the-Menace attitude.

"They all want to be pwesident." He frowns menacingly.

"Yes, because the president gets to make the important calls," I tell him as we walk outside in the gardens.

"I want my dad to be pwesident," he states simply.

"Yes, he is the pwesident."

"I don't want to leave home." His voice cracks, and I stroke the top of his head. Has he overheard someone talk?

"Home is where we are all together, no matter where that is," I assure him.

But my son's words follow me throughout the day. I think about what it would be like to start fresh. A part of me finds it relieving, to be able to have a bit more privacy, but a part of me is not ready to leave here yet—and I'm certain that my husband is too motivated, too dedicated, and too passionate about his job to be ready to leave.

Plus, this house has been our home for three years.

I know the chief usher so well, I've hosted birthday parties for him and went to his son's christening. I know that he handles over a hundred employees, looks out for Matt's and my schedules, runs everything efficiently, and is the head of the household staff and in charge of all the daily operations. Tom makes sure our lives run smoothly, and they *do*.

I'm fond of the chef, who is just like Jessa was when I grew up, loving to make us our favorite cakes and dinners when we have special occasions. Who somehow knows when Matt has had a rough day and makes a particularly tasty dish to bring a smile to his face. And who indulges me in all my kids' luncheons.

I'm fond of Lola and all her stressing about the news and dealing with the relentless press.

Even the Secret Service. All-seeing, all-knowing, tight-lipped, never sharing the information, always not only protecting us physically, but ensuring that our private lives are as private as they possibly can be.

Every room I stand in has meaning. Has a story. Has presence.

The presidency is not just a political agenda, or standing strong against opponents. It's about keeping us together, proud and safe. Taken care of and motivated. It's not only about protecting our rights and freedom, it's about providing examples and inspiration—that is what made America what it is today. I cannot imagine anyone doing a better job than my Matthew Hamilton.

That night after we have dinner in the Old Family Dining Room, Matt Jr. asks his father why he's letting all those men run for president.

"Because it's their right; it's one of the most sacred of our rights, in this country. Our freedom," he explains as we retire to the Yellow Oval.

Matt Jr. frowns in confusion as he listens, then simply declares, "I want you to be pwesident."

Matt laughs, dragging a hand over his face as Matty heads off to run and play with his toys, Jack trailing behind him.

"I'll put him to bed," his nanny, Anna, tells me as she rushes after him.

Matt looks at me then, pouring himself an after-dinner drink and bringing me one as well. "I've been thinking about it. For years, it seems." He looks at me as he takes the seat across from mine. "I've been obsessively counting." He looks into his glass, then at me. "How many days I've been able to be here for you, how many days I haven't. It's a tough call," he admits, with a wry, sad smile. "The day Matt was born—"

"There was no way I would have let you stay with me," I quickly interject.

He seems amused but refrains from smiling. "That's not the only time. On your twenty-fifth birthday—"

"The airport was closed due to the blizzard. How were you supposed to land? All that was not in your control," I assure him.

He exhales, then looks at me curiously, calculatingly, laughing softly. "Charlotte, listen to me."

"I'm listening and you're not making sense."

"Baby," he says, more sternly now. "We need to discuss how you feel about me running. And I need you to be honest with me, honest in ways my mother never was with my father." He's completely somber now, looking at me between drawn eyebrows.

My chest sort of hurts that he even has to ask. I have never wanted him to feel worried about neglecting us; the truth is, he always goes above and beyond. "Were you considering not running?"

"I won't run if it's an issue with my family. You know I love being here, Charlotte. I'm driven to do what I do." He gives me a smile that sends my pulse wild. "But I love you two more than anything."

I'm so in love with this man sometimes it hurts just *because.*

I know that Matt has never wanted to miss out on some important things that he's unfortunately sometimes had to miss out on. I know he's tried harder than any man ever would to make me and our son feel loved, supported, and protected.

"We've both come a long way," I say as we both sit here, looking at each other for a while—and I'm realizing at this moment just how much we've both slowly fought our wars to make this work. "I never thought I could live this life, come to these heights with you—and yet here I am. Not doing too shabby." I grin, and he laughs softly, his eyes sparkling. "And you … you have to know that you've proven more than capable of being both a president and the best husband and father we could ask for," I add, not bothering to hide the admiration in my voice.

"I don't want you to ever feel like I'm putting you and Matty in second place," he says, scrutinizing my face closely, as if searching for the answer. "If for any reason it's crossed your mind, I want you to know that I will choose you both and end it right here."

"No! You can't!" I protest.

I shift forward, scowling at him as I set my glass aside, mirroring his position.

I inhale passionately, then exhale and scowl at him. "Although I am just one citizen among millions, I have had the honor of knowing firsthand what you bring to the table. Integrity. Honesty."

I try not to get emotional, but suddenly putting into context all that he has done for nearly four years makes it difficult.

"I know in my heart of hearts that no other candidate will offer this, bring this … or not quite like you. You are of us. *All* of us. I have you forever, but as a citizen I'd have you as president for just four more years. Make them count. My heart is yours and my vote is yours. Don't deny me all you have to give, or four more years of having this … *honor* … of being by your side while you're doing what you were meant to do." I add, "Please."

He smiles when I end up breathless after my pleas.

He slowly sets his glass aside and comes to his feet. He begins walking around the table, then pulls me to my feet as he clenches his jaw, grabs me by the back of the head, and kisses me. Long and with tongue. "Thank you. I love you. You know that," he hisses, fierce, his forehead against mine, his eyes holding mine deliciously captive.

"Yes," I say, my toes curling the way they do every time he looks at me like that. "But I'm still unsure of how much. Immeasurably, you've said. What is that, even?"

His eyes trace every inch of my face. "It means there's no metric system, no measurement, there's no beginning to it, and no end."

I am completely breathless, and he smiles, noticing that I'm panting, and kisses me again, long and slow. "That's how much," he rasps against my mouth, patting my butt.

We head to the Lincoln Bedroom, where he dials a number through the White House secure lines.

"Carlisle." He speaks the name and looking at me with a smile, clicks the button to put the call on speaker. "I need you and Hessler."

"I told my heart condition to fuck off. That I wasn't going to die anytime soon because I was fucking waiting for this call." I can hear the grin in Carlisle's voice, and Matt and I smile at each other.

"It's done then," I tell Matt when he hangs up. I feel giddy. "There's no way anyone stands a chance."

He shrugs and gets ready for bed, unbuttoning his shirt. "You never know. Better men have lost."

"Yes, but great countries are led by the greatest people—and there aren't many quite like you," I say as I pluck off my diamond earrings.

When I slide naked under the covers with him, I nearly gasp as the warmth of his flesh touches mine.

"Are you ready to hit the trail, wife?" he asks, leaning over me, gazing down at me as he brushes my red hair behind my face.

"Maybe." I grin, then decide to tease him with my favorite slogan from his last campaign. *Born for this.* "Then again, maybe I was born for it."

"No, baby," he's quick to assure. "You were born for *me*." And his mouth swallows any protest I might have uttered. Which, in fact, would have been none.

IT'S ON

Matt

I'm on a roll, and it's not even 10 a.m.

After my daily briefing, hearing what everyone is doing around the world, and making a few calls, I'm in the press room.

I'm ripping it. The pride, anticipation, and adrenaline coursing through my veins already, my intention, desire, and determination to keep my seat and continue serving fueling my every word.

"I must admit"—I look at everyone in the press room—"being president is a tough job. Sleepless nights, tough calls, even looking at your faces every day," I say, mocking the press a bit over their complete obsession with me and my wife. "Man. It's not a job to be taken lightly." I whistle, shaking my head as they laugh. "I've known that since my father took office. It took a toll on our family. I've tried to let it take the least possible toll on mine. Because, you see ..."

I pause, meeting reporters eye to eye.

"If I don't build a better tomorrow for this family I love so much—for this country I love so much—then who will? If I don't ensure and fight for their safety, their rights, who will? If I deny my citizens my every effort, I deny my family, too. I do not want to fail any of you. This tough job has taught me how to be tougher, how to be smarter, and how to be a diplomat, but it never becomes easier. Then again, I wouldn't want easy. Where's the fun in that?"

This is met with laughs.

"Thank you for these four years. For your belief in me. If you will allow it, and the citizenship wishes it—let's make it eight. I am formally announcing my intention"—my eyes meet Charlotte's, and I fucking want to kiss the smile she wears right now—"to run for reelection, and continue to be honored as the president of the United States of America."

CAMPAIGNING

Matt

The crowd is chanting my name as we drive into the first rally in Philadelphia.

"You get the best crowds I've ever fucking seen," Carlisle says. I scan the crowd, wishing she could see it. That always got her excited. Charlotte stayed back at the hotel with Matthew Jr., both of them sleeping in this morning.

"Here we are, sixty percent female, forty percent male. The majority here to see your pretty face. Even married, you have a way with the ladies," Wilson taunts.

My lips twist into a wry smile. "A vote is a vote."

He laughs. "Yeah, I know it bugs the hell out of you—no offense, Mr. President. And don't worry, every president leaves looking haggard as fuck; your beauty will lessen with four more years. If you still draw crowds by now, then it means you did something good."

"Wilson, I'm on a schedule here." I point for him to stop the car.

"Right."

"Hey, do me a favor," I lean into the car as I get out, "check in on Charlotte later. Oh, and tell her Jack hasn't been fed."

"Go about your busy day. I got it."

I step out with Carlisle and Hessler, the rest of the Secret Service piling up behind me as discreetly as possible—some of them disguised as civilians—as we head to the podium and the waiting crowd.

THANKS FOR CAMPAIGNING

Charlotte

'm watching him speak at the rally for Florida small business owners, and for a second, he looks only at me.

"... because not only our aim, but our duty, is to strengthen our country for those who haven't been born yet. And for those we love."

My breath dies, and he slides his eyes away and looks at the members of his team with half a smirk and half a smile.

Nobody notices, though, the looks we share. They have no idea of the real connection we have—that this man is a part of me. Husband and wife, they know what we are, but I'm not sure anyone has a true idea of what he means to me, or what I know that I am to him.

The men are scribbling notes using pens with Matt's campaign logo, and then they're all standing as he rises to leave and starts shaking hands, thanking them. I'm surprised that so many of the male team members approach me to say goodbye as well.

Matt steps to my side as we head out of the room.

"I'd better give you the floor right now," he says, reaching out and sliding his thumb down my jaw. I laugh as we exit the building, but his gaze is still with me as we ride back to the hotel.

We're supposed to freshen up and attend a fundraiser later in the day, and I decide I'll change my heels for flats because my feet are killing me, but I am not missing it for the world.

"My first lady is quite a crowd draw," he says, lifting his hand to grab me by the back of the neck and kiss me. He eases back, leaving me breathless. My husband. He's smiling. He's teasing me, of course, but he has this proud look as if to say *I knew I made the right choice.*

"You, on the other hand, you were awful just now. I think your team wants to kick you off the campaign, Mr. President." I shake my head teasingly. "You're four years older, no longer the young, fresh bachelor you used to be."

His eyes start dancing. "You've aged me, baby, what can I say."

"I mean, at least you made the effort. I don't think they went for it, though—you were far more charming when you were single."

He's looking at me with that strange tender look again, and I'm lying—he is hotter than ever. Nearing forty, so mature, so gorgeous, with no gray hairs yet, no matter how sexy I think he would look with a little gray on that gorgeous head or at the temples. He plucks off his glasses, tucks them into his pocket, and he sends me a warning look that I recognize—one that I suspect he will act on when we enter the suite and he pins me against the wall and kisses the shit out of me.

I'm getting flustered, getting weak-kneed, and I walk into the suite playing a little bit hard to get.

"Is there a reason why you put half the room between us, Charlotte?"

"No. Why? I just wanted to stretch my legs a little bit," I say nonchalantly.

He lifts a brow, slowly coming to stand behind me. "You think I asked you up here to ravage you, wife?" he asks, slipping his hand down and cupping my ass.

"*No*," I groan.

He ducks his head to nuzzle me and I seem to take one last breath.

His smile starts wavering as his eyes begin to darken, and then the smile completely leaves, replaced by a look of pure frustration and raw need. He is too close, so close, his expensive cologne in my nostrils and his eyes looking warmly down at me.

"Charlotte," he says. "We don't have time for this, baby."

"I know. That's why I was here and you were there. But now you're here too, so what are we going to do?"

He reaches out and runs his thumb over my lip. Once. Twice. "I find that the older I get, the more I hate waiting," he confesses, frowning.

I laugh, and walk to the sofa.

"My feet are killing me," I say as I toss my shoes aside and relax for just a second before I need to hurry into the shower.

Campaigning is as exhausting as I remember, and I love it just as fiercely as I recall. Years ago, youth made us believe in the impossible, but it's only those who believe in the impossible who can actually make it possible. And we have. For four years. We've tried, and succeeded, so many times.

Matt gives me a genuinely admiring stare. "I appreciate you being here."

I smile wearily and get a bottle of cold water from the fridge, then come back to the living area to take a sip. "I've always found it inspiring. When I watch you move all those people." I frown a little. "Makes me wonder half the time what's real and what's bullshit."

"Charlotte," he chides. "We don't have a bull in the pen at the offices. None of it is bullshit."

"All politicians bullshit."

He lifts his brows. "I'm not a politician."

"You are now."

I laugh, and then watch him approach.

The air crackles with adrenaline. His satisfaction pulses off him in waves, and my own body responds in kind.

He takes a seat next to me as I lie curled on the side of the couch, leaning forward on his elbows and reaching out to pull my legs toward him. He's close now. Our energies fuse, combine, and seem to multiply the thrill of a successful evening by a thousand.

"I was right."

"Right about what?" I ask.

"Bringing you in that very first day."

"Why did you? Old times' sake? I dazzled you with my bad manners the night we met? Or my huge appetite for quinoa? Or with my letter?"

He just smiles and doesn't answer.

He's smiling as he takes my feet in his hand, tracing his thumb along the arches. For a moment I'm transfixed watching his thumb. The most delicious shiver runs down my spine, to my stomach and the tips of my breasts.

"I'm ticklish."

And breathless and excited and in love.

"I see that."

He lifts his head, slowly cupping one foot by the heel and lifting it up, and up, and up. He opens his mouth, watching me as he nips the tip of my toe. He engulfs it, runs his tongue over the back, sucks gently as he starts running his other hand up my arm, to my face. He inserts his thumb into my mouth, slowly rubbing my thumb with his other hand.

"Matt," I groan. I stop his hand, look down at our fingers. His hands obsess me. Why they obsess me, I don't know, but they're so big, look so powerful. He holds SO MUCH in those hands.

He grabs my shoes and looks at me as he slips and straps them back on, his fingers touching the same toes that are still tingling. Neither of us says a word once my shoes are on, and he keeps his hands on the top arch of my foot for several long, extra heartbeats.

"I love you," he says simply, grabbing my face and pressing a kiss to my lips.

Exhaling, he stands up to get ready, and I glance at the clock and leap to my feet and follow him.

We are traveling extensively. Sometimes Matty travels with us, the times he doesn't choose to remain in D.C. with my parents or Matt's mother.

The crowds follow wherever President Hamilton goes. People want to see him, they want to see his first lady, they want to dote over his son, they want to pet Jack, and they want pictures—goodness, are the media covering us everywhere we go?

Matt is, as usual, a good sport with the press, but I get nervous when I'm walking with little Matty and reporters are snapping pictures and causing Stacey and the guys to work extra to push them all back.

Still, I love being out in the country, seeing the changing scenery. Deserts to forests, cities to small towns, farms and pasture to stoplights and highways. And the people—different and unique, everyone hoping for the glory to keep shining on the United States. Everyone trusting Matthew Hamilton to keep bringing it.

Today we're in Philadelphia, and I get to introduce him to the people.

"Well, it really is such a pleasure to be here," I say, breathless. "What an amazing crowd!" They all clap and cheer. "I know why you're all here. It's because my husband is quite charming and gives quite a good speech." They laugh. "And also, because I know you know that Matthew Hamilton genuinely cares about you, about this country, about what's right. I have witnessed firsthand his dedication, his effort, his complete devotion to this country, and if I weren't already hopelessly in love with him, that would be enough to seal the deal for me right now." More laughter. "The changes he's put into effect these past few years … Millions of new jobs. Better education for our children, a more comprehensive healthcare plan, a thriving economy, and our outstanding free trade, which enables you, as Americans, to have any product for the best price available at your fingertip … this is only the beginning of the more extensive changes he's been working to address … and I definitely hope you sit tight and listen to him share them with you tonight. So without further ado, ladies and gentlemen, I present my husband, Matthew Hamilton, the President of the United States!"

He takes the stage, leans into the microphone. "She's better at this than I am." He smirks, winking at me as I take a spot on the sidelines, and I laugh at the same time the crowd does.

"Thank you, Mrs. Hamilton," he tells me with a nod as he takes in his doting crowd. "She's right. It's a great crowd today ..."

"HAMMY! GO GET IT, HAMMY!" someone shouts.

"I will," he promises, grinning, then falling sober.

"Today, I want to discuss something with you. Last night, I got word that I'm to be a father again. The first lady is expecting." The smile on his face is absolutely dazzling, and so contagious there's not a sad face in the house.

I feel giddy remembering when I told him—how he plucked his glasses off, then just grabbed me to him and swept me clean off the ground. *"You make me so happy, so fucking happy,"* and the rest was smothered with his kiss.

"So it's something I want to talk to you about. Our children," he continues—and pauses. "It is with our children that our greatest potential as a country lies. We are raising world-changers, leaders, girls and boys who can make a real difference. And it all begins with you. With me. With us."

I feel Matty's hand slip into mine, and he's frowning—not too happy he'll be dethroned soon. "You'll still love me best?"

"I'll love you as my *best* firstborn, yes," I promise, and he nods and starts to get restless. "Sit here with me. Watch Dad," I whisper, hushing him, clinging to Matt's every word.

I just love for people to see him as I do, to know the real man, the one behind the façade, the name, and the presidency.

The Matt Hamilton we all love.

I watch out the windows of Air Force One, the clouds beneath me looking like a carpet of cotton candy.

I lay my hand over my belly and think of Matt.

I'm so in love with him and I can't believe I'm four months pregnant with our second child.

The debates are over, the campaigning has been exhaustive but inspiring, and now we're heading back home.

Our little family of three, soon to be four.

I know from looking at my parents that no matter how strong the love, relationships are always tested. Boundaries are pushed, some promises broken, and disappointments happen. That's just life. No road is ever perfectly smooth or straight.

But I also know from looking at my parents that love is a choice. Sometimes the hardest choice of all. And I know as I turn to look at Matthew, his profile showcasing perfect masculine beauty, his lips pursed thoughtfully as he looks quizzically at a stack of manila folders in front of him with his glasses perched on his nose, that I will always choose him.

A realization that comforts me.

I chose him over a normal life. I chose him over privacy. I chose him over insecurity about whether or not I would ever be enough, as a wife, as a mother, as a first lady. I chose him over fear. I chose him over everything …

Love can be passionate, wild, consuming, mesmerizing. It catches you in the wake of what seems to be an ordinary life and it turns it upside down until you are fully living with every cell, every pore, every atom in your body. It makes you live life to its fullest potential. Love heightens all your emotions, until your past life looks like you were living on mute, like you were living with senses that were partly numbed.

This awakening to experiencing everything to its fullest potential is what makes life the most joyful and blissful experience, and also the most painful one. Looking down at the clouds beneath me and the blue sky stretching out before me, I simply let myself embrace it all, whatever comes.

I see myself with Matt. I see myself having kids with him. I see myself stretched out between his legs, reclining on him, while holding hot cocoa in my hands, hearing the crackling of a fireplace.

I see myself holding his face to my chest, quietly soothing him after a hard day. After having to make some tough decisions.

I see him climbing into bed beside me and nuzzling my neck, telling me how much he loves me, how I am his angel.

I see him holding our daughter's hand (yes, it's a girl—we got confirmation just last week!), her red hair in two little pigtails as she skips besides her father, looking up at him with all the love and awe in the world, and him looking down at her as if she were the greatest treasure.

I see myself thirty years from now, sitting next to an old and still ruggedly handsome Matt, talking about how we met, how he won the presidency, how he proposed, the life we've had.

Because even if he wins, four more years as president is not much compared to the years he will be an ex-president, and I his wife. The term is not the only thing that counts. What really lasts is what you did, your legacy for all time.

It's a simple choice, really. I choose him. Always.

And despite his own fears and concerns, disappointments and ideas about his ability to be both president and husband, president and father, president and man … he chose me.

Whatever happens, we chose each other.

It's cold outside, but that's where Matt and I spend the November evening of Election Day. I bring out a small speaker and I play some music, settling for a song Hozier played on our wedding, "Better Love." And we dance, like we sometimes do. I sway in his arms while our team watches television in one of the White House rooms, and Matt Jr. sleeps, and the country waits with bated breath, and I just dance with Matt.

And that's how Carlisle finds us, when he steps outside.

"Well, Mr. President," he says, smiling wryly as he spots us. "Looks like you're up for a second term."

I gasp, my hand flying to my mouth. Matt's hands tighten on me, his jaw clenching, his eyes flashing with happiness—with gratefulness.

He frames my face and plants a firm, fierce kiss on my forehead, then he steps up to shake Carlisle's hand. "I couldn't have wanted to hear anything else."

They shake hands, and Carlisle slaps his back. "You do me proud, Matt."

"Where's Matt Junior?" he immediately asks me.

"In bed. Matt, you cannot seriously wake him—"

"Oh yes I can," he says, already striding inside. I follow him to the bedroom, where he slowly opens the door and steps into the room to find our son's sleeping form.

Matt sits on the edge of the bed and leans down to whisper, "Hey, bedbug," waiting for Matty to stir awake.

"Dad," he just says, grinning a toothy grin.

Matt strokes one hand over his head. "We're staying."

Matty's eyes widen. He'd been worried. No matter how much I assured him that we'd find another home, that his dad has a lot of homes we could move into, he'd argued that none of the staffers he'd come to love would be there, nor the swans in the fountain.

"Jack too?" He blinks, and Matt laughs and grabs his face, kissing the top of his head.

"Jack too."

"Okay," he says happily. "Jack, we're staying!" he says, and we tuck him back into bed and just watch him for a minute in the shadows as he falls back to sleep. Our boy, the apple of our eye. Jack is wagging his tail from the corner of his room when Matt embraces me from behind, cupping my stomach with both hands, his chin propped on the top of my head, his thumbs moving back and forth. He doesn't need to trace the letters "I love you"; the way he holds me says he loves us, all of us, all the same,

THE END

Charlotte

He won. By both the popular vote and the Electoral College again. The White House staffers breathe a sigh of relief. Matt and I wander the West Colonnade, Matt Jr. asleep upstairs. The noises of the White House are so familiar to us, every creak and shuffle, the hum and the bustle. There will be no transfer of power until four years—four more years of Hamilton change are under way, of slow steps forward, continued increase in economy and security.

It's a cold winter day, and hundreds of thousands of people flood the National Mall to watch Matt's second inauguration.

Usually protocol dictates that the operations supervisor organizes the dinners and the entire Inauguration Day, rearranging furniture for upcoming interviews, moving out one president as the next one moves in—all within a few hours. The few hours when the oath is taken, the luncheon is served, and the parade on Pennsylvania Avenue is held. This year, there is no such furniture moving. The first family is staying.

But while that part of the protocol seems to allow the White House staff to breathe a sigh of relief, other parts are still taking place.

Getting ready to welcome the president after the inauguration through the North Portico doors. Organizing a buffet for us to share with our family and friends before the inaugural balls.

Everyone is buzzing—the standard hustle and bustle of the White House seems to be triple its usual speed.

I spend the morning with a stylist and a makeup artist, while Matt has a security briefing to rehash what has been done so far, and where things stand.

We get ready for church service, and Matty and Jack go with us to visit Matt's father at Arlington Cemetery.

I feel a bottomless sense of peace and satisfaction, humility and honor, as we head to the U.S. Capitol, where the inauguration will take place.

I worried Matty would not behave during the event, but instead I've realized that he's as smart as his father, and everything I asked him to do—stand still, pay attention, sing the anthem—he's doing instinctively.

I sit behind Matt as he's sworn in, and I glance at his profile and then at my son's. Matt told me last night that he felt honored to share this moment with his son, that he remembered so clearly the days his father took the oath both his first and second time.

Now I watch Matty drink in his father, as he swears to protect and preserve the Constitution of the United States.

I wore blue last time, and white for my wedding day, and now I went for a wine-colored dress. I look like a flame, Matt says.

You never quite get used to the adoration people shower you with; at first it's almost uncomfortable. It takes courage to receive this love and adoration—to own it, because in a way it means you must reciprocate, must deserve it. I know it has been easier for Matthew to do it than it has been for me. He was born to be commander in chief. You could say he belongs where he is because he was born with America in his veins, but I also believe it's part of his personality. It's what has helped us change and grow so much in the past four years— the knowledge that we are phenomenal, and can do and deserve phenomenal things, but also the humility to accept that there is no perfection, that change takes time and effort, that this country isn't based on one person, but on the joint effort of many. Matt is just the leader.

I could not be more proud of him.

The way he carries himself, the smile he wears, the strong outline of his shoulders straining against his gabardine.

Once he finishes his speech and the inauguration comes to a close, we exit up the stairs, and I hug him. Just a hug, and I whisper, "Congratulations, my love."

Wisps of hair fall on my face, and before I can brush them aside, Matt brushes them behind my forehead first. I laugh at the wind blowing my hair into disarray. The wind is being just as playful with his hair. I brush a lock of hair behind his forehead too.

"Four more years," I say.

"They go by fast, don't they?"

"Too fast."

He smiles. "Let's do it."

His fingers smooth and warm as they touch mine, the effect like a hot burst of fireworks in my veins as he takes my hand, the other already taken by Matty.

"Is my first lady ready?"

"As ready as you are."

After the luncheon and the parade, we head to the White House to relax, snack, and then change for the balls. I go to the bedroom to change into more comfortable heels, and when I head to the Old Family Dining Room, the boys aren't there.

"Oh, Mrs. Hamilton, Junior's with his dad, I think."

"Where?"

"The West Wing."

I head over and greet Portia, worried Matty may be giving her trouble, but she merely grins and motions to the door. "You'll find them both there, Mrs. Hamilton. Also, Alison is on her way—oh, there she is. The president wanted a family picture today."

I just grin, amused, and step into the Oval Office. And there he is, the Ruler of the Modern World, looking out the window, arms crossed, but he uncrosses them as he turns. He sets his hands on the desk before him, arms spread wide, his gaze unflinching and uncompromising—the gaze of the most powerful man in the world. He smiles at me.

I shut the door.

I clear my throat, my lips curving. "Mr. President."

"Mrs. Hamilton." He starts to round the desk.

"You wouldn't happen to know where a rather restless, very handsome young boy went? I can't find him anywhere."

Smiling, he shakes his head and lets his eyes fall to his desk.

Alison is suddenly behind me, her camera flashing as Matt Jr. peeks from under the desk saying, "Boo!"

"Matt, get out from under your father's desk," I chide.

Alison snaps a few pictures.

"But I don't want to. It's my special hiding place," Matt Jr. says.

"We'll make a tent in your room, or in the Red Room—no, the Blue Room. We'll make you the perfect hiding place there."

"But Dad won't be there. It's no fun without Dad."

Matthew laughs and I roll my eyes. "Were you this difficult?"

"Not nearly," he says, glancing at me, his smile fading.

He looks at my mouth, and I realize that I'm gnawing my lower lip. He leans his dark sable head to me as he brushes his thumb over my lip to make me release it. "I want to kiss that lovely lip."

I ease back to look at him. "You're kissing me with your eyes," I whisper.

"To hell with it. My mouth is jealous." He laughs.

He grabs my face and kisses me. It's a quick, dry kiss, PG-13 rated rather than a triple-X kiss, but Matty grins and raises his arms so that we'll scoop him up. Matt scoops him up in his arm and tells Alison, "Catch him while he's still," and Alison is grinning as she starts clicking.

"Jack, come here, boy." Matt whistles to Jack, and I'm shocked to see him crawl out from under the desk too.

"Oh my goodness." I laugh now, and as Jack sits before us, we all turn to Alison's camera lens.

Matthew's lips are curled in a sly grin, little Matt is smirking just like his father does, and I'm blushing—still because of this man, after all these years. No, we don't live in a fairy-tale world, but between all the bad things, there are these moments, these people, these glimpses of who we are—*good.* Who we love. How hard. How true. Which is why we cling to every reminder of that good to steer us back, to find the path to where we want to go. Where we deserve to be. Happy. Free. And loved.

DEAR READERS,

Thanks so much for picking up my new WHITE HOUSE series. I have loved every second of Matt and Charlotte's story, and I hope you have too. There's a third book I have been planning for some time; it's a standalone with new characters, but in this same world, taking place during Matt's second term. I hope to tell you more about it as soon as I am able to. In the meantime, I'm working on something new, another standalone, that I am just dying to share with you in the spring! Stay tuned!

Thank you for your support and enthusiasm for my work,

ACKNOWLEDGMENTS

Amy, as always, thank you for all you do. The White House series is your baby too, and I'm so happy that we could share it with the readers! Thank you for your belief in me, and in them, and thank you to the entire amazing team at the Jane Rotrosen Agency. I'm truly grateful to work with you.

I also could not have done this without my family's love and support, and so many other people who have contributed in small and big ways to supporting my writing.

Huge, huge thank you to my editor Kelli Collins, and Sue Rohan for her expertise, my copy editor Lisa, my proofreader Anita Saunders, and my betas Nina, Angie, Kim J., Kim K., and Monica.

To the fabulous Nina, Jenn, and the entire team at Social Butterfly PR, you ladies are truly phenomenal. Thank you for being as excited about my books as I am and for all that you do.

To Melissa, thank you for everything, and to Gel, for all that you do for me.

Thank you to my foreign publishers for translating my stories so that they can be read across the world.

To Julie at JT Formatting and my cover designer, James at Bookfly Covers, you did an amazing job!

Bloggers, I am ever so grateful for your support and enthusiasm for reading. You always make my day when you choose to share and promote my work from among so many other amazing stories to share, read, and review. Thank you!

And to my readers. You are always in the back of my mind, every time I'm writing. I get to parts that make me smile, or do *other* little things to me, and I think to myself, "I wonder if they'll feel this, just like *this*." It is always my aim for you to, so I am always grateful to be given the chance to coax you into my world.

Thank you for your support and your love. Thank you to everyone who picked up, shared, and read this book.

ABOUT

New York Times, *USA Today*, and *Wall Street Journal* bestselling author Katy Evans is the author of the Real, Manwhore, and White House series. She lives with her husband, two kids, and their beloved dogs. To find out more about her or her books, visit her pages. She'd love to hear from you.

Website:
www.katyevans.net

Facebook:
https://www.facebook.com/AuthorKatyEvans

Twitter:
@authorkatyevans

Sign up for Katy's newsletter:
http://www.katyevans.net/newsletter/

OTHER TITLES
BY KATY EVANS

Made in the USA
Lexington, KY
14 February 2017